LEAVING CAME EASY

LEAVING CAME EASY

The Mysteries of Bella Rose Estate

Book #1

PHYLLIS DEWEY

This is a work of fiction. Names, characters, places and incidents have been fictionalized. Any resemblance to actual persons, living or dead, events or locales is entirely coincidental.

ISBN: 978-1-7364347-0-3

DEDICATION

I dedicate this book to my cousin, Linda Dewey.

I was thirteen when I bravely let her read my first poem. One I had written two years earlier. She was impressed and encouraged me to continue my writing. Many poems, stories, and novel attempts later – this novel has made it for the world to read.

Thank you, Cuz, for your positive words when we were young teens.

May others realize that what a child hears can make or break their dreams and change their future.

Be their encouragement.

Chapter One

Sara and Heather left their attorney's office in silence. Sara's hand gripped the manila envelope containing the legal document that would change their lives. Heather closed the heavy door of the three-story, faded, red, brick building and followed her sister down the few decaying concrete steps to the sidewalk, then blindly walked across the street towards Sara's car. They were both in shock from the news that neither one noticed the heavy traffic passing on the street. Car horns blared as three vehicles came to a screeching halt, avoiding them both as they stumbled. Abruptly aware of their surroundings, Sara nodded an apology to the traffic as they reached the car, opened their car doors, and climbed in.

Shaken, the sisters sat in the car in silence. After gathering her composure, Sara started her car and drove to Bella Rose Manor, where their family had been raised and where life was about to take a turn neither could have imagined.

Their parents had passed away within six months of each other. There was such a thing as dying of a broken heart – the girls had witnessed it. Their father, Glen, died following a fall on a walking trail. The trail that he had carved out in the woods near their home. He had fallen, hitting his head on a large rock, and never regained consciousness. His wife, Susan, found him lying on the ground when she searched for him after being gone longer than usual. He was rushed to the hospital, but two days later, he passed away with his family by his side.

Susan had been so strong for everyone after Glen died. She did her best to stay positive in front of everyone. Inwardly, her heart ached. She wanted to protect her family from finding out some family secrets, so she began to sort through old papers in the attic. Susan had not told the girls, but there were things in the attic that she did not want her children to discover. She planned to get rid of them before they were found. Heather thought it was odd for her mother to be getting rid of things that belonged to her father so soon after he died but did not question her. Susan had always been a bit eccentric and tended to do odd things at unusual times.

On that memorable day, Susan's youngest daughter, Heather, stopped by to see her mother before shopping for groceries. Heather knew she would never forget that day. Thinking nothing of the unlocked front door at her parent's home, and let herself in. Susan could usually be found in the kitchen cooking or the front room reading. Heather had called earlier and knew that her mother planned to be in the attic, and she immediately walked up to the third floor.

The attic, as it had always been called, was a spare bedroom used only for storage. The girls used to love going there as kids to play with the old trunks, old clothes, and hats they found. Their mama had designated a small space in the room for her private writing get-away complete with a writing desk and chair. She let her children play in the room while she sat and wrote. The children were never allowed to be there alone. Heather was always mystified by her mama's writing – because she never allowed anyone to read it.

Heather screamed as she reached the top step and looked down the short hall in front of her. She dropped her purse and ran to her mother, who was unnaturally slumped over against the wall sitting on the floor. Heather dropped to her knees beside Susan while yelling her name. Checking for a pulse, a heartbeat, anything, she found nothing, grabbed her phone from her hip pocket, and dialed 911. She rolled her mother onto her back and started CPR as best as she could remember. The operator's verbal instructions over the phone helped her.

As soon as the EMS arrived and took over the CPR to get her breathing, Heather called Sara, who was out doing errands. Sara answered her cell phone as emergency vehicles sped past her with their sirens and lights going. She could not make out what her sister was saying due to the blaring sirens. All she heard was Mama had fallen. She sped up to follow them and screeched to a halt in front of the manor. She pushed her car door closed behind her then ran into the house and up the stairs. She got there as the EMS team carried her mama down the last flight of stairs on the stretcher out to the ambulance. They had her on oxygen as they sped to the hospital. Heather and Sara followed them to the hospital. The medical team in the ER did everything they could to save her, but she never woke up. She did not know that her daughters were by her side, holding her hands and crying as she took her last breath. The death certificate stated her death as a *Myocardial infarction*. Otherwise known as a heart attack. The girls believed it was from a broken heart. Now, both of their parents were gone.

Together Sara and Heather planned another funeral. They received calls from friends and former guests of the manor. The family mourned – again. They celebrated their mother's life with the many who came to show their respects and love to the girls. Their mother was well known and loved by more people than the girls ever realized.

A couple of weeks after they laid their dear sweet Mama in the ground, they met with their parent's attorney, Randall Williams, to go over the details of the final will. Distraught and still grieving, they were sure the will was going to be a mess. They doubted their mother had taken time to change hers after their Dad passed. To their surprise, she had. Attorney Williams told them that Susan had come in a week after their Dad's funeral to update her final wishes. Mr. Williams recalled Susan telling him she did not want there to be any problems for the kids when it was her time, but she was not going to make it easy on them. Being the eccentric woman she was, her will contained unusual conditions her children had to follow.

Sara and Heather sat in silence inside Sara's car at Bella Rose Manor. It was the place their parents had called home for most of their married life. The place where the girls had grown up. The place they thought they knew. The place that now would change their lives.

No longer would their parents greet their guests. No longer would the kitchen hold large family meals that they had helped their mother make. They no longer would call to talk to Mama nor Daddy, who always stopped what they were doing to chat on the phone with their children. No, now it was Sara's place. And Heather's, of course, but Sara had been the one to inherit the majority interest in the estate, at least for the time being.

The conditions inserted in the will could put a strain on the siblings that neither had ever thought possible. However, they could not fight it. They would have to live with it or ignore their parents' wishes all together, and who could do that? Not them. The family had always been close. Well, Sara and Heather had been. Their brother Andy on the other hand? No one had seen nor heard from him in over three years, but he was named in the will. And that was the first issue they had to address.

They would have to find Andy, or he would have to come home on his own. When their father died, and there was no sign of Andy, their mama said there was little they could do about it. She would have loved to find him to tell him about his father, but now that chance was gone. He may never learn of his father's nor his mother's deaths.

Sara and Heather entered the manor and went to the large kitchen to discuss what their mama had dealt them. The will was not a total mess like they thought it would be, but it was interesting, to say the least, with all the requirements. Sara placed the envelope on the island and stepped over to the kitchen counter to make a fresh pot of coffee.

"Well, Big Sis, how does it feel to be in charge?" Heather asked, trying not to be too sarcastic nor angry. She stood at the island that had been one of the first things her folks had added during their remodeling efforts and waited for the coffee to finish brewing. She looked around as the aroma of the brewing coffee filled the room. The kitchen had been the gathering place for the family her whole life. The window over the sink facing the mountains had been one of her favorite places to spend time with her mother and sister. As always, the place was spotless. She leaned against the marble-topped island as she noticed a small crack along the one edge. She admired her sister for taking care of the place even while they dealt with their grief.

Sara poured them each a cup of coffee, handed one to her younger sister, and sat down before she spoke. "Not all that great, actually. I know I'm the oldest of us all, but I'm finding that it is not all it's cracked up to be. It puts a lot on my shoulders."

"That's for sure. But I promise to go by Mama's wishes and to work with you as best I can." Heather sat down at the island and noticed that Sara was staring at the envelope. "Wait until Ben hears what has transpired. Marc will be excited. He loves being here."

"I'm so glad you will work with me. I want you as an equal as much as you can. I know the will makes it sound like I am in charge, but I'd like to think we are in this together. Think we can, Little Sis?"

"Yes, we can. Let me call Ben and have him bring Marc over so we can fill him in on the contents of the will."

"Sounds good to me. I'll make us some more fresh coffee." Sara stood to make coffee while Heather got on her phone to call her husband. She reached for the coffee pot then realized she had already made a fresh pot. She sat back down. Oh, life had become interesting. She looked around while Heather made her phone call. If they were going to remodel the manor, this room would need some changes. The stove that was there since her childhood would need replacing. It had lasted longer than any stove she ever knew of, but it was time to replace that cast iron thing completely. The newer one that sat next to it would have to go as well. She had always found it odd that her parents had kept them both. She reached for a dish towel to wipe up a coffee spill when she overheard Heather's conversation.

"Ben, you won't believe what was in the will! Can you come over to Bella Rose? Will you stop by and pick up Marc? I'm sure the babysitter is ready for a break."

"Sure, we'll be over in about forty-five minutes. So your mama had made a new will? Are you alright with what it said? You sound upset. What's in it?"

"It's okay. But a lot of things will be changing."

"Changing? What do you mean?" Ben asked.

"I'm not going to discuss them over the phone. We'll all talk after you get here."

"Okay. I'm on my way." Ben hung up and immediately went to his car. He pulled out of their new home's driveway to pick Marc up from the sitter. It took him closer to an hour to get to the manor. First, Marc was not ready to leave the sitter. Then traffic was backed up due to road construction, and it was rush hour. Traffic was much better once he got out of the city limits, and he could relax a bit while he drove the last five miles. He had always loved this stretch of road to the manor. It was relaxing. His grand in-laws had moved here soon after WWII because they loved the countryside and the mountains. The area had been built up with homes and businesses, but there were still many mountain views and open land to enjoy. Bella Rose Estate set back off the main road outside the city limits. The manor itself was beautiful and relaxing. It had some of the best views in the area.

He parked his car and walked around to get Marc out of the car seat and set him down. At two years old, his little legs took him running toward the manor. Ben loved to watch his son run around. So tiny but growing so fast. It was amazing to watch him grow.

With Marc settled with a snack in hand and his toys in the play area, Sara, Heather, and Ben sat down around the kitchen island. Sara opened the envelope and took out the papers that she and Heather had brought home. Mr. Williams had read them out loud and explained the details and conditions. She hoped she could remember it all the way he had explained.

"As you know, Heather and I went to the attorney today. We were expecting the will to be a mess with Mama passing so soon after Daddy. We doubted she had gone to see the attorney on her own. She never told either of us. So this is a total shock." Sara lifted the papers in the air with her one hand.

"We never expected Mama to do what she did, nor do we completely understand it," Heather added while looking between her older sister and her husband.

"So, what does it say? Is it good or bad? Knowing your mother, it can't be that bad, can it?" Ben was getting anxious to hear or read what it said. He was tempted to reach for the pile of papers.

"Okay. I'm going to save you all the details and legalese. What it says is: Bella Rose Estate goes to me. However, several conditions affect us all, including Andy." She spoke and quickly added that last sentence, so Ben would not protest before it was time.

"Andy?" Ben raised his voice. "How can it involve Andy? We've not seen him in over what... three years? How could she include him? He was never here much since he was a teenager." Ben stood up and started to walk around, then sat back down without saying anything else. His mind was too busy.

Sara raised her hand slightly off the table. "Wait. Let me continue. This is the *interesting* part. As I said, there are several conditions that we are to follow. First is the remodeling of Bella Rose Manor that our parents started. We are to complete it and to reopen it. Here is the part that affects you and Heather."

She hesitated and looked at Heather. She was unsure how Ben was going to take this next part. Heather nodded her head for Sara to go on. "Mama added the condition that Heather and you move into the one guest house and help me run the manor." Sara hesitated, waiting for Ben to voice his opinion. When he was silent, she continued. Heather had placed her hand on Ben's arm and squeezed it. Ben looked at her and saw that she was smiling. He knew that no matter what he thought, his wife liked the idea of moving to the family estate property. He'd have to discuss that with her later.

“You know the manor has been handed down to me simply because I am the oldest descendant. According to the will, there is an extra inheritance designated for you if you stay here for five years and help run it. There is also money set aside in a trust fund for Marc." Sara waited again, but no one said anything.

"Now for what you asked about, our brother Andy. Yes, he is named in Mama's will. I know we have not heard from him for over three years. We have no idea where he is, what he is doing, or even if he is alive, although I believe he is alive because no one has heard anything otherwise. But, if/when Andy is found or returns here to the manor, he is eligible to receive his inheritance--if he stays and helps with the manor for at least five years." Sara stopped talking and lay the papers down on the table. There was more, but she wanted to give Ben time to digest the first part. "Those are some of the conditions of her will. I know Daddy's will gave everything to our mother, so it is her will that we have to abide by. What are your thoughts?"

Ben looked up at Sara. "So, you're saying that she wants the manor to stay open; or rather to be remodeled and then be reopened," Ben corrected himself. "Heather and I are to leave our new home and move here, live in one of the three guest houses, and help you run the place? I will most likely need to quit my job to do that. Will there be enough income from guests for all of us to live on comfortably? And we don't get any inheritance until we have lived here and helped you for five whole years?"

Sara sat up to answer his questions and concerns. "Yes, there is enough money set up to support us—even Andy. The funds will be allocated like you would be getting paid for the first five years. Monthly installments if you want to put it that way. But that is the first part of your inheritance. You get your additional inheritance in one lump sum at the end of five years. Until then, it is sitting in an account collecting interest. Marc is also taken care of with his trust fund for school, college, and money to invest. You may be able to keep your job since you own the business and could run it from here if you want. At least for a while."

Ben leaned back in his chair and looked at his wife. "I will definitely have to think about my business. I have employees who are counting on me. They deserve to be taken care of." Ben sat back as he was thinking of his options. He could tell his wife was willing to sell their home and move. The selling and moving should not take too long as it was a newly remodeled house that his construction crew had recently completed. Plus, he thought of something that could work in his favor, but he would bring that up in their discussions about the manor's remodeling project. It could solve a few issues for him.

"I, for one, am excited about remodeling the manor and reopening it in our parent's honor. But Mama did put a lot of restrictions on us," Sara admitted. She did not want her sister and brother-in-law leaving her sitting high and dry to operate it on her own. She had to convince them that they were not the only ones who had to follow some peculiar rules.

"Five years goes fast. Believe me." Sara did her best to sound encouraging. "If you move into the guest house and help me, we can make Bella Rose Manor a major attraction and vacation spot again. Like it was years ago when our folks ran it before closing it for the initial remodeling. It was always their plan to reopen."

She stood up, poured herself a fresh cup of coffee while looking out the window at the mountain view, and continued speaking. "Now it is up to us to follow through. I will be moving into the main house closest to the manor where Mama and Daddy lived. You and Heather can have the bigger one since you have a family. That one is further away from the manor and will give you more privacy. We can leave the other one empty for now while we search for Andy. Or we can rent it out for a while when we reopen if we have not found him."

Heather spoke up. "We can do it. Ben, what do you say? Are you willing to move and help us?" She looked at her husband with her pleading eyes that defeated his will power.

"You know I'm willing to help you and your family with anything you need. Yes, we can do this. I will need to make some decisions about my business, but if that is what your mama wanted, then we have to make it work." He reached over to his wife and pulled her into a hug, kissing her forehead.

"Good. It will all work out for the best for us. I know this won't happen overnight. We all have changes to make in our lives. I am also going to have to move. Luckily, I have only been renting, so it will be easier for me to move out." She picked the papers back up. "Now, there were a couple of other odd things in her will." Sara continued without waiting for any comments.

"What were those?" Ben wondered in silence as his heart sank. What more could there be? Her uprooting their lives was odd enough. No one had ever told him he had to move. Now his in-laws were telling him what to do. Secretly he was not completely happy about it, but he had to stay positive for his family.

Sara took her last sip of coffee, then continued. "We have been instructed not to touch the attic when we remodel. We can only open that up after the manor has reopened."

Ben's curiosity turned to concern. "Why did she add that? That only makes us want to see what's up there. Plus, what if we need to get in there for part of the remodel work?"

"Well, we can't. The door is secured. The attorney and the bank are the ones with the key and instructions to get inside."

"Getting in comes with instructions and a key? Can't we bust the door down?" He was beginning to find the conditions of the will frustrating. He never had like following rules, and this will seemed to have several of them.

"No, we can't, and we won't," Heather added as she took his hand in hers to calm him. "We can, and we will wait. We have enough other things to deal with. We needn't worry or be concerned with what is up there. And yes, Mr. Williams said he had access to the keys to some locks. He did not know what doors they opened, but he said he would give them to us when it was time."

"Okay. I say we have a lot to think about, a lot to get organized, and a lot to start doing. For now, I say we gather up Marc and go find something to eat in town."

Ben stood up, ready to go eat, when Heather added, "That works for me. We can start in the morning to get it planned and organized," Heather said as she stood to get Marc and help him put his toys away. They were blessed that Marc was such a good child. He always had been. Their son, content to play with his toys on the floor, had not interrupted them while they had been talking.

They had a good dinner in town at the new and already successful, locally owned Italian restaurant. Sara ordered her favorite meat lasagna while Heather had the chicken Parmesan and Ben shared a medium, extra cheese, and mushroom pizza with Marc. They all shared the warm garlic bread that came with every meal. Several patrons interrupted them, still offering their condolences. That was the curse and blessing of being a well-known family living in a small town.

That night none of them slept well. There was too much to think about. Sara had to pack up her things and notify her landlord that she was moving out. Her apartment had come furnished, which made packing easier. She was moving into her parent's house and planned to keep most of their furnishings so did not have to stress about buying anything. Heather and Ben had even more on their plate with the need to sell their home, pack, and move. They all had finding Andy on their minds. Marc was the only one who slept through the night.

The next morning arrived like any other day. Marc was up at dawn, waking Heather and Ben up, wanting to cuddle with them in their bed. It was the best part of the day for them. Heather loved her time with her little boy. He was getting too big to be called a baby anymore. Family time was important to her and Ben, but Ben had to get to work. Weekends were his time to lay around, and this was not the weekend. Nor was this going to be a normal day.

Ben got up, and after a quick shower and a cup of coffee, he headed to work. His mind was busy thinking of all the things to take care of before helping his wife and sister-in-law with the manor. He had the idea of his company doing the construction work required if his late mother-in-law had not specified another company. They could all benefit. He would inquire about that and talk to his crew. He could keep his men working and earning a living, at least for a while. How would he tell them that he may have to lay them off because he would have to close his business? One of the men could take over managing it and keep Ben on as a consultant. That way, he could keep his feet in the business. He would have to investigate that possibility. He would love to help at the manor, but he did not want to give up on something he had spent so many years building. He was proud of his hard work and becoming a success in such a short amount of time. There was so much to consider and straighten out. He shook his head as he walked into his office.

First, he planned to meet with his men this morning and get them busy with their current job. There was no need to get them worried yet. He did not want to lose any of them if he did not have to. They were all great workers. He was blessed to have them. He was finding that so many people did not want to work that hard anymore. One of the good employees he had known since grade school. His latest hire had moved his family from Colorado to be closer to her family. They had two children to support; one had special needs. He could not take his job away. Donovan had been with him for the last three years and had been promoted to foreman quickly. Ben had even hired his wife as a part-time receptionist to fill in when his regular one had to take time off. Cecelia had also been a great help providing designing tips for some of the homes they built. Maybe Donovan would be the one to take over the business. Ben would consider that option. He knew his former classmate was not the one to be the leader. Some people were born to lead; others were born to follow. Some had more business sense; others had more common sense. They all worked well together in his business.

Chapter Two

Unable to sleep, Sara got up and drove to the manor to think. She sipped her first cup of coffee as she watched the morning light of the sunrise appear over the distant mountain and shine through the window illuminating the kitchen. It had been a long time since Sara had seen that beauty. The morning's silence was daunting as she remembered the years when guests would talk among themselves while her mother prepared their breakfast in this space. It was common for Susan to cook for twelve people and, on occasion, several more. The ghostly sounds of children playing in the great room and parents chatting while sipping their coffee, making plans for their day, made her smile. Many of the guests had made new friends as they learned about each other during their vacations at Bella Rose Manor. Some of those friendships had lasted for years and scheduled their visits to align with their new friends. They came from all over the country and some from other countries. It had been an amazing place at one time, and Sara felt blessed to have grown up there. She turned and smiled as she visualized everyone being there from years past. She felt blessed with the memories.

Bella Rose Manor had been in their family for three generations since her grandparents, Robert and Rose, moved to the area right after they married. They bought the land and built a simple one-bedroom log cabin on top of the hillside. Their property line led down to the main road that wound around through the countryside into the small town. The forest surrounded them on either side with a view from the back porch of distant mountains. The trees' height had hidden some of the original views during the summer, but it was still breathtaking. They had a small yard with flower gardens in front of the house, and a vegetable garden had occupied space on the log cabin's side. The driveway had been all dirt with ruts that needed repairing after the spring rains. It was indeed a piece of heaven in the country.

As time passed and their family grew, her grandparents had built a second log home. This one had three bedrooms to hold their family and a larger kitchen. It was far enough away from the first cabin to maintain privacy. The views were about the same for both. The original single-family building became the first guest house they rented out for extra income. It was a quaint log home, remodeled over the years. Her parents had lived in it when they first married, and after their children had moved out, and was now where Sara would be living. Her grandparents later built the manor between the two log homes. Her grandfather had several trees removed for a better view from the estate's back deck and then added a large wrap around deck for people to enjoy all views while sitting outside. It was not only a place people came to stay and recharge; it had become a local destination for a short, day trip.

After her grandparents died, her parents, Glen and Susan, built a concrete overlook area, including permanent concrete benches and a fire pit, a few yards below the manor. They also constructed a third guesthouse beyond the front of the house just off the driveway. They widened and paved the driveway, called it Bella Rose Lane, and convinced the county to add an official road sign at the bottom so those traveling the main road could find them easily. They also added a small picnic area with two wooden picnic tables about halfway down the lane with parking for anyone who wanted to enjoy it. Rose bushes, small evergreen trees, and floral areas, embedded with white stoned gardens, framed the lane. The front landscape featured roses, benches, walkways, and a small waterfall feature. It was a great place for guests to sit and relax while enjoying the views. There were many sights to see, nature to experience, and beauty to breathe in the ten acres. A few hiking trails jutted out from the lane as well. Currently, they needed improvements before guests could use them.

There was never a charge to visit the overlook, the garden, or have a picnic even for non-guests. Often, the locals would stop at the manor and offer to help clean up the grounds each spring. Some offered to help with a project to pay for enjoying the area without the exchange of money. Many local residents rented the dining room to area residents for large parties for a fee.

Sara had returned home five years earlier to help her parents run the manor. They had offered the one guesthouse to her, but she said she wanted to be on her own – close enough to help – far enough to have a life of her own. This allowed them to continue renting the house to guests. So she had rented a small house between the manor and downtown.

She sat sipping her second cup of coffee when she began to feel overwhelmed. It was sinking in that she was now the owner of the estate. Its future success depended on her and her sister, but she felt the pressure. There was Ben, Heather's husband, who was there to help. And then there was Andy, their missing baby brother - if they could only find him. While she waited for Heather, her thoughts drifted to all that the manor had to offer its guests.

The manor had eight bedrooms, each with its own bathroom. The main entrance opened into the spacious great room where guests often gathered and enjoyed talking with other guests. To the left of the great room was the office where guests registered, and all the business of running the estate took place. The library, with its wide variety of books, sat between the office and the kitchen. A game table with padded chairs was set up for board games, and a couple of smaller sitting chairs were placed near the bench window for guests to sit and relax or read. The large kitchen with a dining area sat in the back of the manor with the dining area opened to the great room. The large hand-carved mahogany dining table could hold eighteen people. For larger crowds, they added folding tables and could feed up to twenty more people.

A wide staircase led to the second floor at the rear of the great room, where the hallway also began leading to the four bedrooms on the first floor. The other four bedrooms were on the second floor with a narrower staircase leading from that hallway to the third floor where there were two more rooms. One which was currently used for seasonal storage, the other across the hall, was what the family called the attic. Susan's will stated that no one was permitted inside until after the remodel, and the manor was making a profit.

Sara contemplated all the things they had to do to honor their mother's final wishes. She could picture her father shaking his head at the way his wife had written her will. It was not how he would have done it, but it was Susan's way. Sara finished her coffee and stood up and went to start writing a list. She had inherited the list-writing trait from her grandmother, who was so well known as a list maker that it had been mentioned at her funeral. Those memories made her smile as she opened the door to the office and walked inside. She took a seat at the desk and opened the top center drawer searching for a notepad and clipboard. When she then opened the top side drawer searching for a pen, she noticed a pile of keys lying beyond the organized dividers. The keys had no identification on them or the attached simple round metal key ring. There were two more keys that were old skeleton keys, also with no identification names or marks either. Sara picked them up and wondered what they opened. They could have belonged to her grandparents or even her great grandparents. She had no idea what they may be for. They could have been keepsakes from a time gone by and kept for sentimental reasons.

Sara jumped when the doorbell rang and tossed the keys back in the drawer, quickly closing it. She grabbed the clipboard, notepad, and her pen as she headed for the front door, closing the office door behind her as she went. She had not noticed how late it had become.

Standing outside the front door were two well-dressed, older ladies from the church where her parents attended. She knew the ladies were there to pick up a few things her mama had set aside to donate a week before she had died. Sara had contacted them about it when life began to settle down after the funeral. Sara let them in and offered them some coffee or tea and to visit. They graciously declined her invitation, adding that they had other stops to make. Sara directed them to have a seat and told them she would be right back with the box of donations. Sara returned to the living room with the box and handed it to them. She said she would have more to donate when she and her sister went through her parents' things. The ladies stood and thanked her, saying they looked forward to her call. They invited her to visit their church sometime. She politely thanked them even though she had no intention of visiting.

Going to church was not her thing. A few minutes later, the ladies had the box loaded inside their silver SUV and went on their way. After they drove away, Sara realized she had not even looked inside the box her mother had set aside to donate. She hoped it was not something she should have kept. She shrugged her shoulders and soon forgot about it.

Sara was glad the ladies had not wanted to stay. She had too much on her mind for a long interruption. She knew that if they stayed at least an hour sharing their stories about her parents and how they were so active in the community and church, and how everyone loved them. She was not in the mood for their chatter. She knew better than anyone what her parents were like. She missed them so much that hearing about them from others at the moment would have only enhanced her grieving, and that was something that she was trying to block out. She was doing her best to be the strong older sister.

Sara closed the door after they drove away, picked up the clipboard, and started a list. The first of many lists she would be making. Even her lists had to be organized. Sometimes she hated that family trait.

Heather had stayed home with Marc when Ben left for work. She sat on her sofa, watching Marc play on the floor, thinking of all she had to do. Before they moved to the guest house at the manor, she would have to pack up everything in this house, clean the house top to bottom and contact a Realtor. Having a toddler underfoot did not make it easy. She was grateful he still took long naps. A tear fell down her face when she thought about why she had to move, why she had to disrupt her family, why Ben may have to give up his business, all because her mama said so. Then she smiled as she realized it was her mother's way of making sure her children stayed close to each other. Her way of keeping family together, the way she thought it should be.

Heather, like her older sister, was organized and wrote notes and lists. She remembered her mama writing a lot over the years, although her mother wrote more than lists and notes as her sister and she did. She remembered her mother's long writing sessions and getting tired of playing in the attic before her mother was tired of writing. Heather often wondered what had ever happened to all those writings over the years. She made a mental note to ask Sara if she knew where the writings were or even remembered their mother's writing. If they were in the attic, it would be a while before they could get to them. Her mother had made sure of that.

Six weeks later things at the manor were beginning to take shape. The remodel was continuing, Heather had started moving things into the guest house for her family while they cleaned it out, and Sara was marking things off her lists as they were completed. The first thing she marked off was moving into her new home. It was a little hard to do as it was full of memories of her parents, but she was happy to be there. She estimated that in another few months everything would be done so they could reopen.

One Friday night, after Ben and his crew had been working on the remodel for several weeks non-stop, Sara told Ben and Heather it was time they had a night out. She suggested they take Marc to the babysitter, allowing them to have an official date night, adding that she was also going out to meet someone. Ben and Heather were thrilled at the thought of a night out, a break from the recent chaos.

Heather was excited about her sister going out on a date! It had been five years since the divorce; she figured it was past time that her older sister moved on with her life. She hoped life was finally going to change for Sara. She deserved love and to be loved. She had suffered enough through her bad marriage, divorce, and, more recently, dealing with death, grieving, and taking over the manor. That was a lot to deal with. She was still young – time to enjoy life again. Heather hoped whoever her sister was meeting would bring her that – love and joy. Heather repeatedly asked Sara for the name of her date. Sara assured her it was not a date, but simply a meeting with someone she had not seen in several years. There was something in the way she said it that made Heather think otherwise.

"Please tell me it's not your ex!" Heather responded.

"God, no! It's not my ex!" Sara said as she shuddered.

"Okay, because if it were him, I'd have to have you committed!" Heather laughed but was also serious.

"No worries there. I'd commit myself first. Now go home and get ready for your date with your husband."

"I'm going. We're going out to eat in Kingsport, and then we'll be home. That way, Marc isn't kept up too late at the sitter. We'll talk tomorrow."

"Sounds good. I may be out late or not. I'll see how it goes. As I said, I've not seen this person in several years. We may find we have nothing in common anymore. Or we may talk 'til dawn." Sara swung around to go home to change. She hoped her sister had not noticed her grin.

Ben arrived home from work, changed clothes, then he, Heather, and Marc were out the door. He had made reservations and did not want to be late. It was the first time in a long time that they had been out on a date.

Sara finished getting ready. She was proud of herself for keeping her secret. She did not want her sister to know she was meeting Andy, their baby brother. The brother who had disappeared for over three years. He had called her out of the blue the week before. He said he wanted to come home, that he was tired of running. She asked if he had heard that Mama and Daddy had both died. He told her that he had heard the news a couple of weeks before. That's when she became suspicious. The thought crossed her mind that he only wanted his inheritance. Ha! Was he in for a rude awakening when he would hear the only way he could get it! She agreed to meet him in a public place before allowing him to come home. She did not know what he was like anymore or what his motive was. She had to be cautious. She had seen him at his worst and his best. She also knew he had been an alcoholic for years, so she was careful where she agreed to meet him. She could not handle being the cause of him becoming drunk again if he was still drinking or even providing the temptation if he was sober.

Sara left the house and headed for the Downtown Cafe. She had not been there in over a year, but she knew the new owners who had purchased it six months earlier. The hostess greeted her as an old friend even though they had never met. Sara asked for a table near the front so she could watch for Andy. She was fifteen minutes early and doubted he would be there already. He was always late. She snickered to herself as the thought crossed her mind that Andy would be late to his own funeral. God, she hoped so; she'd had enough funerals in the last several months.

The waitress brought her a menu and took her drink order of sweet tea. As Sara was looking at her menu, she realized she would have to develop a menu for the manor. Luckily it was just breakfast and brunch foods that she would have to deal with. Maybe snacks and sweets to have available in the kitchen would be a nice gesture to add. Sara made a mental note to remember that thought.

The waitress returned, setting the sweet tea on the table, and asked to take her order. Sara replied that she was waiting for someone and would wait. The waitress nodded then walked away, leaving Sara to her thoughts.

Sara looked at the clock hanging above the front door and continued watching for Andy. Several customers came in and were seated while she waited. A few couples left that had been there when she arrived. About the time Andy should have arrived, the door opened, and a young man walked in, hesitating as he looked around. Sara looked at him and was about to call her brother's name when he waved, then walked to a table nearby to join a lady and three little boys. Sara sighed. Although it had been several years, and he could have changed a lot, she figured she should recognize him. However, that man was not her brother. She continued to watch the door.

She was getting hungry, so she motioned for the waitress, placed her order, and then continued to wait. The more she watched the door and the clock, the more she knew it would be like watching and waiting for a pot to boil. It was not going to happen. Her food arrived, and she ate it without tasting the flavors. Her baby brother had once again broken her heart. It seemed that he had been a disappointment to the family since childhood. She remembered that her father never bonded with him as he had with her and Heather. You would think that a father and son would be close, but that was not the case in her family. Andy started to rebel as a preteen. Sara was staring into space when the waitress stopped at her table to clear the dishes and ask if she needed anything else. Sara shook her head, "No, Thank you. And thanks for letting me sit here this long. I guess my brother is a no show."

"You are welcome. So sorry he was a no-show. If he stops by later and asks for you, is there a name and a message I can give him?"

"No, he knows how to reach me."

Sara stood to leave. She left a large tip for the waitress, whose name she learned was Rose, like her grandmother, and headed for the door. She turned as she opened the door. "Rose, tell Andy that Sara still loves him" Rose smiled and nodded, "I sure will, Sweetie."

Sara took the back road home without realizing she had driven at all until she parked her car. She shook her head to clear her mind, time to get back to reality and the work at hand. She checked the clock, figured they would be home soon and hoped they were having a good time. She would wait until morning to call them and let them sleep in a little. She snickered when she realized Marc would have them up early no matter how late they stayed out.

She thought of her brother and wondered where he was. Why had he called her to meet and then not showed up? Was he even in the area, or was it a joke he was playing on her to find out if he had inherited anything? Was that all that interested him? She hoped he had simply chickened out. Maybe he would call her later to apologize or to explain and ask to reschedule. Deciding to stay up a while to see if he called, she poured herself a glass of wine and sat by her window, enjoying the silence.

Chapter Three

Sirens sounded in the distance. The blaring sound drew closer as the sounds of screams and moans grew louder and louder mere feet away. He smelled smoke and could feel the heat. He noticed the guardrail was now a mangled piece of metal. Ben strained to open his eyes. He wanted out of the nightmare. Sharp pain in his chest halted his attempt to sit up.

The vehicle had landed on its right side, pinning the passengers inside. The two visible tires on the driver's side were still spinning. The driver's door was hanging on only by the top hinge. A small tree and a few bushes lay flattened from the car's force as it flipped over the steep embankment.

Joe and his wife, Nicole, came upon the wreckage seconds after it happened. Joe pulled his Black Jeep Wrangler onto the shoulder. Before he came to a complete stop, his wife had opened her door and jumped out. He was on his phone with 911. They both rushed to the edge of the embankment. One look at the sight told him it was bad. The screams from inside the car and the hissing of the car itself made it difficult for Joe to hear the 911 operator who was asking for any details Joe could tell him. Nicole was climbing over the steep embankment to reach the car. The recent rains had not been kind, and she was sliding as she went. Joe was right behind her while he continued to talk to the 911 operator.

"We need an ambulance here fast! It's not good! I can't see anyone yet. I only hear screaming! We're almost to the vehicle." Joe's responses to the 911 operator's questions were short, loud, and demanding.

He had given the location as best he could. They were on a country road with no houses around. He had grown up nearby, but at that moment, he could not think of how to describe where they were. It was highway 36 headed north, past the old BBQ place. He couldn't remember what had replaced the BBQ place. He hoped the 911 operator, or the rescue team knew where he meant. He added that they would see his black Jeep Wrangler at the side of the road.

"I'm almost there! Tell them to hurry!" Nicole yelled back at her husband. She only had a few more steps to go before she could help whoever needed her.

"They are on their way; please stay on the line. I've got fire, rescue and the police headed your way." the operator said in a calm voice.

Joe held on to his phone while he continued to ease down the embankment to the car. Smoke continued to rise, and the screams he once heard grew quieter. He knew that was not a good sign. He also knew that his wife would do anything and everything she could. She was a nurse and good at her job. Whoever was hurt would be in good hands with her.

Before the rescue teams arrived, other people had stopped to help. One gentleman was slowing traffic as best he could. He had taken the flares out of his car and set them out as a warning. He knew this was not the first accident on this particular stretch of curvy road. He had heard of a few and been a witness to one. Joe was close to reaching Nicole to help her when the ambulance, police, and fire truck arrived. The screaming had gotten even quieter. More volunteers had stopped to see if there was anything they could do. Vehicles were now backed up as the police directed traffic so the rescue teams could do their work.

Nicole and Joe reached the car as a man, covered in a lot of blood, crawled out from the wreckage. Nicole reached for him as he crumbled to the ground with a moan. "Get my son and my wife. He's two. Car seat," the man whispered, taking a small breath. "His name's Marc. Her name is Heather," He added with his next short breath. Then he lay his head back and closed his eyes. Nicole lifted the man's head, trying to get him to open his eyes.

"Stay with me. Stay awake. Help is on its way." She checked his pulse, and though it was weak, she sensed in her heart that he would be okay. Joe saw a blonde-haired lady slumped over, pinned against her door in the front passenger seat. He saw a little child still buckled in his car seat in the back passenger seat. Both were crying. The lady was moaning between her cries.

One EMT was right behind him. Two more EMT men had caught up carrying a stretcher. One of the men who had helped bring the stretcher down took over for Nicole, who was with the man on the ground.

"You'll need another one of those," Joe said, pointing to the stretcher. "There's a lady and a two-year old boy trapped in there," he said as he pointed to the car and backed out of their way.

One of the EMS attempted to move Nicole out of the way. "I'm a nurse. I can help if you need me." She yelled above the noise.

"Sorry, ma'am. I didn't know. For now, please step back."

Chaos took over the scene. Joe and the other volunteer stood back and watched. There was nothing they could do now, and they did not want to be in the way, nor did they want to leave.

The first EMT, who had said that his name was Bob, managed to reach the child and ease him out of the car. He checked him over and did not notice anything wrong with him. Nothing seemed broken. He had blood on his forehead, but the bleeding had stopped for the moment. The car seat had done its job and protected him. Bob attempted to remove the car seat, but it would not budge. He carefully eased the boy out and hoped he had no other injuries. He turned to Nicole. "Can you handle him while we get his mother out?"

"Sure," Nicole said as she took the boy and wrapped her arms around him. She turned his head away from the car so he would not witness what was going on. His cries had slowed down to quiet sobs as he rested his head on her shoulder. Nicole lifted his head to make sure he stayed awake. She saw a small lump forming on his forehead. She caressed his back to keep him calm. He tried to turn his head to look at the car, but Nicole called his name to get his attention. She wanted to keep him away from seeing the car's condition and his mother as they worked to get her out. That sight was something no one, especially a child, should ever have to witness.

Joe noticed the screams were no longer coming from inside the car. He heard a moan from time to time, but that was all. What should have been a quiet night was anything but that. EMTs, fire rescue and other helpers were calling out instructions to each other as they worked as a team. The lights from all the rescue vehicles broke the darkness of the night. It was taking everyone working together to get the woman out. Her cries were becoming less and less frequent.

A wrecker arrived at the scene, ready to pull the car up. More police had arrived. Everyone was talking on their radios to each other with instructions and details.

"We need Medi Vac here, STAT!" Bob yelled on his radio. "Tell them to land across the street. There is a field there where they can land. We'll get her up there." He turned to the men who were standing close by. "Now we need to ease her from this car. Help me position the backboard under her as we get her out." He spoke quieter after yelling for the Medi Vac. Bob cut her seat belt and placed a neck brace around her neck.

The two men were able to get her onto the backboard and then out of the car through the driver's side. It had been the only way out. The one EMT adjusted the neck brace while the other one secured her to the backboard. Then they lifted her onto the stretcher and strapped her in so she could not fall.

Joe watched them carrying the lady on the stretcher up the hill by ropes and a pulley attached to the firetruck. They disconnected the ropes and carried her on the stretcher to the helicopter that Robert had requested when he first saw the victims' injuries. As soon as the helicopter's door latched, it lifted off the ground and flew the few short miles to the hospital.

Joe had noticed the silence coming from the lady on the stretcher as the crew carried her. Whoever the woman was, she was not making a sound. It was almost eerie after hearing her screams when he and Nicole arrived on the scene earlier. He knew that head injuries bled a lot and hoped it was nothing more serious, but there was so much blood. He said a quick prayer for her, even though he believed she was already gone. There was no way she could have survived that crash.

Nicole had climbed to the road with little Marc in her arms while his mother was being rescued. She had sung to him along the way to keep him calm. The driver was taken in an ambulance while the rescue of his wife had taken place. A second ambulance arrived to take the little boy, and Nicole handed Marc over to the medic. She looked at Joe, who knew what she wanted, and nodded his approval. Nicole turned to the ambulance crew.

"May I ride along? I am a nurse and have been with him since we arrived."

They nodded to let her join them, then assisted her as she climbed in and reached for the boy's hand as she sat as close as she could without being in the way of the EMT.

Joe reached his Jeep as the ambulance carrying the little boy and his wife sped off for the hospital with the siren blaring. He took a deep breath. His adrenaline was starting to slow down. He was stepping into his Jeep when a State Trooper approached him.

“I need to ask you a few questions for the police report.”

"Sure. Officer Bakker," he said as he read the officer's name badge. He shut his door and leaned against his Jeep for support. He did not trust his legs to hold him at that moment.

"What can you tell me about the accident? Any details will help. Was there another vehicle involved? Did you see it happen? Anything will help us." Office Bakker held a notepad ready to jot down Joe's interpretation of the accident.

Joe stood, leaning on his Jeep, waiting for the officer to stop asking the ramble of questions.

"All I know is we came around the corner there," Joe pointed behind him. "And I saw the twisted guardrail. My wife and I noticed smoke or steam coming up over the embankment, and I immediately pulled over and called 911. My wife climbed over the edge to get to them to help. It all happened so fast." Joe fell silent as he envisioned the scene.

"Okay. Anything else you remember? Do you remember any other vehicle, a deer, or a bear that would have caused them to swerve, overreact?"

"No, sir. Nothing that we noticed." Joe was rubbing the back of his neck while he tried to visualize anything else that he may have seen. "You can check the 911 call for what I may have told them. I can't remember it now."

"Okay. We will be reviewing the 911 call. That's protocol. Here is my card. If you can think of anything else, please call. We need to talk with your wife." He handed Joe his card, then asked him the best way to reach him and wrote down all his information on the police report form. "You are free to go. We'll be here awhile. We have to clean up the area, analyze the wreck, and search for more details while the wrecker lifts the car out. I will touch back with you later."

"Thank you, Officer Bakker. I'm headed to the hospital to check on them and pick up my wife. She rode in the ambulance with the little boy."

"They are lucky you came along to help. Thank you. Are you alright to drive?" the officer said as Joe turned to open his door.

"Yes, I'm fine."

Joe sat for a while in his Jeep, collecting his thoughts. He glanced at his watch; it had been an eventful couple of hours. His mind started to have *what if* thoughts. What if they had taken another route and weren't there to rescue them? What if they had actually been a witness to it? What if they had been the ones that wrecked? What if, what if, what if. He knew there was no sense in thinking that way. There was nothing that could be changed at this point. He was thankful they had not been involved in it but more thankful to have been there to help. He lifted a prayer for them all, especially that the female survives for her child. A child always needs its mother. He knew too many kids who were being raised in single parent households. They always managed, but he knew having both parents made life so much easier on the children.

Chapter Four

To stay awake while she waited for a call from her brother, Sara had gotten up and washed the dishes from her morning breakfast. Yes, she was one of the few who still washed them by hand, even though she had a dishwasher. She only used that when she had company, which was not often. She was single, lived alone, and did not dirty many dishes; it was easy to hand wash them. Plus, it gave her time to look out the window and enjoy the beauty outside. It reminded her of helping her mama do the dishes when she was little.

It was their private time together to talk every day. At least it was until her siblings were old enough to help. Then her mother would give each of them a turn helping her after the evening dinner. Ah, good old family time. Now gone. She reached up and wiped a tear that had escaped from her eye.

Looking out the window after putting the last dry dish away, Sara's thoughts went to the upcoming weekend. Heather, Ben, and Marc were coming to do the final cleaning of the house they would be moving into the following week. Heather planned to decorate before they moved in to avoid doing it with all their furniture and boxes of their stuff in the way. Sara had gotten a kick out of Heather when she called it *stuff*. She was sure it was important *stuff*. Her sister was not one to keep a lot of excesses around. Heather was so unlike their mama and herself, who tended to hang on to memorabilia. Sara enjoyed mementos and had a few knick knacks on display, with more packed away.

Sara was still deep in thought about the weekend when her phone rang, startling her back to reality. She glanced at the clock and figured it must be Andy finally coming to his senses.

"Hello, I was waiting for you to call me." She answered as her heart rate returned to normal. She waited to hear her brother's voice and his explanation.

"Hello, is this Sara Fairchild?"

"Yes," Sara replied, wondering who wanted to know. It was not Andy. And most people who called knew her and knew her voice. They would not need to ask if it was her. Thinking it was one of those annoying robocalls, Sara almost hung up. They usually did not call late at night, so she waited.

"Mrs. Fairchild, this is Officer Robert James of the Sullivan County Police Department. I'm calling to let you know that there has been an accident. Your brother-in-law, Mr. Kane, wanted me to call you to let you know."

"Is he alright?" Sara cut him off before he could go on.

"Mrs. Fairchild, he wanted me to let you know that his wife has been airlifted to the Mountain View Medical Center."

Sara fell into the kitchen chair upon hearing his words. "Airlifted? Officer, how bad is she? How is Ben? Was the baby with them? Can I talk to Ben? What happened?"

"Mrs. Fairchild, Mr. Kane, and the baby are being taken by ambulance to the same hospital." You can meet them there. We can send someone out to pick you up and take you if you wish."

"No, I'll be fine. I'm on my way," Sara said as she was standing back up, gathering strength in her legs to move. "I'll meet them there. Thank you for calling." She hung up the phone, grabbed her purse and keys, and was out the front door.

She had never driven so fast in her life. Well, maybe, but this time her adrenaline was high, and her heart was pumping faster than she remembered it ever being. She was glad the police were not around to stop her and that the few traffic lights she came upon were green. Her thoughts raced as well, trying to remember what the officer had said about her sister. Had he said anything other than she had been airlifted? She couldn't remember.

She pulled into a parking spot near the emergency entrance to Mountain View Memorial and rushed inside. She was out of breath when she approached the receptionist area. "Sister, Heather Kane. Just brought in by Medivac. Where is she?" She managed to get out before taking a breath.

"Ma'am, take a deep breath." Another nurse came around the desk to ease Sara to a chair. He wanted to get her calm before they had another patient on their hands. The ER already had their hands full. Sara fought back.

"My Sister! I need to see her!"

"Ma'am, my name is Nate. We need you to please have a seat. I'll go check with the ER doctor and have him talk with you." He let go of Sara's arm when she finally sat down. As he turned to walk to the exam rooms, he glanced at the other nurse behind the desk. She shook her head as Nate walked past the nursing station. It was going to be a long night.

Sara looked at the clock. What was taking the nurse so long? Why couldn't she see her sister? Where were Ben and Marc? She started to stood up to ask about them as the nurse walked back in from the exam areas.

"Ma'am, can you come with me please?" Nate said as he reached to help her stand. He never knew how people were going to react to some news and had learned to be there to lend a helping hand of support figuratively and literally.

"How is she?"

"The doctor has asked me to take you back to see your sister to talk with her. The doctor's name is Dr. James. She will let you know the details."

By then, they were a few steps from where the exam curtain blocked anyone from seeing who was behind it. Nate called out for Dr. James to let her know that Sara was there.

"Yes, Nate. Thank you." Dr. James said as another nurse pulled the white curtain back to let Sara step closer to her sister.

"Mrs. Fairchild," Dr. James began as she walked with her to the head of the bed so she could see her sister while she spoke.

"Hi. I am Dr. Susan James. I am the doctor taking care of Mrs. Kane. She has been in a bad car accident resulting in injuries requiring surgery. We've taken x-rays, done a CT scan, and an MRI. Currently, she is resting comfortably with the help of pain meds. She's drifted in and out of consciousness. Tests indicate a concussion, and the bruises on her forehead were most likely caused by hitting the dashboard. There is no sign of a brain bleed; the Chest x-ray shows a couple of fractured ribs. We are also dealing with a compound fracture-dislocation of her right ankle. Due to the fracture's extent, we will need to set it with a plate and screws. We're waiting now on the OR."

Sara did her best to take it all in. A nurse she was not. So some of what the doctor was saying was not registering. She caught the words, no brain bleed, and ribs broken. She could not wrap her head around a plate and screws to fix a broken ankle. But she accepted that the doctor knew what she was doing.

"Does she know what is going on?" Sara asked as she gently stroked Heather's head.

"We have been talking to her, but she has not responded," Dr. James replied while writing in Heather's chart. She then pointed to Heather's arm as she continued speaking. "You can see she also has a laceration on her arm, which I have already stitched together.

Sara took Heather's hand. "Heather, it's Sara. You were in a car accident and are in the hospital. You have a broken leg, so they have to take you to surgery, but I'll be here when you get out," Sara said as calmly as she could. Inside, her heart was breaking to see her baby sister like this. She looked so frail and in so much pain. Sara did her best to keep from crying. She had to be strong.

Heather moved her fingers in Sara's hand while struggling to whisper, "Ben? Marc?"

Sara squeezed her sister's hand and looked at the doctor. "Where are her husband and son?" she asked, feeling bad that she had completely forgotten about them when she saw Heather and realizing she had more than her sister on her hands. Whatever tears she had felt were replaced with more concern and fear.

"They are being taken care of in another exam area down the hall. I heard they are okay. Nothing major."

Heather moved her head enough to show that she had heard. She may not remember later, but she knew for now. Then she drifted back to sleep.

"Can I see them when you take my sister up to surgery?"

"Yes, Ma'am. I'll have a nurse take you to them." Dr. James nodded her head toward Nicole, who was standing to the side while the doctor had examined Heather and spoke with Sara. Nicole gave Dr. James a nod. One the doctor understood. Nicole was not officially involved with this case, but she had become involved while she was off duty. As a favor, she would take Mrs. Fairchild to see her brother-in-law and nephew.

"Mrs. Fairchild, you can come with me. They are going to take Heather up to OR now so you can see Ben and Marc," Nicole said as an orderly entered the room to take Heather for surgery.

"Heather, I'll be right here when you are done. I love you." Sara squeezed her sister's hand as she stepped away, letting the orderly roll her gurney out of the exam area to go to OR.

Nicole led Sara to the next exam room. She told Sara that Marc was in another exam area across the hall with other doctors looking after him. She added that she could take her to see him. Sara wanted to see Marc first, but Ben saw her as they passed the divider curtain and called her name. He gave her a small wave and lowered his eyes as she went to him and reached for his hand.

"Ben, what happened?" Sara asked with concern. "How did the accident happen? How fast were you going?" As soon as the words were out of her mouth, she knew it was the wrong thing to say.

Ben looked up at her, cutting off whatever she was going to say next. "I wasn't going fast at all," he protested. "I know that part of the road. I know it's a dangerous curve. We were driving along on our way home from picking Marc up from the babysitter. I felt a bump. It all happened so fast." He then looked into Sara's eyes and held her hand a bit tighter. "It was not my fault." His tone softened as he let loose of her hand. "How is Heather? How is Marc? No one will tell me."

Sara hesitated to tell him the truth, but he needed to know. "Ben, she's not good. They are taking her up to the OR to operate on her broken leg. She has a concussion and a couple of broken ribs."

Ben looked away. Sara noticed his tears before he turned. "How's Marc?" he managed to say while trying to hide his tears.

"I have not heard. I was on my way to see him when you called my name. Let me ask about him. I'll be right back." Ben nodded his head and wiped away his tears. Sara turned to find Nicole patiently waiting for her by the curtain opening. Sara stepped away from Ben and met up with her saying she was ready to see Marc.

"Of course, he's right here." She opened the curtain that was a few feet from where Marc was.

Sara saw the nurse checking the monitors and wires connected to Marc.

"How is he?" Nicole asked the nurse in a whisper, doing her best not to disturb Marc.

"He's a trouper. We are watching him to make sure nothing develops from that bump on his head. Are you the nurse who was with them?"

Nicole glanced at Sara to see if she had heard that last comment. Sara did not react. She was already holding Marc's hand and stroking his hair. He seemed so small in that big bed. So innocent.

"How is he?" Sara asked. She had not heard Nicole ask the same question a few minutes earlier.

"He is doing very well, considering. We gave him some pain medication that has relaxed him, so he is sleeping. He has a bad bump on his forehead, but there is no indication of a concussion or any other injuries."

"Thank you. I need to let Ben know. I'll be right back." Sara let go of Marc's hand, reached down, gently kissed his forehead, making sure to avoid the large bump. She did not want to wake him; he needed his rest.

Sara turned to go back to Ben when she heard, "Code Blue! ER 2." Sara stopped in her tracks as medical staff ran past with the cart straight to where Ben was! She did not know many medical terms, but she knew 'Code Blue' was a life-or-death situation. She started toward him. Nicole held Sara's arm to keep her from getting in their way. She knew it was not good. He had seemed fine. He had been alert at the accident site. Injured some, yes, but not anything that would cause him to code. He had been awake and talking with Sara! There must have been more to his injuries. Shock? What more would this family have to deal with?

"What's going on?" Sara asked Nicole. "What happened? He was fine a minute ago!"

Nicole led them to the waiting area. "Sara, it will be okay. He is in the best hands", she said calmly as she held Sara's forearm as she sat beside her.

"NO! I was just in there with him! He was fine!" Sara tried to stand up, but Nicole held her arm tighter.

"Sara, stay here and let them work. You don't want to be a distraction to them." Nicole knew they had been working on him a bit longer than a quick resuscitation should have taken. That fact concerned her. She saw the medical staff walk out of the room and nod at the nursing station nurse. A sign that it was okay to go back in. A few minutes later, the nurse came to let Nicole and Sara know they could see Ben. Nicole stood and inquired about Ben's condition.

"They got him back. The doctor is in with him now. Not sure what caused him to *leave* us. But they revived him, rather quickly." She had added the word *quickly* so only Nicole could hear her. She was not at liberty to tell Sara how bad things may be.

"Thank you," she nodded.

Sara and Nicole walked to Ben's side. He was lying on his bed with his eyes closed.

"Okay. He has stabilized," the doctor said as he finished checking Ben's vitals. "We're going to run more tests to see what's going on. He may have internal injuries we hadn't seen. Or it could have been from shock."

"Thank you, doctor. Can I talk with him?"

"Of course. But keep his stress level to a minimum. Until we figure out what is wrong, we need to take precautions."

Sara pulled up a stool and sat down next to Ben's bed. "Hang in there, Ben; we need you. Your family needs you. Your son needs you. Heather needs you!"

Nicole nodded to Sara and pointed to the curtain's opening as a way of saying she was leaving. Sara nodded back and whispered, "I'll be okay. Thank you," she smiled.

Her thoughts started jumping from one thing to another as Ben slept. Would she really be alright? Could she handle all of this? How was her sister? In all honesty, how was Ben doing? Was Marc going to remember any of this later in life? She took a deep breath as she felt a tear slide down her cheek. So much had happened in the last 24 hours. It had already been a very long night. It was going to be a very long day. It could be a very long month, maybe a very long year – again. She had already buried her parents and lost touch with her baby brother again. Now she was hoping and praying that her sister and brother-in-law would survive. How would she survive without them? She laid her head back against the back of her chair and closed her eyes. The hum of the machines lulled her to sleep and dreamland.

Chapter Five

Daniel woke up in a small, smokey, and musty hotel room. He gradually opened his eyes, straining to see through the darkness. His head hurt. He felt nauseous. He attempted to get up and nearly fell to the floor. The room was spinning. He held his head as he lay his head back down on the pillow and closed his eyes.

What was going on? His head was not clear enough to make any sense of where he was, nor why he felt this way. He closed his eyes tighter in an attempt to make the headache go away. He waited while his mind woke up. He could not believe what was coming to his mind. He forced his eyes to open again, and this time looked around the room.

He hoped it was all a bad dream. He rolled over on the bed and forced himself to sit up while he opened his eyes all the way. There on the small round wooden table by the window was what he feared he would find. One bottle was lying on its side. The other was standing tall and proud.

"Look at us," the two bottles of Jack Daniels seemed to say. "Look what we did, glad we could help," they mocked. If he could stand up, he would take both bottles and throw them as far away from him as he could.

He hated himself – again.

Daniel had once been a handsome young man with dark brown natural wavy hair, blue eyes, and a muscular build. He was of average height at an even six feet. Although he never pursued a long-term relationship with anyone when he was younger, the women loved him. He enjoyed the attention and friendship. He was in college when he had his first lasting relationship. And even that one had lasted less than a year.

He had gotten in with the wrong crowd in college. The drinking and drugs took their toll by the time he graduated. He was impressed that he had even graduated and was more impressed to have secured a good-paying job. He knew a few of the kids he had partied with never made it that far. Two of them had died from overdoses. Daniel had given up drugs after his closest friend died of an overdose. He eventually found sobriety through AA and support from new friends.

After college, his first job was in the hotel business and provided him financial security, his own apartment, a new car, and love. He was a success. Life was good. At least for a while.

Then he started drinking again. He enjoyed showing off his beautiful girlfriend and his status by going out to bars and clubs and buying drinks for his many friends. Soon this way of life took its toll, and he lost his job after just two years due to his drunken behavior and missing so much work.

It did not take long before he lost his car, his apartment, and then his girlfriend. He felt hopeless with no place to go, and no one who wanted him. He saw no way out of his rut. He continued drinking and rarely was sober.

His refuge was a men's shelter in town. It was a place to receive a meal, sleep at night, and meet other people - homeless people. He also met with counselors who came each week to talk with the men, encourage them, and help them find work to get them back on their feet and off drugs and alcohol.

Daniel had avoided talking with the counselors at first. He was so distraught he rarely looked up. He had no ambition to start over. No goals. No desire to improve. He had decided that being a drunk was all he would ever be.

Then a new counselor arrived one day and befriended him. The counselor took the time to talk and encouraged Daniel to tell his story while he patiently listened. Daniel opened up one day when he asked if there was a way for him to start his life over. He wanted to stop drinking, to find a new job and a new life. The counselor was more than willing to help him out.

Daniel started attending AA meetings again and got sober. He found a new job as a caterer at a local restaurant. He saved his money, found a tiny apartment, and bought a used car. Life was looking good again, though not for long.

Now here he was. At the bottom – again. Why? How? When had life gone downhill? Daniel was still trying to clear his head and think straight as he stood up and staggered into the bathroom to take a shower. He was going to face this day if it was the last thing he did.

On his way to the bathroom, he bumped into the table by the front window. He picked up the two bottles that lay almost empty on their sides. On the way to the wastebasket near the bathroom door to throw them out, he lifted the one to his lips. Before taking another swig, he saw his reflection in the mirror. Reality stared back at him. He poured the remains of both bottles down the drain and dropped the empty bottles into the wastebasket.

He took a long hot shower, got dressed, tossed his belongings into his suitcase, and walked out the door where he met the brilliant sunshine of the day. Taking a deep cleansing breath, he headed to the hotel lobby to check out of his room. His mind was becoming clearer, but he had no clue where he was.

According to the address on his receipt and the brochures in the lobby, he was in Pennsylvania. He shook his head when he realized he had somehow driven to familiar territory—that of his childhood.

He took the time to inhale some breakfast in the hotel dining area just as they were closing for the day. He had not realized it was so late. There was not much food left, but the black coffee tasted good going down, plus it helped clear his head. The pastry was stale, and the banana had brown spots on the peel, but he ate them anyway. After eating, his head felt clearer, and overall, he felt better. He refilled his coffee cup and headed to his car. He wanted to get on the road and make it to his destination. Knowing he was in Pennsylvania, he assumed it was for a vacation to where his parents had vacationed when he was a kid. He had not been there in years. It would feel great to go back and enjoy a few days at the lake.

He was starting to feel positive again. He did not know why he had been drinking the night before but decided not to dwell on it. He put his suitcase in the trunk then walked around the car to check the tires and make sure the car was okay. It was an old habit that he started after watching his Dad do the same thing every day before heading to work, and every time the family went anywhere.

As he reached the front passenger side of his car, he noticed dents in the right front fender. His beautiful white Toyota Camry that he loved was damaged. He took a deep breath as he tried to figure out who may have hit him during the night. He had parked right outside his room. Why had he not heard anything?

His eyes stared into space as it all started coming back to him. He leaned his hands against the hood of the car to steady himself. He understood now why he was traveling and why he had been drinking in his hotel room. He had been drinking earlier that day, possibly for days before that. He looked again at the dents. No one else had hit his car; he had hit something. That is what caused the damage to his car. He had been in a car accident, one where he had kept going. He did not remember when or where. He shook his head as he looked to the ground.

A drunk driver. A screw-up--Again! A tear slid down his left cheek.

He knew the damage to his car was not too bad and assumed the other vehicle had not suffered too much either. He thought it could have been a tree or pole. That would explain why he had not stopped. But what if? What if he had caused more damage to another car? Or hurt someone? He closed his eyes. He could not picture where he had been. He could not even visualize another vehicle. In his heart, he knew he had caused an accident. Now what was he going to do? It could not have happened too far away from where he was.

The more he thought about it, the more he realized that if it had been nearby, the police would have found him by now. Maybe no other vehicle had been involved, and there was no reason to worry.

Daniel took a deep breath. "Nothing I can do about it now," he thought. "Time to head to the lake." Daniel started the car and headed north.

The roads heading North into Pennsylvania were a challenge with the potholes, rough pavement, and road construction. He chuckled, remembering his parents saying that there were two seasons in that state, Winter and road construction. He noticed that some areas were pretty with fields of grass, pasture with barns and farm animals, while other areas along the way looked dirty and dark even with the sun shining. He remembered why he had not been back since he was a teenager traveling with his parents. He had lost interest when he found other things to do closer to home. The drive had become boring, and he found no fun in the things his parents thought he would enjoy doing. He found no joy in doing the same thing every year.

His parents had spent two weeks every summer at the lake. He could only remember the faces of a few people they had met during the years he had been with them. He hoped none of them would remember him, especially the businesspeople. His appearance had changed over the last fifteen years due to drugs and alcohol. Even his hair that he currently wore short and dyed blond was different.

He made a stop for gas and then stopped for dinner at a small mom and pop restaurant just off an exit. Noticing a billboard for a local bar, he hesitated before he parked his car. He so desperately wanted a drink and glanced at the billboard one more time before he parked and walked inside the restaurant, avoiding the temptation. He avoided eye contact with anyone as he followed the hostess to a booth in a quiet corner. He ordered comfort food of meatloaf, mashed potatoes, and corn, then waited, hoping no one noticed him. He ate in silence, doing his best to not bring attention to himself. He ordered a coffee to go before paying his bill in cash, including a good tip, and quietly walked out to his car to continue his trip.

His eyes began to feel heavy as darkness overtook the day. Fatigued and not liking to drive at night, he opted for a hotel room. He was too tired to drive the final miles to his destination. Stopping would also give him a chance to think about the accident and his future.

He felt mentally lost as he closed his eyes, hoping for a good night's sleep. He tossed and turned. He had a lot on his mind. His craving for a drink was not helping. He had done all he could to avoid going to the bar down the hall. His room was so close to it he could hear the clatter of glasses and laughter of the patrons well past midnight. He was proud of himself for not giving in. In his earlier years he would have gone in and had a few to start. Seeing his damaged car and not knowing how it happened had affected him. He knew he had been sober for several months. He could not remember why he had a drink, nor if his drinking had caused the accident, although that could be why he was running, again. He opened his eyes, realizing he was not on vacation; he was running – backward.

He envisioned the lake. The gentle waves of the water. The warmth of the sun. The rocking of the boat. He saw sunshine, felt the heat on his face. Sleep finally won and produced dreams of happier times.

Chapter Six

Sara woke with a start, momentarily confused. As soon as reality dawned, she returned to Marc's room so he would see someone he knew when he woke up. Being a two-year-old alone in a hospital must be scary. She hated that she had fallen asleep but smiled, seeing nurse Nicole sitting by her nephew's side, holding his hand when she entered the room.

"Hi Nicole," Sara said in a quiet tone. "Thank you for being here." Sara noticed Nicole was wearing her name badge but that she was not in typical nursing scrubs. "Are you his nurse tonight?"

"Oh, no. I'm off duty. I normally work on the rehab floor, not in the ER, except for special cases." She looked at Marc, then turned to Sara and added, "I was there."

"Where?"

"At the accident scene."

"Oh," Sara replied with a deflated breath. Several visions flooded her mind. She immediately had so many questions she could not figure out which one to ask first. "You saw what happened? Talk to me." She pulled the chair up to Marc's bed, took his other hand but looked straight at Nicole.

Nicole stopped holding Marc's hand and rubbed her fingers over her forehead before turning her attention to Sara.

"Mrs. Fairchild," she started.

"Please, call me Sara, and it's Ms, not Mrs."

"Okay, Sara. I don't know what the police have told you."

"They didn't tell me much of anything. Except that there was an accident, and that Heather, Ben, and Marc were on their way to this hospital. Heather by the Medivac with Ben and Marc going by ambulance. I told them I was on my way, and I guess I cut him off before he could tell me more. No one has told me any details of the accident. I've been too busy to ask for more than their conditions and what is being done for them. What do you know?"

Nicole hesitated before answering. "Well, my husband Joe and I were driving home and saw what turned out to be steam rising from the embankment. I yelled for Joe to stop as he was already pulling over. I ran out of the Jeep to get to the vehicle while he called 911. Joe and I reached the car before the medics and did what we could. They took over as soon as they arrived. When they pulled Marc out of the car the medic handed him to me while they worked to get Heather out. Ben was out of the car by the time I reached it, but he was not talking much. He was in shock and collapsed near their car after saying that his wife and son were inside. I asked to ride along in the ambulance with Marc so he would not be alone with the EMT. They let me ride along because I was a nurse and had been there for him at the accident site." She hoped that was enough information. She wanted to spare Sara from the full details.

Sara reached for Nicole's hand. "Thank you," she whispered.

"No thanks needed. I'm glad we happened to be there at that moment. We were on our way home and decided to take the back road instead of the main interstate. We usually avoid going that route because it is such a dangerous road. But something was telling us to take that road today. Now I know why."

"The officer told me that the accident was on Highway 36. That is a dangerous road. I've heard of several accidents there. They need to do something about it."

"I agree, which is why we take the other road most of the time."

"Did you see what happened? Did someone run them off the road? An animal? Anything?"

"No, they were already down the embankment when we arrived. We didn't notice any other vehicle pass us or coming from the other direction. It could have been a deer Ben tried to avoid and swerved too far. That happens sometimes. There are only woods in that area, and deer, even bears, are known to live in that stretch of woods."

"I hope they find out what caused it. Ben told me he felt a bump before the accident but has no idea what the bump was. That was all he knew."

"I'm glad none of them are worse or that no one died! I've seen enough of that working here."

"Yes, I'm sure you have. Sara lowered her head, imagining if things had been worse and what she would do if they were. She pulled her mind back to reality. "Have you heard how Heather is doing in surgery?"

"No, I've not heard." She glanced at her watch. "They should be done soon. They are pretty good at notifying the family."

The door to Marc's ER room opened before she could say more. "Mrs. Fairchild?"

"Yes, it's *Ms* Fairchild, but that's me," Sara replied as she turned to face the voice. It was Nate, the nurse who had met her when she first arrived at the ER.

"The surgeon called and said everything went well in surgery. Heather is going to be taken to recovery and then up to her room. The doctor will be down in a few minutes to talk to you."

"Thanks. When can I see my sister?"

"As soon as she is out of recovery and in her room, we will send for you," the nurse said as he turned to go. Having a second thought, he turned back to Sara. "Is there anything we can get for you? You've been here quite a while. Is someone else here with you? Someone else we could call?"

Thanks. I'll be here. And, no, I'm fine. Nicole has been here for me." She then turned to Nicole and smiled. The nurse nodded his head and walked out of the room.

"When are they going to move Marc to a regular room?" Sara asked Nicole with concern. "He's napping, but otherwise they said he was okay. I would think by now they would know if there were other issues besides the bump on his head."

"I agree with you; they should know something by now. Let me talk to the head nurse. She should know some details."

Nicole walked out of the room. She looked back at Sara and Marc with concern, then turned toward the nurses' station. It was going to be hard to say goodbye to little Marc. She had grown fond of him in the several hours she had known him. She blinked to keep from shedding a tear. It was surprising how fast you could get attached to someone. That was her only hindrance to her nursing career. Nicole whispered to the nurse at the nurses' station, asking about Marc's room transfer, Ben's condition, and any information she could get on Heather.

"Slow down. One patient inquiry at a time." The nurse said as she raised her head above the computer monitor. "They are preparing a room at the children's wing for Marc. The nurse will move him over there shortly. Ben is improving, but we want to hold him for observation. Since he collapsed at the scene and then almost losing him here, we need to monitor him. Now for Heather, let's see." The nurse was looking at the computer for updates. "Her surgery went well. They had to put some screws into her leg to hold it in place. They also, oh my," she hesitated and looked up at Nicole.

"What is it?" Nicole strained to catch a glimpse of the computer monitor over the nurse's shoulder.

"Dr. George stitched her arm where she had a deep laceration. And it looks like she has another laceration on her face that needed several stitches. She has several injuries," she said, then immediately shut down that screen as if it was all she saw.

Nicole could tell there was more on the chart. Sara's family was not her case, nor was the ER her department, so she did not ask any further questions. She was only there to help Sara.

"Thank you. I'll let Sara know. If there is anything else you can share, I'd appreciate it. Sara is the next of kin, so you can let her know any updates." She tilted her head and raised her eyes at the nurse.

She knew there was more going on with one of the three patients, although she did not know which one. Nicole left the nurses' station and walked back to Marc's room to give Sara the updates on everyone.

"Okay," Nicole said as she pulled up the other chair to sit near Sara. "Here is what I found out for you. Ben is improving, but they want to keep an eye on him in the ER for a bit. They are getting a room ready for Marc in the children's wing. Heather has come through surgery and will be in recovery for a while, which they have already told you. They will let you know when she is transferred to her room so you can see her. In the meantime, we can stay with Marc, so he isn't afraid."

Sara smiled slightly. "Thanks, Nicole. You are a Godsend. I'm not sure what I'd do if you weren't here. I feel like my world is caving in around me."

"No, it's not caving in. They will all be okay. You will be okay." Nicole patted Sara's forearm to reassure her.

"Mrs. Fairchild?" a quiet voice sounded from outside Marc's room.

"Yes, come in," Sara called out through the door. She had given up correcting everyone about her name. She assumed they were quiet because Marc was asleep, even though he was now awake and squirming in the bed. The doctor walked in and was surprised to see Marc sitting up.

"Wow, look at you," he said to Marc. "You're awake!" He lifted Marc's arm to check his pulse, felt his head for fever, and checked his eyes. All seemed to be fine. "You are doing great, little one. Are you ready to move into your own room?" Marc smiled and nodded his head as he looked at his Aunt Sara. Without saying a word, she knew what he was thinking.

"No, Sweetheart, it's not your room at home. It is a different room here at the hospital. I'll be right by your side; no need for you to be afraid. I won't let them take you anywhere without me. Or nurse Nicole," she added, smiling at the angel who had been there for her. Nicole was a godsend.

Marc reached his arms up to Sara for a hug and started to cry. She embraced him as he cried. She was careful not to move him much due to the IV still being attached to him.

"Mommy?" Marc asked while looking up at Sara. She wiped away his tears. "I want my Mommy."

"Oh, Sweetie," Sara held him a bit tighter as she spoke. "Your Mommy is in another room. Another doctor is taking good care of her. She will come to see you as soon as she can."

She wondered how she was supposed to tell a two-year-old that his mom was hurt so bad that it may be several days before he would see her. She was doing her best to hold it all together for herself, let alone for Marc.

"I want Daddy." He started to cry more as he buried his head into the bend of her neck.

"He is with another doctor. Let's see if we can stop in to see him on our way to your new room. He will come to see you as soon as he can too."

Marc wrapped his arms tighter around her. He started crying harder and louder. Sara was at a loss of what to do and what to say as she held him tighter with one arm and rubbed his back to calm him down with her other arm. She sat on his bed with him on her lap and rocked him like she had when he was a baby.

Nicole put her hand on Sara's shoulder. Sara looked up at her, saw her wink, and then noticed her other hand behind her back. "Are you okay? What do you have behind you?" Sara asked.

"Shhh," Nicole said, her index finger raised to her lips.

"Marc," Nicole whispered as she bent a bit closer to the little boy she had become fond of curled up in Sara's arms. His sobs quieted down. He raised his head to look at her while he wiped his eyes. Nicole smiled as she brought her right hand out from behind her back and handed him a cute little tan teddy bear wearing a blue bow tie. She held it out to Marc. He reached out, took it into his arms, and hugged it close.

His grip loosened from around Sara, and she laid him back on his pillow. She rubbed his head, careful not to touch the bump, reassuring him that he was safe with her. She smiled up at Nicole.

"Thank you. I have no idea what I would have done without you here."

"I am glad to be here. I will stay here as long as you need me."

She looked at Marc holding his teddy bear and smiled when she realized he had stopped crying.

Chapter Seven

The blaring sounds of sirens came from the distance growing louder as they got closer. It blended with the sounds of screams and moans rising from a few feet away. The sounds of squealing tires, metal crunching, and breaking trees preceded a sudden thud that whipped her head back and forth and with pain pulsating through her leg. Heather had a nightmare again. She hated it, but he could not shake it.

She kept her eyes closed as she had in the past. She knew she was supposed to be working on her memory of the accident. Yet her recurring nightmare was as far as she had gotten no matter how she tried. She always awoke from it with the vehicle's sudden stopping that gave her a noticeable physical jolt. She could not remember any more details of her dream either when she first awoke from it, or later when she tried to delve back to relive it.

She knew she had been in a car accident. She knew her husband and son were okay. She had learned all this by asking her nurse, her doctor, and her sister. They had been reluctant to tell her any details at first. They wanted her to remember everything on her own, but the doctor told them they could fill her in with a few details to encourage her.

Dr. James had become her regular doctor after treating her in the ER. She told Heather and her family that she was sure Heather's amnesia would dissipate in time. Her memory loss was due to her head injury and concussion.

She closed her eyes harder this time. She searched inside her head, looking for more details, more answers. She knew the police wanted answers. But there was nothing. It frustrated her that she could not remember the accident nor her first week in the hospital.

Heather took a deep breath as she woke up and looked around. She knew she was being released to go home today. Her doctor had told her there was nothing more they could do there that could not be done as an outpatient, so her sister was taking her home.

She wondered why Ben was not coming to get her to take her home to their house. Why had she not seen him in a few days? Or had he been there, but she could not remember? She looked around her room to see if there were any clues for her. A note from Ben. Anything. Maybe he was preparing for her return and was going to surprise her when she got home.

Her room at the rehab facility resembled a typical private hospital room. Her bed, positioned near the bathroom, the TV hanging on the wall facing her bed, the nightstand by her bed, and a spare reclining chair made up her room arrangement. The large window to her right still had the curtains drawn, and she could not tell if it was still dark out or if the sun was up. She glanced at the clock that hung on the wall next to the TV and saw that it was 10:15 AM, which meant the sun should be shining.

She sat up in her bed as she heard voices outside her door. She hoped it was the doctor getting everything ready for her to get out of this place. She was tired of being in there. Hospitals were not fun! Heather swung her feet over the edge of the bed, preparing to stand up. She wanted to look outside to see the sunshine. That was when she realized she could not remember the last time she had looked out, let alone been outside. She did her best to think back, then shook her head. It did not matter when it had been. She was getting ready to go home and be with her family. She could deal with her memory at home. She reached over for the crutches so she could stand up and walk, or hop, over to the window when she heard a knock on her door.

"Come in," she answered as she sat back down on her bed and rested the crutches against the nightstand. Dr. George, and her favorite nurse, Nicole, walked in. Dr. George was a tall, slender woman who wore heels and, to some, looked intimidating. She wore her shoulder-length, dark brown hair in a bob cut with one side pushed behind her ear.

Heather liked Dr. George, but it was Nicole that held a special place in her heart. She had been the one nurse she remembered seeing the most. She felt there was a deeper reason she felt connected to her, but, like her other memories, she could not recall why. Nicole was spunky, cheerful, and always had a smile, even on Heather's worst days that raised her spirits. She was a short-haired blonde, with uncommon dark brown eyes, who wore the perfect amount of makeup, and was the sunshine in Heather's life. Heather smiled when they came in.

“We're here for your final check-up before we let you escape this place," Dr. George said with a smile. "You are free to go as soon as we get this paperwork signed." She leafed through the file in her hand. "I imagine you are more than ready to go home. Do you have any questions for me? Any for Nicole?" Dr. George set the medical forms on the rolling table at the foot of the bed then moved the table so Heather could read them and sign them.

"I'm feeling fine, considering. The only issue is that I hate using these crutches. I don't plan to use them forever! I can't remember everything yet about the accident, but you told me it would take time. And you told me that I didn't need to be here if I promised to start outpatient therapy as soon as possible. I guess the only question is, 'where is a pen?" Heather smiled and reached out her hand for a pen.

"Yes, Heather, we are releasing you to complete your recovery at home. However, if you have any concerns you want to discuss, I want you to call my office and tell me. I am keeping you on as my patient until you are 100% better and back to the person you were before," she cut herself off before completing her train of thought. Heather did not need to know the extent of her condition, not yet.

Nicole had been listening while getting Heather's belongings from the small closet for her to take home. She wanted to assure Heather that everything would be fine, even if she was not sure it would be for this beautiful young lady. Thanks to Sara, Nicole had learned a lot about Heather while she had been under her care. Sara had been there every day helping her sister. Nicole hoped in a way that Heather would never remember all the details of what she had endured. Life would be easier if those memories stayed hidden.

There was another knock at the door and the three of them, Dr. George, Nicole, and Heather answered in unison. "Come in."

They were laughing when Sara walked in with a suitcase and looked at each of them with raised eyebrows. "Why is everyone laughing? Is there good news about my sister?"

Heather stood up on one leg, put her right hand on her hip, looked at her older sister, "I'm right here, and I can hear you. I'm doing just fine. We're all laughing because we all said to come in at the same time. Now let's go home." She reached for her crutches before she fell over. They all smiled. Heather was getting her sense of humor back. That was a good sign.

Sara turned to her baby sister and smiled. "I know you are here, just wondering if there are any improvements or anything new, I need to know, such as if you are up to running a marathon."

Dr. George shook her head from side to side. "No, nothing new to share except that is a definite no to marathons just yet. I am discharging her into your care for her further treatment and home rehab exercises. Be sure she continues with the follow-up appointments. Call me if there are any major changes or anything that concerns you." Dr. George finished double-checking the form. "I look forward to her complete recovery." She added that last statement while looking straight at Sara.

Sara could read between the lines and sensed the doctor was not sure she would recover completely. She knew that Heather may have some emotional setbacks when she saw her full medical report. After all, Heather was not aware that it had been two months since her world had changed in a split second and how much of her world was different. Luckily Heather did not remember all of the accident nor all the details about her life after the accident. Physically she was stable enough to resume her everyday life. Mentally there was a lot of work to do. They all hoped that being home would help her more than staying in rehab.

"Okay, Sis, let's get your stuff packed and get out of here," Sara said as she lifted the suitcase onto the bed and opened it. "Dr. George, is there any paperwork or forms I or Heather need to sign?"

"No, it's all signed, sealed, and delivered, as the saying goes. Thank you so much for being able to take care of your sister. At least she has you."

Nicole, who had been quiet, turned to Sara. "I'd like to continue to help you if I could. Here is my card with my contact information. I can come out to help you or be available to talk on the phone. Ms. Heather here is one special lady." Nicole handed her card to Sara and then reached out to stroke Heather's hair. Heather jerked away.

"Sorry," Heather said. "I just don't want – oh, never mind what I want, you just startled me."

"Thanks, Nicole. I will post this on the refrigerator in case we need it," Sara said with a smile as she dropped the card into her jacket pocket. Nicole nodded and headed out the door. See you again soon," she said as she closed the door.

"Okay, Heather, let's finish up here," Sara said as she closed the suitcase she had been packing. All the things had fit in it except a few floral arrangements and a small cactus plant. "Let's see about getting everything in one trip. The faster we can get out of here, the better. You've been here long enough."

"I agree; a couple of weeks is long enough," Heather said as she put on her green cardigan sweater. Sara shook her head as she looked away from her sister and glanced at the floor. It was going to be a long journey for the two of them.

Nicole knocked on the door as she automatically walked back in, pushing a wheelchair for Heather's escort down to the car. Hospital rules. "Told you I'd see you soon," Nicole commented with her usual smile and sparkle in her eyes. "Now, if you're ready, let's get this show on the road and get you on the road to recovery."

"Yes, let's go!" Heather said as she stood up on her one good leg. She turned and sat in the wheelchair, placing the crutches on her lap facing the floor. They left the hospital's rehab ward after one more look as they headed for yet another world of the unknown.

Who knew what being home would be like for her. Sara was concerned. She knew that she had a lot to deal with once they left the confines of this place. The place that had been Heather's home for longer than Heather realized. Her rehab had been slow and painful. But at least now she was walking again. Even if it were with crutches, those would only be temporary if she continued working hard in her outpatient therapy.

A lot of thoughts ran through Sara's mind as she drove from the parking lot to the curb at the hospital's rehab entrance. How was she going to manage it all on her own? How was she going to explain things? She knew Heather would be full of questions. She had a lot of questions herself. Why did their parents have to be gone? Why was she the one left holding it all together? Six months. A lot had happened in those six months. And they still did not know where their brother was.

She cleared her mind as she pulled to a stop to pick up her younger sister to take her home. Now was not the time to worry.

Nicole helped Heather out of the wheelchair, who then hopped to the car. She hated her crutches and had mastered the art of hopping short distances while in rehab.

Sara walked around to the passenger side of the car. Heather had already settled herself into the seat, including connecting her seat belt. Sara caught Nicole before she went back inside with the wheelchair. "Thank you so much for all you have done over these last couple of months. You have been there for my entire family. You have spent most, if not all, of your spare time with Heather or members of my family. Please thank your husband for letting us borrow you."

"He's been out of town working but should be coming home tonight. I have missed him so much. It was my honor to be with you and your family. I've grown to like you all very much. I hope all goes well, and Heather has a complete recovery."

"Nicole, you and Joe are welcome at Bella Rose Manor any time. Stop by to say hi or come and spend a vacation with us – when we get it up and running again. We have our work cut out for us once we get home." She tipped her head toward Heather. "I will have her up and running around helping soon." We were so close to finishing the remodeling when the accident happened. Life stopped for a while for all of us."

"She will do fine. Another couple of weeks and the walking cast should come off. She'll need physical therapy for a while to get her strength back in that leg, but she's young and has done well so far." She turned the wheelchair around to go back into the hospital. "Take care, Sara. I will be stopping by. We may indeed make a reservation when we are both home and free. I'll hold you to that invitation."

"I look forward to it. Have a great rest of the day. Say hello to Joe for us. I've not met him, but he must be a wonderful man." Sara reached out to Nicole. They hugged goodbye. Nicole said goodbye to Heather then took the wheelchair into the hospital so someone else could use it. She turned and waved as Sara pulled away and headed home.

Chapter Eight

Heather adjusted well to living with Sara, and following her physical therapy, was off her crutches within the first month at home. Her lacerations healed with only the scars to show for her injuries. She had discussed plastic surgery with Dr. George but had decided against it. Her scars were a part of her life story. And what a story she now had.

Heather had been excited to be going home. She knew Ben and Marc would be there to greet her. Instead, neither were there, and she soon resolved herself to the fact that Ben had taken Marc and walked away. He had already filed for a divorce and full custody. She had been kept in the dark about it while she was in rehab. Now that she knew the truth, she did not understand why he would do such a thing to her and her son. What had she done that was so wrong? The accident was not her fault. True, her injuries had left scars, and she had a limp, but she was the same person inside that she had always been. At least she thought she was. Except, of course, part of her memory was still missing. She still could not remember all the details of the accident. She could not remember what happened immediately before the wreck.

It was not until later in her discussions with her doctor that she found out she had been pregnant and lost the baby. That was when she realized that Ben must have left because he felt guilty. They would be having a baby in a couple of months if it had not been for the accident. She sank into a depression for a few weeks when she learned she had lost the baby. She still felt sad when she thought about it. They had always wanted another child. Now her doctor said they might not be able to have more children. Plus, with Ben gone, it was doubtful she would be a mother to anyone except

Marc. She did not even have Marc at the moment. She would not even have custody of her only son if Ben won the custody battle in their divorce.

A divorce she was determined to fight. She told Ben that she would not sign the papers. She wanted him to go to counseling and that she would go too if it would help. Ben thought about it, then agreed to attend counseling. He also agreed to let Heather see Marc whenever she wanted. He still loved her deep down, but his wife was right; he could not get rid of the guilt. Her injuries were his fault. It was his fault that her face held scars that would be visible for the rest of her life. It was his fault she may never walk normally again. His fault she had lost the baby. How could she ever forgive him?

Sara and Heather worked on the manor as soon as Heather got home and could move around enough to help. They wanted to get it up and running as they had planned before the accident. Ben held to his agreement with Sara and helped his crew continue the remodeling. He kept his crew working on other projects during the slow down following the accident.

Life was getting back to normal. Heather believed it could be completely normal if Ben would tear up the divorce papers and they reunited. She had the patience to wait. Ben remained living at their other house after his discharge from the hospital. Heather moved out of Sara's house and into her own at the estate as soon as she was mobile. It should have been with Ben and Marc, but that was not in the cards for the time being. She still held onto the hope that he would come back to her so they could be a family again.

A light snow had fallen overnight, glistened in the sunlight like iridescent glitter across the yard. It was winter's attempt to hold on a while longer. They hoped this snow was the last of the season because their soft reopening was in a month, and they needed good weather. Sara was already taking in reservations for the soft opening and a few for the grand opening weekend.

The official grand opening was the second weekend of April. The girls originally wanted it the first weekend of April until they noticed the date was April first. They were not superstitious, but they never knew about those things and did not want to jink themselves.

Leaning against the stove while waiting for the cinnamon rolls to bake, Sara looked around the kitchen and smiled as she, Heather, and Ben enjoyed the freshly brewed coffee she had made. Heather and Ben may not currently be together as a couple, but they had not divorced either. Marc was enjoying his milk in his favorite sippy cup while sitting in his booster seat. He was full of giggles and laughed as he made a mess of the cinnamon roll while eating it. The events of the accident seemed a distant memory for him. Yes, Sara thought to herself, life had changed, but it was still good. Marc was growing and had healed completely. Ben was back to normal, and Heather was well on her way to a full recovery, except for her scars and limp that would be there for life.

After breakfast, the girls cleaned up the kitchen while Ben went outside to brush the snow off the front porch. Marc walked off to the play area where his toys were in the toy box.

"Are you ready to do this?" Heather asked Sara as they met in the great room to do a walk-through checking on what needed completion.

"Are you kidding? I've been ready. It's the manor that wasn't ready. Let's get started."

They interlocked their arms and walked to the foyer to start the final tour, visualizing it as their guests would. They had taken Ben's offer and hired Cecelia, who worked for him, to help with the decorating. She was good at it, and Heather was grateful for the help. Cecelia was unable to do the walk through with them, so they made notes.

They separated their locked arms and began their inspection. The replaced front door was now a beautiful red wooden door with side windows. The first note Heather made was for wreaths to hang on the front door. She added the idea to change them with each season. She also added that the front porch needed plants and chairs. These would create a place for guests to sit outside and visit while enjoying the view.

The ladies turned from the foyer and walked into the great room where a sofa and two loveseats were already in place. A recliner sat in a corner with an end table. Two cane rocking chairs sat on either side of the stonework framed fireplace at the far end of the room. A local stone mason had created the frame around the fireplace. The wooden mantle was hand-carved from local chestnut by another local artist. Heather noted that they still needed an area rug in the center under the coffee table. She wanted to showcase the hardwood flooring that went throughout the living space on the first floor but wanted the carpet to add warmth.

Then came the dining area that opened into the kitchen. The girls had debated keeping it as a separate space from the kitchen but opening it up made more sense. They wanted it formal, yet family friendly, as well as comfortable. A large table sat towards the back of the dining room with a smaller table along the room's side. They could feed forty people in that room or make it cozy for a few guests. Sara made a note to ask Cecelia about more artwork on the dining room walls. The kitchen area was complete with all the new appliances, countertop, and fresh painted walls. The center island with the tall chairs around it made it perfect for their family gatherings to continue as they had been when the girls were young.

Next, they walked through part of the great room to go to the office and then the library. To their right was an area they had set up for the kids to play. It was set apart from the seating in the living room, but close enough that the parents could keep an eye on the kids as they played.

Between the kitchen and office was the library, convenient for all the guests, adjacent to the great room. The room's focal point was the cushioned window seat adorned with pillows with a view of the side garden. It had a simple valance window treatment allowing guests to sit and read while enjoying the view. Bookshelves lined one complete wall and were full of various books, photos, and local art pieces. A sizable built-in cabinet filled with board games with a table in front of it occupied most of the left wall. Guests were welcomed to sit to play games or put a puzzle together or read. A bit old fashioned for some, but great for memories for families as well.

The office, with its front-facing window, had Sara's antique desk in the middle facing the office door, a large file cabinet along the back wall, with an additional table along the sidewall for paperwork and files. A hidden closet in the corner held the safe with shelves for office supplies. Both rooms were ready for opening day. Sara had been using the office as soon as they completed it.

Next, they inspected the guestrooms. The girls had named each guestroom after a different quilt pattern. A quilt made in that pattern would lay on each bed. A matching quilted wall hanging would hang on the wall above each headboard. Decorative throw pillows lay across the head of the bed. A cut-glass vase crafted by local merchants sat on each dresser and would hold fresh cut flowers for each new arrival. Each guestroom also had a wicker trunk on the floor at the foot of the bed. Inside were two extra blankets, two extra pillows, and a small lap quilt.

To make their guests feel a part of their own family and a part of their history, the girls included a small notebook and pen that rested on the trunk. They would encourage each guest to write a review of the manor, comment on their room, or write whatever they liked in the notebook. Each notebook had a brief handwritten story of the history of the manor and the family that owned it. It was those personal touches that would help make Bella Rose Manor a favorite place for travelers to stay.

Heather continued taking notes of the colors of each room and what was missing. She made a note to contact the quilters for an update on their delivery. The last update she had was that the local quilting bee was hand quilting them.

They headed upstairs to the other guest rooms when they finished with the first floor. On the second floor, the four rooms followed the décor of those on the first floor.

The third floor had only two rooms that could be used as guest rooms as they each had private but smaller bathrooms. Recently one was used for seasonal storage and the other room, now locked, was the *attic*. Heather and Sara remembered their mama writing in that room and how they would play there while she wrote. This room was the room they could not enter until after they reopened and were making a profit. Of course, they still had to find Andy before that could happen. Heather went to the office after their tour and contacted local merchants to update her orders and order a few new items. She hoped they would all arrive on time. Everyone was excited about the manor's reopening. It had a long history in town, and the town businesses had all suffered some when it closed. Soon they all would benefit from the guests. She also called Cecelia to discuss the decorating details and set a time for her to help with all the finishing touches.

Chapter Nine

Daniel awoke from his first good night's sleep in longer than he could remember. What made this better was that he woke up sober. Taking a deep breath, he sat up and swung his feet over the edge of the bed, then stood up and walked to the window, separating the curtain panels enough to peer out without anyone being able to look in. Then he noticed his car and sighed. His shoulder slumped from the reality of his current life. So much for being sober, he thought. Life was not all that great after all. What did people think when they told him he needed to get sober? Reality sank in when he was sober, but life was the pits when he drank, dealt with hangovers, and could not remember things. It was time to get his head on straight and figure out what he was going to do with his life. Time to start small. Time for a shower and a hot cup of coffee. Then he would work on the bigger picture of his life.

Daniel sat in the hotel lobby drinking his coffee and watching people as they checked out and left. They were moving on with their lives. Today he was going to start doing the same. He hoped that going back to the better days of his childhood was a good thing. He was about to find out. He took the last sip of his now cold coffee and tossed the disposable cup in the trash by the front desk. He checked out, got his receipt, then walked out through the automatic doors to his damaged car.

He tossed his suitcase into the back seat of the car. Getting into the driver's seat, he put his sunglasses on, started the car, placed his hands on the steering wheel, and with his head ready for answers and a new start, he pulled out of the parking lot and onto the road. He drove the back roads for the last hour of his trip, observing old sights along the way. He was not on a deadline, had no schedule and no one knew he was coming nor knew where he was. He had been a recluse for over three years and stayed in a stupor. He drove on, lost in his thoughts. Finally, he turned onto the final country road that would lead him straight to his future, whatever it became.

He continued his journey following the twists and turns of the road past the woodlands, the vast pastureland of cows, horses, hay fields, cornfields, and more woodlands.

He finally saw the sign he was waiting to see, *Lake Wallenpaupack.* The distance was indicated but he paid no attention to it. He just knew he was getting closer to the place of his childhood summer vacations with his parents. It may have been the last place he had ever smiled. He did not remember much about the history of the area anymore. He knew the lake was man-made and had replaced several farms and homes. Besides that, he only knew it as his parent's summer getaway. It was his place to swim and hang out with summer friends. Most of the people who spent summers there were from the Northeast area of the United States. He and his parents were the odd ones since they were from Tennessee and headed north in the summer. He recalled his grandparents' stories of taking his father there on their vacations and that his father had kept up the tradition.

He stopped by the side of the road a few hundred yards before exiting Route 84. He knew there were other exits he could take, but the one he was going to take took him down the one road he wanted to drive. He was so close but needed time to think about how his life was about to change. He wanted it to change. He wanted this destination to be his place to think. To start over if that was possible. He enjoyed making friends there as a child. Now he hoped it would give him a new sense of who he should be.

He restarted his car and headed for the exit that would lead him to Route 507 and his destination. The last road was full of twists and turns. So much of what he was seeing was different than he remembered. There were new businesses and new homes. Heck, there was even a new school. He had never gone to school there, but he had made a few friends who had. He hoped none of them were still living in the area. He did not want them to know how he had messed up his life. They were most likely all successful businesspeople now.

He was shocked when he arrived at the small resort where his parents used to stay. It was not at all what he remembered. It was a total transformation. Where were all the trees? Where was the little house? Now there was a huge parking lot, boats in storage in the back of the lot, a three-story hotel to the right, and dirt. He knew it would be different but was hoping some of the old had remained.

He pulled into the large parking area. There were no parking lines as the parking lot was dirt and gravel instead of the expected blacktop. He stopped his car in the middle of the lot while he took it all in. It was not the quaint little hideaway he remembered as a kid.

Even the changes he saw seemed already outdated. He noticed the cabins were still across the road. At least they were still there, although they looked updated. He looked to where he thought the small house had been and realized it was still there but now had an addition. The newer section had two floors with a deck that seemed to wrap-around both sides. He saw the woods behind the house where he had loved to play. It had been a great place to find snakes, to run and hide among the rocks and play. He had heard that kids used to sleigh ride down the steep hill in the wintertime. He even remembered the tale of one year when the kids had been able to ice skate down the steep hill, across the road, and onto the lake. Now that had to have been a cold winter! He had never experienced a winter there.

He eased his way to the hotel and parked his car near the entrance. It was time to start his new life, to find answers, to sit and reflect. His time to unwind, regroup, and figure out his past and present life. Part of him wanted a good stiff drink. He smiled when he could not see any bars within sight but wondered if the one he remembered was still operating.

A bell rang as he entered. Scenic paintings of the lake decorated the walls of the small lobby. Pieces of driftwood adorned a few end tables, and a sofa and two rocking chairs sat near the wood fireplace. He rang the bell on the desk. A young lady walked through the curtain that separated the registration desk from the back office. Her name badge said her name was Karen.

"Hello sir, how may I help you?" She asked. She looked at him while pressing keys on the computer to get the registration page onto the screen.

"I'd like a room, please," he said. He pulled out his driver's license to show his identification before she had time to ask.

"For how many nights?"

"May I rent it by the week?"

"Sure. Most people do in the summer, but since it's not quite the season, most of our guests have been only stopping by for a night or two. You're welcome to stay as long as you like until the end of May. Then we start getting booked up and I already have most rooms reserved."

"Good enough. I'll stay at least two weeks. Do you take credit cards?"

"Of course. Do you want a king or a queen bed? We have both available. There is no smoking in any of the rooms; I hope you are not a smoker."

"That is perfect. I'll take a queen bed. It's only for me. No family, no kids." For no logical reason, he had added about the no kids even though she had not asked.

She snickered. "Okay. It wouldn't matter if you had a wife; kids would require an extra bed."

"Sorry, most people ask if it's for one or two people. I was saving you from asking."

Karen finished typing in his information and handed him the key to his room. "Your room is on the second floor at the end. It has an extra window giving you have a view of our *wonderful* parking lot and the lake." She handed him the key. Daniel took the key from Karen and looked at the number, room thirty-six. He shuddered.

"You okay?" Karen asked. She had been watching him and noticed he shuddered. "It's a bit chilly out, I know. I shiver once in a while too."

"No, I'm fine. I'm not cold. Something about that number. I'm fine." He walked out of the hotel to his car.

He walked to his room, laid his one suitcase on the floor, inspected the room, then sat on the bed and leaned back. The room looked nice. It looked like it had been remodeled recently. Compared to the outside of the hotel, the room looked up to date and welcoming. It had a large flat-screen TV, microwave, small refrigerator, queen bed, small round table with two chairs. The curtained shower had a curved extended shower rod providing more room to take showers. The white towels were thicker and larger than standard hotel linens. It smelled clean and looked nice. Comfortable without being elegant. He was going to like staying here. He did like the lake view. Karen had rented him one of the suites that also had a small kitchenette.

He returned to the hotel lobby to ask if there was a good place to eat nearby. He remembered his parents cooked in the cabin and rarely went out to eat, except for pizza. He recalled the place they frequented for ice cream. He could not remember the name, but knew it was popular.

He found Karen sitting behind the registration desk, working on paperwork. She stood to greet him when she heard the doorbells ring. In response to his question, she told him that there were a few restaurants within a few miles, depending on what he wanted to eat. He made a mental note of the ones she mentioned. He thanked her as he headed out the door to his car to find a place to eat and then to drive around to see what was new.

He anticipated that a lot more had changed than he had noticed on his drive. He drove past Lake Marina. It looked new or remodeled. He did not recall it being there when he was there last time. He continued looking for someplace that he did remember. He was hoping that the laid-back peaceful place of his childhood would be the place he would find himself again. The more he looked at all the changes, the more he thought it was a mistake. It was so different, so built up. It was a bit depressing. He smiled as he came to a stop sign and looked to his left. There was the Dike. He remembered that.

He pulled into the parking area facing the water. The lake was still as beautiful as ever. The ice from the winter months had thawed, but it was not warm enough for any boats on the water. He noticed the one island of the seven he knew were part of the lake. He worked his way through a few small trees and brush that had fallen over the winter and stepped onto the dike. He walked to the first of several benches inviting visitors to relax and enjoy the view. The wind made it too cold for him to sit, but he did stop to look for a few minutes. He was beginning to feel at home. Maybe this would do the trick. He would give it time and not judge against all the advancements to the area. Maybe, just maybe, something good would come from it.

After dinner at the Lake View Diner, he drove to the little town a few miles further away. The one with a single red light. He turned the last corner into town and smiled at the beauty that was before him. There were only a few other cars on the road. Older buildings lined the main street. He did not know which businesses were new or which ones had been there when he was a child, but he thought the town looked like a quaint little family town.

His family had not spent a lot of time there, but he did recognize a couple of the buildings. He decided to explore more later in the week.

He made a U-turn at the first street and headed back to the hotel instead of driving through town. The evening was starting to settle in. He noticed the sun starting to set when he reached the dike. The beauty made him smile. He remembered swimming in the lake after dinner and watching the sunset when he was a kid. The bonfires they had in the evenings along the shore. The stories the other kids shared. The stories his parents shared with other adults as they all watched the lowering sun reflect against the water. Those had been the good old days. Before his drinking days. Days before heartache, disappointments, and adult life. He took a deep breath and concentrated on his driving. Having another accident was the last thing he needed, even sober.

Those were his thoughts as he passed a bar located a few blocks from the hotel. The temptation was real. But he was determined. He parked close to his hotel room and went up to his room.

He jumped when the phone rang in his room as he stepped inside and closed his door.

"Hello?" Who could it be? No one knew he was here.

"Hi, Mr..."

"Call me Daniel." he interrupted her as soon as he heard her voice.

"Daniel," She corrected. "This is Karen at the front desk. I am calling to ask if you needed anything before our shifts change for the night."

"No, not that I can think of. Thank you for the recommendations earlier. I did grab a bite to eat at the Lake View Diner. It was pretty good."

"You're welcome. Lake View is one of my favorite places to eat for a quick bite. My Cousin owns it. She took it over. Well, never mind. I am just being a chatterbox. I'm sure you need your rest. I wanted to make sure you didn't need anything. There will be a new person at the desk for the overnight shift, but I'll be back on duty in the morning. We have a small breakfast for our guests if you are interested. It is available from 6 AM to 9. We have coffee and pastries during the week. We offer a full breakfast with hot foods on the weekends."

"Thanks, I'm good. I may be in for coffee in the morning. Have a good night."

"You too," she said as they both hung up. She shook her head and turned to go back to the office and talk with her evening replacement.

"I hear we have a new guest," Renee said as Karen walked through the doorway to fill her in on the newest guests and anything she needed to be aware of for the night shift.

"Yes. Daniel. He prefers to be called by his first name instead of his last name; must be a Southern thing. He came in from Florida. There is something different about Southerners. They seem to be more personable," Karen turned away from Renee as she spoke.

"Southerners? Or is it this one?" Renee teased. "Well, I will do my best to take care of him tonight for you, she said and then shook her head. "Well, that's not what I mean! Don't take that the wrong way! He's too young for me. I'd say he's more your age."

"Southerners in general." She tried to sound convincing. "How do you know how old he is? When did you see him?" Karen said. She turned to glare at Rene.

"I saw him when he returned from getting dinner or wherever he went. Why is your face red?"

"Oh. No reason. I didn't realize it was," she said, trying to hide her face more. She filled Renee in on the few other guests they had, then headed for the front door and her car. Time to call it a night.

She glanced over at the hotel, focusing on Daniel's room before she left the parking lot. There was something different about him. She hadn't talked with him for very long, but she could tell something was special. She hoped to find out more as time went on. He was only there for a week, maybe two. That was not much time to get to know someone. She was going to do her best while she could. Tomorrow was a new day. She was not scheduled until around noon but planned to be there in time for coffee and a pastry. She'd make up some excuse to Renee about why she had come in early.

Daniel had been looking out the window as Karen was leaving. He noticed her hesitate and glance his way for a moment before she left. He hoped she had not seen him looking. He estimated her to be just a few years younger than him and wondered if she had grown up here or had moved here later in life. He could not picture her as a preteen. She would have been cute because she was a beauty now. Her long dark red hair worked well with her blue eyes. He could not tell if she had tinted contact lenses or if her eyes were naturally almost turquoise. He caught himself smiling as he thought that someday he would have to find out.

He sat on the bed and flipped through the TV channels. He needed something to do. Finding nothing of interest on the TV, he looked at the time on his cell phone. It was still early. In his former life, he would have driven until he found a bar. The urge was still there, but he had found his will power. He finally stopped at a TV channel, left it there for the noise, and then drifted off to sleep. He woke up when the 11 o'clock news was on. He heard the weatherman announcing warmer temperatures for the next day and predicted to last all week. A local report showed a few Robins in someone's yard. Another photo showed crocus and hyacinths blooming. He knew they had already been in bloom back home and that the Robins showed up in his hometown as early as February.

He wanted to hear the rest of the weather report to get an idea of what he would do during his stay. He promptly fell back to sleep when a commercial came on. He slept through the report of a robbery in town. He never saw the news that a former local summer resident's daughter had made a miraculous recovery after a near-fatal hit and run car accident a few months earlier. Nor that the authorities were still on the lookout for the driver of the other car. Nor did he hear the updated weather details about a storm headed their way the following week.

Karen had stopped at the grocery store on her way home. A quick stop to get something for supper and to buy a bottle of red wine. You never know when a special occasion would arise, she told herself. She rarely drank but tried to have something on hand for those who did. She usually joined them for a glass. Her friends had drained her supply at the New Year's Eve party she hosted. She heard sirens and watched the police speed by as she left the liquor store. She watched for where the police may have gone as she drove home but did not see anything. At home, she put the wine in the refrigerator and ate leftover lasagna from the night before. She put her dirty dishes in the dishwasher and cleaned up the kitchen. Then she went into her living room and sat down to read a book.

She turned the TV on to wait for one of her favorite shows to come on. She often forgot about it but hoped to catch it this time. Then she got engrossed in her book and missed it anyway. The next thing she knew, the 11 o'clock news was even almost over. She was about to turn the TV off when she caught the updated report of a former summer guest's daughter. The story was about her miraculous recovery. They also added that the authorities were still on the search for the hit and run driver. Then she listened to the report of the robbery in town. That must have been the sirens I heard earlier, she thought as she turned the TV off. She made sure to lock her doors and close her curtains. Then she went to bed. The next thing she knew, her alarm was sounding, and it was time to get up to face a new day.

Chapter Ten

Sara and Heather had finished with their tour. Heather had made the calls needed to schedule deliveries for the remainder of furnishings and essentials for the manor. Everything was falling into place. Sara made a fresh pot of coffee as they sat down at the island in the large, beautifully remodeled kitchen. Everything was new—stainless appliances, a larger oven, microwave. The cabinets had been refinished in white to coordinate with the new counter tops. The island was now large enough to seat six and had additional drawers and shelves for storage. They had replaced the stools to fit with the rustic décor. Guests would be welcome to use the kitchen anytime they wanted. Each day, breakfast was provided for their guests, with Sara and Heather sharing that responsibility using some amazing new recipes they had found. They still had the recipes their mama and grandmother had used and would use those as well.

"It's been a wild few months, hasn't it?" Sara asked as she set their coffee mugs down on the center island.

"That's for sure. I can't believe all that has happened. Sometimes it feels like a dream. Then I look at the boot still on my foot or look in the mirror, see the scars, or think of Ben. I'm so glad he was willing to go to counseling. We are doing joint marriage counseling, but he has started private counseling as well."

"When did he start that?"

"About two weeks ago. Ben said he needed more than just our marriage counseling. Our counselor recommended a colleague of his, and Ben seems okay with it. He told me it was going well. However, he won't talk about the details. Says that maybe someday he will, but for now, it's something he has to work out on his own with the counselor."

"It's wonderful that he's willing to work through it. I'm so glad he stopped the divorce proceedings. And that he lets you see Marc any time you want. A lot of men would not do that."

"Oh, believe me, I'm glad too. I would be devastated without Marc in my life. He is my reason for living. I am a believer that he helped pull me through at the accident. I heard him and knew I'd have to be there for him."

"I understand. I may not have any kids of my own, but I love Marc so much. I was looking forward to the three of you moving into the other guest house. I'm glad you are there now but having the three of you there was the plan. I hope it will still happen."

"Me too. I have to start working on that house, so it's ready for them. I enjoy living there, but it won't be *home* until Ben and Marc are there."

Ben, who still was living in the old house, had just finished his coffee when he heard Marc calling from his bedroom. It was going to be another long day for them both. He had to take his little boy to daycare while he went to work. Then he had his private counseling session with Dr. McBride. He was hoping the doctor would tell him that everything would be fine, but he knew better. Not until he...

Marc's cries interrupted his train of thought. Ben went to his son's room and saw him climbing out of his little bed, dragging his one constant – his security blanket. The Mickey Mouse fleece blanket his grandmother had made for him right after he was born. It went everywhere with him. He had thought it got lost after the accident, but the towing company had rescued it and returned it. The owner's wife had even taken the time to wash it first. In the middle of the chaos and pain, a stranger had gone above and beyond for a little child. It was the little things that make the most significant difference.

Ben picked up Marc and gave him a tight squeeze. He was the bright spot of his life. After taking him to the bathroom and changing his clothes for the day, it was breakfast time. Quick waffles from the toaster were on the menu. That, plus a sippy cup of milk made for the perfect morning for a little guy.

For once, Marc didn't cause any delays by playing more than eating. Ben looked at the clock to make sure they would not be late again today. He smiled as he let Marc out of his booster seat, cleaned up the dirty dishes, and watched Marc head for a pile of toys.

"I love you, little guy."

"Me too," he said as he reached the toys and sat in the middle of them.

"No, son, we have to go now. Time for daycare and for Daddy to go to work."

"Mommy."

"No, you have daycare today. You'll see Mommy soon."

Ben was still struggling with his feelings for his wife. He still loved her; after all, she was the mother of his child. But something had happened to him when they had the accident. He just could not put his finger on it. Counseling was helping. He had canceled the divorce and was going to marriage counseling as well as individual counseling. He had no problem with Heather seeing Marc, but not to the point of spending the night. Not yet.

Ben dropped Marc off at daycare and headed to his office. He had a few more days' worth of work on a remodel for a client before they could move back in. He was so glad that they had completed most of the remodeling of the manor before the accident. And now, all the work there was almost done as well.

He had considered it an honor to be a part of transforming the old building into the modern one he and his crew had finally completed. They had done a total upgrade from head to toe. He knew Sara and Heather were busy putting the final touches on the manor before their opening. He was supposed to move into the guest house with Heather, and then he would be the maintenance man for the estate. Heather had moved into the guest house alone after healing enough from the accident. He was not sure he ever would. It was time for some serious counseling sessions. He had some major decisions to make and was not sure what he wanted. Maybe today he would be able to work through the last of his issues. He could use some good news.

This session was going to be the last one, he hoped, even though he knew in his heart that they had not resolved all the issues. The truth was that they had not even addressed some of them. He would do his best to fake it without bringing up any other issues about his life. Then again, Joe was pretty good at his job. Not much got past him. Ben found out that Joe had been there at the accident and had witnessed what Ben had gone through. It helped Ben to know Joe understood him.

Ben arrived at Joe's office a few minutes early. He signed in for his appointment as the receptionist informed him that the doctor was running a little late. He sat down to wait. The room was comforting. Light teal was the main color scheme with accents in pale yellow and gray. A bookshelf filled with books sat in the corner. A child's table with chairs sat in front of the bookshelves. He knew that Joe and his partner were also counselors for children going through rough family situations. He glanced at the brochures that filled a rack by the receptionist. The topics covered suicide, alcoholism, depression, chronic illnesses, marriage, and couples counseling. He realized that the office handled a wide variety of mental health issues.

Ben was contemplating how best to lie when Dr. McBride came to the door and called him back to his office. Ben shook the doctor's hand as they walked through the doorway leading to the hallway.

"How are you doing, Ben?"

"I'm good," Ben responded, keeping it simple.

"Only good?"

"Good is good. Things are looking up."

They reached Dr. McBride's office, and Joe held the door open to let Ben walk past him. He switched the closed sign to "In Session" and closed the door behind him. He walked over to the desk, picked up Ben's file, then sat down, facing Ben who sat in the large armchair.

"Ben, be honest with me; how are things going?" Dr. McBride asked as he flipped to a blank page in his file.

"Things truly are going good, Doc. Marc and I are adjusting to life together. Heather and I are getting along and sharing time with him. Work is going well. I have a new contract to remodel that old building on State Street. Have you heard what's going in there?"

"No, I've heard a few rumors going around, but nothing specific."

"Well, I'm not at liberty to say what it is yet, but it will be amazing."

"Okay then. Now, let's get back to you. You told me that you had some emotions creeping up. Emotions that hit you at the worst times and make you feel angry. You said you were not sure you should go back to Heather if you still had anger issues. Are you still having those? Can you explain them in more depth?"

Ben looked around the room before answering. He noticed the abstract paintings on the wall, the solid light gray curtains at the window. Were those new? He noticed the cream-colored area rug under the desk. Finally, he responded, "No, I've not had any of those in the last week. I'm hoping they are gone."

Dr. McBride took notes. He knew the episodes were still happening. Joe knew body language spoke louder than words, and this was the case with Ben at the moment. When Ben told the truth, he would look at him. With his patient looking all over the room while responding, Joe knew Ben was hiding something. Each person was different, but he had gotten to know Ben over the last month or so. He knew his little quirks when he was in session.

"Ben, be honest with me, when was the last episode? I cannot help you if you won't be honest with me. You know everything we talk about is confidential. It's the law. Unless you give me written permission to reveal even the slightest thing we talk about, I cannot tell a soul."

Ben lowered his head. His ideas of faking being well were being taken over by his honest desire to talk about what was bothering him.

"Doc, I had one two nights ago. It was horrible. I keep reliving the accident, but there is more. It's like the accident was a reminder of something else that happened in my life, and while I can see it in my dreams or nightmares, it's not clear. The pictures in my mind seem clouded over, like a distant fog."

"Tell me what you can recall. Are they the same visions each time? What do you see? How does it make you feel when you wake up?" Joe leaned back in his office chair to give Ben a feeling of not being forced to talk. He wanted him to feel relaxed enough to open up more.

"Yes, it's the same vision, nightmarish. I'm confused when I wake up. I'm hurting. I physically feel like I've been hit, run over, in a big fight. Something." Ben closed his eyes and lowered his head.

"Okay. Let's try something. Keep your eyes closed and try to envision your nightmare. I do not want to send you for hypnosis unless that's the only way to help you, and I will if you want. But let's try this first. Okay. Now, with your eyes closed, think about the accident. What happened?"

"We were driving along, headed home. This car came out of nowhere and went to pass us. He was so close that I took my foot off the gas and moved over. I guess I moved over too far or hit the ditch. The next thing I know, we were over the embankment, and Heather was screaming, Marc was crying. I crawled out of the car and saw a lady reaching for me. I told her I was fine and to help my wife and son. Then a man appeared to help as well as the EMS. The next thing I know, I'm in the hospital. I guess I lost consciousness. When I asked about my wife, they said she was in surgery. When I asked about Marc, they said he had a bump on his head but should be fine. I remember falling back to sleep and..." Ben stopped. He raised his head but kept his eyes shut.

"Go on," Joe said quietly so not to disturb Ben's visions, but to encourage him to continue talking.

"I saw visions that night." Ben took a deep breath, then shook his head as if trying to shake the sight out of his head. "I was in another accident. I was lying on my back. The car was beside me, but I was on the ground. There was blood all around me. I heard screaming." Ben gasped, then continued. "It's my mother."

He continued to piece together the vision as if it were currently happening to him, his eyes now opened but transfixed into blank space. He begins to speak as though he were there. "I hear other voices but don't see anyone. My face is cold. It is snowing. I hear more screaming. I lift my head and turn it. I see my mother pinned in the car. She's crying. I try to get up, but I can't move. No one is coming to help. She is moaning now, not crying. I keep calling out to her. I am yelling for help. Finally, someone comes and goes to her first. I don't hear her moans anymore. I hear a helicopter."

Ben stops talking. He gripped the arm of his chair and squinted his eyes shut as if trying to see more details. He moved his head from side to side as if he was looking for something. He broke into a sweat.

"I wake up in the hospital," Ben added and then stopped talking, gasped for air, and opened his eyes. He continued his blank stare, then closed his eyes because he wanted to see the vision again. He could not pull it back. He felt worn out. Ben wiped his face of the sweat that had dripped from his forehead to his cheek. He opened his eyes, looking at his hands, feeling the pain in his arms and hands from tensing. He stretched his fingers out to relax the muscles.

Dr. McBride did not say anything. He wanted Ben to remember as much as he could on his own, without being prompted. To interject anything at this stage could cancel out his train of thought, and the door that just opened in his mind may close for good. He waited in silence.

"Doc?" Ben continued while still staring into space. He was not focused on anything that is currently there in the room. He looks back into his mind and memories. "Doc. I was three when that happened," he hesitated then added, "That was when my parents died!" He opened his eyes wide and looked right at his doctor before closing his eyes again.

Silence.

"That's, that's, that's when..." He stopped talking and gasped for more air.

"When what?" Dr. McBride finally interjected in a whisper. He had been taking notes while Ben had been describing his vision.

Ben opened his eyes. He sat up in his seat and leaned toward Joe. He wrinkled his forehead in confusion as he realized what he just discovered about himself. "Doc." He hesitated again as he made a connection. "I was adopted when I was five. Everyone told me my parents had died when I was young and that there was no one else to take care of me. I spent two years in foster care before the last foster care family adopted me. They said they both died in a car accident."

Joe took notes while Ben continued recalling the pieces of his childhood trauma.

"No one ever told me that I was there and saw it; that I had watched my mother die! Odd though, I never notice my father being in the vision. Was my father there? If he was, where was he? Why was I told that both my parents died in that car accident if he wasn't there?"

Ben stood up and walked to the window. He looked without focusing on anything outside. He was visualizing what was on his mind. He was trying to see more of the vision, trying to find his father. He turned around and went back to his seat when the inner image was no longer there. He shook his head as if to clear his mind and looked to Joe for his input.

"Ben, I believe you have made a breakthrough. The new accident sent memories to you that you had suppressed since childhood. This accident reminded you of losing your parents. You connected it to this accident and were afraid of losing your wife and son. But, they survived. You survived. This accident brought up the similarities between the two. Heather, being trapped in the car for a while, her screams reminding you of your mother.

That is also why even though you were physically okay, you lost consciousness at the scene and again at the hospital when they told you about Heather being in surgery. You were afraid of her dying. Your body went into shock, which caused your mild heart attack and your coding at the hospital.

Ben interrupted him. "Is that why I have a hard time seeing Heather hurt and scarred?"

"Yes, the scars may remind you of seeing an injury on your mother. Maybe you saw the cuts on her face or body before they took her away. You see your mother in Heather. Your subconscious does not want to relive the reminders of that childhood accident or the years that followed. That is why you are avoiding seeing Heather. You are keeping Marc away, for the most part, so he does not have those reminders when he sees her. You are afraid that he will have nightmares."

"Can I get over this? Can I keep Marc from having the nightmares of what he saw?"

"You may never get over it, but we can work through it. As for keeping Marc from the nightmares, only time will tell. He was only two when it happened, so he may not remember it at all. Or like you, it may be years before he does. His experience afterward is not the same as yours. He still has his loving family. For now, let's work on you."

"Okay, what do we do?" Ben leaned back in his chair and let out a long breath as if he had been holding it for a while. He felt drained.

"First, let's discuss your feelings about losing your parents and people not being honest with you all those years. Let's get you and Heather in here to discuss why you are behaving the way you are toward her. Once we do that, I believe we can get the two of you back together as a happy, functioning, normal family."

"I feel so much lighter. I feel drained, but like I just let go of a heavy weight that I didn't even realize I was carrying. Let's get this started."

"We will need to start this on another day. Your time is up. He hated doing that to his patients. He knew some needed more time. Setting limits was rough on them as well as him. I can check my calendar and see when I can get you in next. I will aim for tomorrow or the next day to work this out while it's still fresh in your mind. He looked at his schedule. "Yes, I have an opening the day after tomorrow at 4 PM."

"That's perfect!" Ben stood to leave.

Joe stopped him before he reached the office door. "I have homework for you. When you get home, I want you to write down any thoughts you have about what you've just learned. It does not matter if you think they are helpful or not. Write it all down. More memories, your feelings about what happened when you were a child, and your feelings now. Write it all down, whether it makes sense or not."

"Okay. I will do my best." Ben was reaching for the doorknob. His head was reeling with emotion. He still felt some confusion, but he felt there was hope now for him and his family.

"Being able to work out the things that bother us makes life better. Having things stuck deep inside eats away at us." Joe sensed Ben's feelings as he opened the door. They shook hands, and Ben left to pick up Marc. He would make them dinner and start writing as soon as he had his son in bed. He also wanted to call Heather.

Heather and Sara were sitting at the dining room table, eating dinner while going over the last of the details before opening day. It had been a long day of planning and visualizing how the manor would look with all the guests. They were both smiling when the phone rang. Sara answered it.

"Yes, she's here." She said after she had only gotten a hello out.

"Heather, it's for you. It's Ben. He sounds excited." She handed the phone over to her younger sister and left the room to give her some privacy.

"Hi Ben, how are you?" she asked while taking the last bite of her supper.

"I'm fantastic! You won't believe what happened today! I made a breakthrough at Dr. McBride's office!" He blurted out before she had time to interrupt.

"That's great, Ben! I'm so happy for you." She tried her best to be excited. He may have made a breakthrough, but what did that mean for them? Was it going to bring them back together as a family?

"Thanks! I have another appointment the day after tomorrow to discuss it further. Then the doctor wants to see the two of us together so I can talk to you about it and explain why I have been behaving the way I have since the accident. I believe this is the breakthrough that we need!" Ben's mind was racing, causing him to talk faster than usual. He had barely taken a breath, trying to get everything said before she could say much.

Heather sat back in her chair. She was smiling but still was concerned. "Oh, Ben, that sounds so wonderful! I miss you and Marc so much! I know I see you and him for visits, but it's not the same. When is the appointment for us to go together?"

"That is not scheduled yet. I will let you know after my next meeting. Oh, and Heather, I love you so much. I want us to be a family again. I am so sorry I thought I wanted a divorce. Thank you for making me stop that process." Heather could tell he was smiling as he talked.

Those were the words she wanted to hear. Now she was getting excited. "I want to be a family again too! How is Marc doing?" Heather smiled as she sat up straighter.

"He's fine. He misses you too. We'll see you in a few days. I've got to go. I love you, babe."

"Love you too. Have a good night." She hung up the phone and stared at it. Was she dreaming? Or was life about to become the way it should be? She leaned back and smiled. She lifted a silent prayer thanking God for the answered prayers. She knew it might be a bit too soon, but it was a start in the right direction.

Chapter Eleven

Ben sat in Dr. McBride's waiting room for his last scheduled private counseling session. They were going to discuss his breakthrough from two days earlier. Ben had written down his thoughts as Joe had suggested. The memories he wrote brought tears as he recalled the years he missed with his birth parents. Ben wrote of trusting his adoptive parents and the story they told him. He believed that his parents had died in a car accident. He did not remember their funeral. Was he too young to remember? He wondered if anyone took him to their funeral. Or had he blocked it out of his memory? Maybe the children's home did not take young children to funerals, even when it was their parents. Since he had become an orphan with no other family, Children's Services had taken him to a home for orphans. He grew up believing he was the only person in his family. Why would he think otherwise? Could he possibly have other family members that were still alive? Had they lied about that too? Something to investigate. He hoped Joe would be able to help him find answers.

He had spent his life trusting people. Now he was uncovering that he had been lied to as a child. How many other people had lied to him over the years, and why had he been gullible enough to believe them at their word? But what did all that have to do with his feelings for Heather after the accident? Why had he thought he needed to distance himself? Why did he think he had to keep Marc away from his mother for those first several weeks? Why was he protecting his son? He did not have a good reason; he just did it. He also realized he felt the accident was his fault, although it was not. His recent discoveries explained why it was difficult for him to see Heather's limp and scars. He hoped he could overcome that.

He blamed himself for losing their baby that they had not known about until receiving the doctor's report after the accident. When they found out about losing the baby, she said she had not known she was pregnant and he believed her.

Dr. McBride entered the waiting room and apologized for making Ben wait. They walked back toward his office.

"That's okay. It gave me more time to think. I wrote a few things down, and then more things came to mind. I am still trying to connect the two accidents and figure out why the one when I was a child would cause me to act the way I do towards Heather. I would think I would want to be there for her." Ben was already talking nonstop before Joe had even closed the door.

Joe and Ben sat down as Ben handed him the notes he had written. Joe skimmed over the papers to read what Ben had discovered and what his thoughts were regarding them. When Joe finished, he responded to Ben's original comments.

"I am glad you had time to think and write a few things down. As you remember more from your childhood, everything may make more sense. You automatically put up a wall in your mind, and even in your heart when you had your accident involving Heather and Marc. Without consciously thinking about it, you were preparing yourself for losing her. You had lost your mother in a car accident that required her to need airlifting to the hospital. Heather had to be airlifted as well. You heard her screams and moans, the same way you listened to your mother's. You thought she was going to die as your mother had. Even the doctors were not sure she would make it at first. That wall became hard to remove. Now that you know the connection, I hope you can reach out to her and let your love for her replace that wall.

"You are right. I did put up a wall. I was not protecting my wife. I was protecting myself. My God, how could I do that to the woman I love? How could I keep her son from her? I've got to tell her!" I've got to tell her how much I love her! I've got to tell her I'm sorry." Ben stood to leave.

"Hold it right there. Sit back down. We're not done yet." Dr. McBride stood by the door, blocking Ben from leaving. He loved it when his patients had finally figured out the answers, but there was always more to discuss before he let them loose into the world.

"Why not? I've figured it out! I need to make it right."

"Ben, sit down." Dr. McBride pointed to the chair. "You have begun to connect the dots. You have a whole picture now to finish as you connect more dots. Take a moment. Think about your recent behavior and the distance you've put between the two, correction, the three of you. That wall was solid enough that you thought the only way out was a divorce. You have stopped those proceedings, but has she forgiven you? She does not know about the accident of your childhood, and what happened to you as a child, does she?"

"She knows I was adopted as a child and that my parents died in a car accident. That is all I knew myself until the other day."

"Now you have to be able to sort out your feelings and to tell her what you have discovered. It may affect your relationship more than you realize."

"How so?" Ben slumped back into his chair.

"You now have more to deal with than your attempt to get Heather back and going on with your life. You have a lot of back history to handle. It will not be easy for you. She has had a lot happen in her life recently. Now she will have your history to deal with as well."

Ben leaned forward and put his head in his hands. "You are right. What if she decides she can't handle it all?" He became quiet. He looked at his hands, then up at the window. Then he looked down at his hands. "Okay. Let's talk this through. Where do I start?"

"We start with what you are going to tell her. Telling her you have it all figured out and that you want her back would be easy. She is going to want to know the details of what you figured out."

"I want to tell her everything. Where do I start?"

"Okay then. You tell Heather everything. But you have to do it gradually. If you blurt everything out at once, she may get as confused as you were. There is a lot to take in, starting with what you learned about your childhood. She has been with you long enough to love your adoptive parents. Which brings up another topic we can discuss later. You have to decide if and how to talk to your parents about this new-found truth."

Ben was shaking his head. "So much to take in. I never want Marc to go through this. We will tell him the truth as he gets older. In the meantime, I need to organize my thoughts so Heather can take it all in and understand. I haven't even thought about my parents. I'm not sure they can handle me knowing that they lied to me. They aren't in the best of health."

With the help of Dr. McBride, they worked out what Ben would tell Heather and how. Just telling her he loved her, and he was sorry would be a start. He had already told her that on the phone the other day. The hard part would be explaining the accident when he was a young child and how in his mind, it connected to his current behavior. He felt relief that he had answers and hoped he could move forward.

Chapter Twelve

Sara and Heather were busy cleaning the manor for the soft opening. They only had a week to make any necessary changes, set all the furniture where they wanted it, and make sure each room was perfect. They were waiting for a few last-minute items to be delivered. Cecelia was there to help set everything in place. Ben was there to deal with any maintenance issues, touch up painting, whatever they needed him to do.

Ben had also offered to be there on opening day. Since he had the breakthrough with his counseling, he had been around more often. He and Heather's first joint counseling session was scheduled a few days before the manor's opening.

Heather arrived at the counselor's office, hoping to see Marc there as well as Ben. She was a few minutes early with no sign of either of them. Dr. McBride saw Heather in the waiting room and waved to her as he approached. He went over to her and told her it was good to see her again.

Since the accident, when he and his wife rescued her and her family, he had not seen her. She thanked him for being there and apologized for not remembering him. He said that was okay; he had not expected her to. He was just glad she had survived. He glanced around for Ben and not seeing him, excused himself to ask the receptionist if Ben had called saying he would be late. Ben walked into the waiting room before she had time to reply.

"Sorry that I'm late. My car broke down about five miles away. I've been nursing it all the way here. Is Heather here?" He noticed her when he turned his head, and suddenly got nervous. They had been around each other and spoke at the manor, but never about what they were going to discuss here. He was about to share details of a life that he had not even known about less than a week before. A life he was still trying to understand.

Heather stood up and met Ben and Dr. McBride in front of the receptionist's window. She had overheard Ben talk about his car.

“Hi Ben, I hope it's nothing too serious with your car.”

“It shouldn't be. Something mechanical going on with it, I hope. I'll get it looked at after we finish here. Or tomorrow.”

The three of them walked into Dr. McBride's office. After everyone was in, Dr. McBride closed the door and turned his sign to “In Session.” He was impressed when he saw that a conversation was already taking place between Ben and Heather. This may go easier than he thought. He smiled as he sat down at his desk. Ben and Heather were sitting side by side on the sofa and opposite Joe.

They stopped talking when Joe sat down. Heather wondered what was going to be discussed. Ben began feeling apprehensive about what he was going to tell his wife, and maybe a little worried about her reaction.

Joe opened the conversation. “Heather, as I said out in the waiting room, it is so good to see you again and that you are doing so well. There were a lot of prayers lifted for you all.”

“Thank you, Dr. McBride. I'm very thankful and very blessed.”

“Please, call me Joe." He smiled. He always preferred the more personal connection in his work with clients. "I know Ben has told you of his recent breakthrough. We believe it was time to bring you in so the two of you can talk while I work as a mediator. He has discovered a few things that may help you both understand his behavior. I'll be here to help explain anything if you have questions. If you don't need my input, I will sit here and listen. I hope the two of you can get your lives back on track and your family back together. We can meet for as many sessions as you believe you need to deal with that transition.”

Heather looked at Ben. She was interested to hear what he had to say. The way Joe presented the situation, she was not sure what Ben had to share. She hoped it was all good, but now she was concerned. She pushed her hair behind her ear, revealing her scar. The accident had changed her appearance, but not the person she was inside. She saw that Joe noticed, but he was professional and did not react.

Ben turned away from Joe and faced his loving wife. The woman who had stood by him while he took a giant step to open his own business. The woman who had given him their beloved son. The woman who deserved the world from him. The woman who he had rejected for reasons he still did not quite understand. There was no excuse for the way he had reacted. It was the way it was. He hoped she could help him work through it. He was, after all, still in love with her.

"First, let me say I am so sorry," Ben started. He hung his head in a humble sign of sorrow. "I'm sorry for treating you the way I have since the accident." He raised his head to look at his wife—the woman he loved with all his heart.

Heather watched him as she listened to his words and how his emotions revealed his true feelings. She let him continue talking.

"I was so scared after the accident. I was afraid of losing you, of losing Marc. I was afraid you would blame me. Afraid you would hate me for causing your pain, for causing Marc pain. I spent weeks trying to figure out why I was feeling that way. I thought you were going to die there along the side of the road. Then I thought you would die on the way to the hospital. When they took you into surgery, I held my breath and almost lost my own life. But they brought me back to life again. Once you were out of surgery and going to be okay and I could see you, all I saw was the injuries – the broken leg, the cut on your face, the injury to your arm. I heard the doctor tell me that she was uncertain you'd be able to walk normally again. She even mentioned that you might lose the use of your arm. I was so scared."

"But I'm okay," Heather interrupted as she moved her legs and her arm to prove she could function normally. She moved her head and let her hair cover her scar.

"Let me finish. This isn't easy, but I have to tell you. You see, what I discovered through my sessions is that the accident and seeing your injuries brought back long-buried memories from when I was three." Ben saw her confusion on her face.

Ben continued to tell her of the accident when he was three years old when his parents had died. He told of his foster care, his adoption, and how he had been told that his parents had died in a car accident.

"I know all that. You told me that when we were still dating. You told me your parents are your adoptive parents. You told me your biological parents had died in the accident. What did our accident have to do with that?"

"It wasn't the full truth. I found out that a lot of that was a lie. I had flashbacks after our accident, and seeing you, seeing Marc, gave me nightmares. In my nightmares, I saw my parent's accident. I realized that I had been in that accident and had watched them die. You see, before our rescue, I heard you screaming in pain and fear. That triggered my brain to recall those same sounds I heard when I was in the accident with my parents. I heard the screams of my mother. And then her silence. And then I lost her. I had minor injuries like Marc received. Through my counseling sessions, Joe helped me understand that I put up a wall to save myself from the pain of losing you. I thought you were going to die. I couldn't face that. I wasn't mentally able to face it. I didn't want Marc to have the same nightmares when he was older. The sights, the sounds of death. I know you survived, but I couldn't bring myself out of those feelings. My memories were in my subconscious, so I didn't attribute them to my recent behavior." He stopped and looked at Joe for reassurance that he was making sense.

Joe leaned forward to help explain it to Heather. Her face had a look of total confusion and disbelief. She was leaning back on the sofa. Her body language indicated a distance from Ben, revealing her doubt about the story he was telling.

Joe saw the disbelief in her eyes. "Heather, our minds are a powerful force in how we react to things. Things, such as tragedies, may happen in our lives and we automatically block them out because we don't want to face them, like him being in the accident when his parents died. He heard his mother slowly die. He did not remember it until the other day in our session. No one told him the truth about the accident over the years. They lied to him when it happened because they weren't sure he could deal with the truth. Later, after lying to him all those years, they may have thought it was too late. Anyway, when the accident happened with the three of you, it triggered those memories. Ben was afraid, and the only way his mind could deal with it was to run. Unfortunately, he ran from you instead of to you. He didn't understand why but felt that was the only thing he could do. There is more that he is dealing with."

Heather looked at Ben as he took a deep breath. "In my memories of the accident when I was three, I remember hearing my mother. I remember seeing her. Seeing her hurt. Remember I said that both my parents died in that accident? Well, I can't remember seeing or hearing my father at the accident scene. I honestly don't think he was there. I keep trying to relive the scene, as hard as it is to visualize, but he is not there. I don't remember seeing him in my life after that. I doubt I attended their funeral because I was so young, and whoever was in charge of me must have felt it best to keep me away." He hesitated while he again tried to think back. He was hoping that somehow talking about it would bring up a memory he could count on.

His wife kept her eyes on him. She was absorbing this new revelation. "Oh, Ben. I'm sorry, but I'm not sure how to take this. I'm confused." Heather stopped talking as she tried to digest his story and how she should react or deal with it. Finally, she had her thoughts together. "You say you have these memories and that you realize they are what caused you to feel the way you do now. That distancing yourself from me was the best thing for you to do. But how does that affect us now? Is this new development supposed to erase the emotions between us over the last few months?"

"I would love that, but I know it is too much to ask. We may never have our old normal again. We can build a new normal. I love you, Heather. I love our son and our family. I want us to be together again. I know it will take work. I know I still may have the nightmares, from what Joe says. But I also know that if you are with me, we can work it all out."

"Ben, I love you too. I never wanted you to be away from me. But, what about the nightmares? How do we deal with them if they continue? Have you been able to take that internal wall down?"

Joe answered Heather's question. "We can discuss all that here before you leave today, or you can come back to discuss them on another day. Either way, for your relationship to work, you will need to work at it. You have a lot to deal with. Be open with each other about your feelings, fears, thoughts, love for each other, and your son. You both have Marc to consider. He loves you both. He is still small and doesn't understand some things. Right now, it is the way his life is, and he doesn't know it should be different. He may ask about your scar and your limp when he gets older, Heather. He may ask other questions as he remembers the accident. He may never remember the accident. Or, like Ben, he may remember it much later in life. It would help if you were honest with him when he is young. Tell him about the accident. That will hopefully keep him from going through what Ben has been going through these last few months."

"Heather, what do you say? Can we work on this? Can we go on with our plans for the life we had planned before the accident?"

"Ben, it will take work, but I love you. I have never stopped loving you. I didn't understand why you had not moved into our home at Bella Rose, nor why you filed for a divorce. I was angry, thinking I had done something, other than this scar and my limp, to send you away. Knowing it wasn't me is such a relief!" She smiled, reached for Ben's hand, then nodded her head.

Yes, she wanted him back in her life. She wanted the life they had planned. She wanted to grow old with him. She knew it would take more work than she had planned, but she had married him hook, line, and sinker, for better or worse, sickness and health, till death. And she hoped that death was a long way off.

They both stood up, and for the first time in over six months, they hugged as if they would never let each other go. They kissed like it was their wedding day. Joe remained sitting and watched love in action. He loved it when things worked out for his clients.

When they finally let go of each other, Joe discussed with them the next step. He offered counseling to them as a couple if they wanted it. They said they would like at least one couple's session and set up a time to come. He then brought up the one thing that had not been brought up. "Ben, you realize that since you don't remember seeing your father at the accident scene nor afterward, and the fact that you now know of the lies, that your father may still be alive. You may want to consider investigating that further. You need to figure out how to talk to your adoptive parents about what you know. It could be that they never knew the truth either."

Ben nodded. He had thought about that. "I know. But for now, I only want my family back. I want Heather and Marc and I to be together again."

"That sounds good. We can discuss other things during future sessions. Now you two go out, pick up your son, and start your life the way it should be. Know that it won't be the same as it was, but it can be better. No secrets." He ended the session with assurance from them that they were starting a new chapter in their lives.

"And to start that chapter, you, Ben, are bringing Marc and moving into our home at Bella Rose where you belong – with me." They were both smiling with their arms around each other as they walked out of the office.

Joe watched as they left. If only more of his clients were that easy to work with. He walked back toward his desk and hoped that it would work out for them. He felt there was more going on with Ben than he had discussed. Maybe there was more to that nightmare. He picked up Ben's file and put it in the O*pened File* drawer. He was not ready to put it in the closed file.

Chapter Thirteen

Daniel opened his eyes to sunlight streaming through the separated curtain panels. He had left a space in the curtains hoping to wake with the light of day instead of setting the alarm clock. He smiled as he stretched and took a deep breath before throwing the covers off and getting up. He looked out the window to feel the slight warmth of the sun before closing the curtains. He started a pot of coffee on his way to take a shower. He looked forward to a cup of hot coffee as he dressed for the day. He did not have a lot of plans for the day except to make it another good day.

He remembered his conversation with Karen the evening before as he sipped his coffee. He had only been at the lake for three weeks but surprised himself when he opened up to Karen about his recent past. The thing that surprised him the most was how good it had felt to be open about being an alcoholic. She had taken it all in stride and mentioned the local AA meetings. He thanked her but added that he was doing fine without the meetings.

He told her he had hit bottom about six months prior and had headed south to Florida to live with an old classmate. Five months later, he realized he was not making as much progress in his life as he wanted. He talked with his old classmate, who suggested revisiting his favorite childhood place. So, he headed to Pennsylvania to find some peace and figure out his future. He hoped his friend was right and that revisiting the place of good memories would help him. His memories of that time in his childhood were happy memories for the most part. He needed that. He needed to be happy again. He had quit coming there as a teenager when he had rebelled against his family. He hoped the memories of the preteen days would bring his joy back.

Karen had been a great listener from the time he arrived. He was looking forward to seeing her again that day, right after his job interview. He had no plans to move to this area, but he did need to replenish his money reserve. He has spent his life moving from one place to another since he had been a teenager. His parents brought him home as soon as he was found the first time he ran away. The older he got, the better he became at hiding. He assumed they either could not find him or that they had given up when they did not track him down this last time. He believed their life was easier without him than for them to chase after him and bring him home. They must have known he would plan to run away the first time he got a chance.

His job interview was at a local marina he remembered from his childhood summers. Even though there were other marinas in the area, he remembered this was the one his Dad frequented to rent a boat. At that time, it was the only one that had rentals for tourists. The marina was currently advertising for maintenance and handyman positions. Jobs would include repairing boats, cleaning, and repairing the docks on the cove. The job was temporary because it was seasonal. Perfect for Daniel.

Daniel admitted that he was not much of a construction worker during his interview, nor was he a mechanic, but he assured the owner that he was willing to learn. He told Mr. Carr that he would do his best at whatever job he was given. The interview did not take long. As he was about to leave, feeling good about the interview, Mr. Carr added, "Daniel, Sorry to hear about your parents. It was so hard to hear of their deaths."

"Thanks," he said as he walked out the door. He hesitated then and turned back to face Mr. Carr. He had not remembered mentioning them during his interview.

Mr. Carr saw his confusion and explained, "I remember them when you used to come here as a kid. If you're wondering how I knew."

"Ah, yes, when I was a kid." He nodded his head then continued to look at him for a moment longer with his eyes opened a little larger. He did not say anything, but the man who he hoped would hire him, with no experience, must have understood.

"No worries," was all Mr. Carr said.

Daniel left relieved and happy with the job possibility but wondered if he could keep it if he were hired.

Daniel returned to the hotel after stopping for a few groceries at the local, family-owned market. He was glad he did not recognize anyone there and that no one seemed to recognize him. He was still surprised to know that Mr. Carr remembered him and was unsure how he felt about it.

He had stopped sponging off Karen for meals and was tired of eating out. While he enjoyed chatting with the locals, there were times when he liked the quiet. With his potential new boss remembering him, he wondered how many others would start to remember him. As much as he had come there to relive his childhood memories and happier times, he had hoped to do it under the radar of others. That was why he had only let Karen know so much about him without telling her everything. She was so easy to talk with; it would have been easy to say too much. She never questioned what he told her and never asked for more details. She had learned a long time ago from her other guests that it was best not to ask too much. If a person wanted to share something, they would, in time.

He called Karen to invite her to dinner. It was his treat. He was doing the cooking. “You can cook? You never told me. I've been doing the cooking all this time.” She let the rest of her thoughts dangle in midair.

“Yes, I've been keeping secrets from you.”

“Secrets, as in plural. More than one?”

“No, just one,” he coughed. “I can cook. Okay, maybe two.”

“What's the other one?”

“I'm a good cook.”

“Ha! We'll see. What time is dinner?”

“How does seven sound?”

“It sounds like a number to me.”

“Very funny.” He changed his tactic. “How would you like to come over to the hotel room at seven o'clock this evening for dinner?”

“Sounds good to me. I'll be there. Is there anything I can bring?”

“Nope, I have everything I need. It's a date.”

“No, a date is numbers and days on a calendar,” she replied with a smile he could not see.

“Well, whatever you call it, I'll see you later.” He was careful in his word choice this time.

Karen arrived at the hotel room precisely at seven o'clock. She had set her wristwatch precisely so she would not be late. Since their conversation about dinner time had been sarcastic and silly, she did not want to be early nor late. Being late was not her nature.

Daniel opened the door wide and motioned for Karen to come in. “Welcome to my home, the home of Daniel.”

“Technically, it's a hotel suite and not yours, but thank you,” she said as she walked through the door into the living room. The area was open to the kitchenette, and she saw the small table already set. The kitchen counters were clean, and the fabulous aroma of Italian spices filled the air. Daniel was thankful that Karen had rented him a suite. When he knew he would stay long enough to look for a job, he was grateful for the extra space and the kitchen space. There had been one available, and Karen was happy to rent it to him.

“Sure smells good. Are you sure you cooked? Where's the mess?”

“I cleaned up as I went. With it being an open space, a messy kitchen is a distraction. Believe me, I'm not always this tidy, although my mama tried to teach us to be. He motioned for her to have a seat as he pulled the chair out for her.

“A true gentleman.”

“I try. That, by the way, I learned from my Dad.”

He then brought over two salads with a side serving of her favorite Blue Cheese salad dressing.

“Thank you. You remembered my favorite!”

“Of course I did. It's mine also.”

They sat in silence as they ate. Although Daniel and Karen usually had no trouble communicating, this evening felt different. Maybe it was being in private instead of out in public making a difference. However, they had eaten in private at her place before. This time it was his rented, temporary home. Maybe that was the difference.

When they had finished their salads, Daniel took their bowls to the sink and returned with the lasagna and garlic bread fresh out of the oven. He set it down in the center of the table and served them each a large square of the lasagna. Karen helped herself to a piece of garlic bread. She was impressed with his cooking after taking just one bite of the lasagna.

"Oh my, this is amazing! Did you make this from scratch? You should be a chef! I may hire you to be my personal chef!" She savored her next bite.

Daniel saw the look in her eyes. He smiled at her with a gleam in his eye. "I don't know you well enough." He took a bite of his food and agreed. It was good. A chef? Yes. However, not her personal chef. He took another bite.

"What would you like to know? You have asked before, and I never did tell you much about me." She was ready to talk about herself now. She had talked about the area, her work, and her guests at the lake, but nothing too personal.

Daniel thought for a moment. What did he want to know about her? "Tell me something few people know about you," he finally said.

Karen continued to savor her meal, momentarily avoiding any further conversation. She was mentally occupied, thinking of what she was going to share with him. There were many things about her life that people did not know even though she had grown up there.

"Let me think about that, and I will tell you."

They finished eating, including the dessert of a simple chocolate mousse he had also made. Daniel built a fire in the fireplace after dinner. The early Spring was still chilly enough to enjoy the warmth it emitted. They sat on the sofa as they continued with small talk about the weather, the spring season, and more about the lake. He told her about his job interview and said he thought it had gone well. Finally, Daniel broke the small talk by telling Karen it was time for her to spill the beans about herself.

"Okay." Karen repositioned herself on the end of the sofa so she could sit with her legs under her as she faced him. She took a deep breath. "Are you sure you are ready to hear this?"

"Of course. I wouldn't have asked if I wasn't."

"Here goes. You are talking with a thief."

She waited for Daniel to react, but when he did not even flinch, she continued. "Yes, I'm a thief." She hesitated. "No reaction?"

"Not yet, continue. There has got to be more to the story. You're not in jail, you have a great job, and you haven't stolen anything from me – yet."

"When I was a little girl, I had a girlfriend who lived down the road not far from us. She was two years younger than me, and a lot braver or daring is a better word to describe her. She and I walked to the gift shop and started to look around. She looked up at me and said, 'watch this.' Then she took something off the shelf and put it into her pocket. I was stunned! I gave her such a look. She shook her head at me and told me that she did it all the time, that it was easy. She then egged me on to give it a try. I kept saying no, but she told me I wouldn't get caught. I noticed where the owners were dealing with another customer and not facing us. We were standing in front of the jewelry display. I had been eyeing a jade and gold ring for a while. I forget how much it cost, but to me, it was a lot. I picked it up and put it on my finger. It fit! So I took it off and put it in my pocket. We kept walking around for a few more minutes and then innocently walked out. She had been right; it was so easy to do. I quickly owned the ring I had wanted for so long, but I couldn't wear it. I didn't want anyone to ask me where I bought it. I especially did not want my parents to know about it. They knew I didn't have any money and wouldn't believe me if I told them someone gifted it to me."

She looked at her ring finger as if to still see the ring. "But, I felt guilty, so, so guilty. I hated feeling that way. But I did like the ring. The strange thing was that my parents belonged to a faith that we were not supposed to wear jewelry at all! Even if I wanted to chance wearing it, I couldn't wear it around them or out in public, and certainly not if I ever walked into that gift shop again. So I put it in a small box in my dresser."

"Do you still have the ring? Or did you eventually get caught?"

"No to both questions. I held onto the ring for the next four years. I went away to a boarding school over a hundred miles away when I was fifteen. I lived in the dorm and went to school on campus. Months later I continued to feel guilty. I finally told one of my new friends about it. She told me I had to give the ring back. I tried to reason with her that the owners never missed it. The truth was, I was afraid to get arrested and sent to jail. Or that my parents would kill me. I was more afraid of what my parents would do to me than going to jail. But I knew she was right in the end. I needed to give the ring back, no matter what happened. So, the next time I went home, I went to the gift shop and handed the ring to the owner. She looked at me and the ring and asked why I was handing that to her. I told her my story. Well, almost. I never ratted out my friend. I had no idea if she was still stealing things or not. We had stopped hanging out together soon after our joint thievery. Anyway, I gave the ring back. At least I tried. The owner told me that it had been so long that I could keep it, if I wanted to. I told her that I couldn't keep it; that it had bothered me for four years. I wanted the guilt to go away. She took the ring back and thanked me."

"She thanked you? That's amazing."

"That surprised me too. The store owner said that my four years of guilt had been enough punishment. She wasn't going to punish me, report me, not even tell my parents; and they were close friends."

"Wow, you were lucky. So glad it worked out for you." Daniel was about to say something else as Karen continued.

"Oh, wait, there's more to this story." Karen stood up to stretch her legs. Sitting on them for so long hurt more than when she was a kid. She stretched, then got up, walked to the window to look out. She smiled at the beauty outside, then grinned, knowing how her story took a turn. She returned to the sofa and sat back down to continue her story.

"Go on," Daniel motioned for her to continue. He was curious to know the rest of her story, especially when he noticed her grin.

The more he spent time with Karen, the more he wanted to know about her. Trouble was, he knew that one day he would have to tell her more about himself. He was not prepared to do that, and to be fair to her, and more so to himself, he would not push her to tell him anything else.

"I went away to college right after my high school graduation." She hesitated, then added, "When you think about it, by my leaving home while in high school, I left home when I was fifteen. My father hated me being away from home. But Mom wanted me in the boarding school. I spent the summers at home, which helped." Karen hesitated and stared into space.

Daniel was mesmerized by her story and did not interrupt her.

"Sorry, short Rabbit Trail there, I have a habit of those... the Rabbit Trails." She shook her head and chuckled as she remembered something. "Back to the real story. I decided to make business management my major. After my experience returning the ring four years after the fact and how nice she was about it, I knew I wanted to be like her someday and work in the business. I wanted to make a difference in other people's lives like she did. I did well in college. I came home for a while after graduation and moved back in with my parents for a short time while I searched for a job. I had worked in the mall across town from the college campus and knew the world of retail. I even moved up into management early in my career. But it wasn't satisfying. I wanted more. So I moved home to figure it out."

"What did you figure out? How did you get here?"

"I had no idea what I wanted to do with my life until the owner here saw me one day enjoying some spare time at the lake. She came over, and we started talking. She told me that she and her husband would retire later that year and needed someone to run the business, actually to take it over. They would still own it, at least for a while, but they didn't want to be hands-on anymore. They wanted to entrust it to someone who would run it the way they did. Someone who would treat their customers and renters with compassion and understanding. Someone smart and strong enough to also handle the business end. She told me they wanted someone they knew they could trust and not have any worries. I told her that I would be sorry to see them go and wished her good luck finding the perfect person. She told me she already had – ME!"

"Wow! That's how you got here?"

"Yep. The owners stayed in charge when I first took over and only traveled short distances to be here if I needed them. I had increased their profits in just two years, and they approached me about buying it from them. So, I did, along with a silent partner."

"That's amazing. They found a good one in you."

"Thanks. Yes, especially since," she hesitated, "I stole that ring from here. It proves that no matter what someone has done in their life, it is never too late to make amends and set things straight. I learned that the fear we live with, not knowing how someone will react, is worse than facing that fear head-on and releasing all that anxiety. It was such a relief when I returned that ring, and it changed my entire life. Before I returned the ring, I spent several wasted hours playing scenarios over in my head. So strongly that at times I pictured myself spending life in prison. I had a hard time shopping in any store for a while, thinking everyone was watching me and that they all knew I was a thief."

"You can't get life for stealing a simple ring." Her story was an inspiration and had him thinking.

"No, but your imagination runs wild when you are a kid. When you're guilty of something you think no one will understand or that no one will give you a second chance, you think the worst."

“True,” he said. Then added, “I guess.”

They sat in silence for a few minutes. Karen looked at her watch and stood up. Where had the time gone? She had to get up early the next morning. A few early arrivals were coming for an early-in-the-season vacation.

“Oh my, look at the time. I need to get going. I've been a bit long-winded with my life's story, but you did ask. You have to promise not to tell anyone. No one knows about my past and stealing that ring. Well, no one but the previous owners and now you.” She suddenly felt vulnerable. Would he tell? If he did, who would he tell, and what difference would it make. If he told her customers, her silent partner, her investors, would they think less of her? Would they not trust her? “Please don't tell anyone,” she pleaded.

“I won't tell anyone. Believe me; I have my own stories.”

“I'd love to hear them. Maybe next time you can tell me something about yourself that no one else knows. Deal?” She held out her hand so they could shake on it.

“I'll have to think of which story to tell you,” he chuckled as if he had several to tell.

“I'm sure they will be interesting,” she said as Daniel walked her to the door.

“See you tomorrow.”

“Yes, see you tomorrow. Thank you for a delicious meal and a great evening.”

“You're welcome. I hope we can do this again.”

They stood facing each other for a long silent moment, as their eyes met. Karen smiled and turned and walked out the door.

Daniel watched as she left. He didn't close the door until he saw her get in her car and drive away. He leaned on the door, thinking about what she had just shared. How was he ever going to open up to her and tell her his story? His were so much worse than hers. He shook his head, then headed to the kitchen to wash up the dishes. He wanted a drink. No, he silently told himself, thankful there was no alcohol in the hotel room.

He finished cleaning up the room. His phone rang as he was walking back into the living room area. It was Mr. Carr telling him he had the job if he wanted and that he could start in the morning.

Chapter Fourteen

Daniel arrived early for work. It was one of the many things his parents had instilled in him. Always be on time, always give your best. Larry, as Mr. Carr asked to be called, met him at the docks. Larry wasted no time getting to the details of the job. He explained to Daniel the work that needed completing before the guests arrived. He went on to explain the variety of customers and guests they dealt with throughout the season. There were the early arrivals, who liked to beat the crowds, the families who had to wait until schools were out, and those that preferred late summer and early fall with the cool nights and autumn colors. There were those that rented a cabin versus those that only rented dock space or a boat while enjoying the lake. Daniel did his best to take in all the information. Larry added that the first place they would be working was the landscaping at the cove to make it safe for guests.

"So, Daniel, how have you been doing?" Larry asked when they were taking a lunch break. "Again, I'm so sorry to hear about the loss of your parents. Such a tragedy to lose both of them so close together."

"Yes, it was quite a shock." Daniel avoided making eye contact. He did not want to discuss it. "I'm still trying to digest it all. It was so sudden. Something no one would expect." He tried to brush it off.

Larry picked up on it and added, "It may help to talk about it. I'm here if you need someone to listen."

"I came here to remember the better times with my parents. It was always the three of us when we came here in the summers. I loved it. The lake, the friends I made, the fun. No stress. I remember my parents being more relaxed when they were here." Daniel was talking, but his eyes and mind were in the distance. Memories were flowing, and for some reason, Daniel found it easy to talk to Larry. He had not planned to share his thoughts while at work. He was beginning to share some of his life's story with Karen, thinking that was enough. Yet here he was, opening up with Larry even more.

Larry was quiet while listening. He sensed that Daniel wanted to talk, so he did not want to interrupt him. There was a time and place for everything; this was the time to listen. All the work that they had to do could wait. Lunch break deserved more time occasionally. He had been good friends with Daniel's parents and felt compelled to help Daniel. Listening was the first step in helping him as he had helped his parents. It was not up to Larry to interject what he knew about them. Especially not their issues. It may come up in time, but now he would merely be there for Daniel to listen or help. The choice would be up to this young man he had hired.

Daniel shifted his body to get a better view of the lake. Their lunch break time was over, but Daniel continued sharing with Larry.

"I remember when I was in grade school when Mom and Dad were both busy working. Mom was the one who helped with my homework, took me to game practices, and drove me to school functions. I always thought the reason Dad never spent time with me was that he was busy at work. I remember him spending time with my sisters every night when he was home, but not with me. Mom spent time with all of us. Special occasions were a big part of our family, with large family dinners during the holidays. Christmas was amazing. The house could fit a lot of people. I was a bit older when I finally realized that all those who stayed at our house weren't family. They were paying guests. They paid money to be there." Daniel stopped to take a drink of water. "I didn't mean to tell you so much."

"That's okay. I told you I was here to listen any time you wanted to share." Larry encouraged him to continue.

"We lived with my grandparents when I was real young. Eventually, my grandparents and parents made some renovations to the place. They built on additions for more people to come and stay. Dad even quit his job to help Granddaddy run it. Mom helped Grandmom cook and clean. We still came to the lake each summer. The tensions from home had lessened, but it was still always easier at the lake. It was less stressful for them since they did not have to worry about the guests and everything being perfect. I don't know what made the difference with my Dad. He tried to get closer to me when I was a teen. Except I was too much of a rebel by then. His attempt seemed forced, adding to the fact that I didn't want a relationship with him. That was the first time I took off. I disappeared for a while. I got in with the wrong crowd. I started drinking and getting into trouble. Nothing put me in jail, thankfully, but it was close a couple of times. My parents found me and took me home, but later I took off again. This time they reluctantly let me go."

Larry offered Daniel another bottle of water. He could tell they were going to be there a while. His plans for the day were changing. Work could wait. Daniel needed to talk to someone. His wife would understand when some work did not get done. She would even be forgiving if he were late going home. That was something she loved about him. He was always there for others, as well as his own family. Larry loved his wife because she was so understanding.

"Yeah, I know, I messed up pretty bad at times, yet somehow it all turned out okay. Then I hit bottom again about three years ago. I made a bad business deal and lost it all. I took off to find a better life and ended up hitting the bottle again. I traveled around the country, staying for short periods in each place, but always stayed the wanderer, always the drinker. By the time I heard the news of my Dad's death, I was too late for the funeral, but it woke me up. I wanted to get my life straightened out for my Mom. I was attending AA meetings and was getting clean. I was heading home. Then a friend showed me the news that my Mom had died of a heart attack. I was devastated. I had to go home."

"So, did you go home?"

"No, I tried, but I was stupid and stopped at a bar a few days before, and that was it. I hit bottom by the end of that night. All I could do was run – again. I was no good to the family."

"So, you came here to reconnect?"

"No, not immediately. I went to Florida for a while, and then I came here."

Larry reached over and touched Daniel's arm. "Anytime you want to leave here and go home, I will understand. You don't have to stay. I can always find someone to help me get this place ready for the tourist season."

"No, I'm not ready yet." He had a small smile on his face.

"Why the smile? Something I should know about?"

"I met Karen."

"Ah, it figures it would be a girl. Karen is a fine young lady. She's made quite a success for herself. You can't go wrong being her friend."

"It may be more than that. I really like her. The trouble is, she doesn't know much about me. I've kept so many things secret from everyone all these years. It's not easy for me to open up about my life."

"But, here you are, talking to me about it."

"You're easy to talk to. Why is that?" Daniel turned and looked at him. He was back in the present day. He took a deep breath as if he was clearing out all his memories and demons.

"I'm not sure, but your Dad and I used to have long talks as well."

"Yeah? What did you talk about?"

"Lots of things. I'm not going to bore you with the details. Know that your Dad loved you the best he knew how. He had a hard time showing it so that you would know. I'm sure someday you will understand."

"I hope so." Daniel stood up and dusted off his jeans. "Time's a wastin', time to get back to work."

"Okay, son, let's get some work done before dinner time rolls around." Calling him *son* was a natural thing for Larry to do. He was glad Daniel had no reaction to that part of the comment. They picked up their mess from lunch and headed to the next small cove to clear more fallen and blown brush.

Larry watched as Daniel put his all into getting the job done. He was a good worker, but he could tell he had a lot on his mind. Distractions were not a good thing. He would have to keep him busy and focused.

Larry thought back to the years when Daniel's family spent summers there. He remembered the conversations with Daniel's dad and the time he shared with both his parents while they were at the lake. He knew Daniel did not know about those years. It may be years before he found out if he ever did. Larry hoped that if he did learn of those times that he would be able to handle it.

Larry invited Daniel home for dinner at the end of their workday. Both physically and mentally exhausted, Daniel asked for a rain check.

Daniel returned to the hotel, looking for Karen as he entered the parking lot. He was a bit disappointed but also relieved when her car was not in the parking lot. He needed to get some sleep. He had a lot on his mind but hoped sleep would come quickly.

Chapter Fifteen

Sara and Marc were having a great time playing with all the toys in the play area of the great room of the manor while they waited for Heather to return from her counseling session with Ben. She hoped things were beginning to work out for the two of them.

Most of the Bed and Breakfasts they were familiar with were designed for couples. Sara and Heather purposely added the play area to Bella Rose Manor as it would be set up for families with children except for a few weeks of the year that would be designated for couples only; such as New Years, Valentine's week, and the third week in June to accommodate newlyweds on their honeymoon.

She heard car doors close and watched Marc as he jumped up from the floor and ran to the front door when he heard them.

"Mama!" he was jumping up and down. Then Sara heard, "Daddy!" She knew things were going to be okay. Ben was home. She hoped.

"Welcome home!" Sara said as she greeted them near the door. How did it go?"

"It went very well, Sis. Ben and I have some things to work out, but life is amazing!"

Sara smiled when she saw their faces aglow with young love and Ben's arm around his wife's shoulders.

"Good to know. I assume you are moving into the guest house?"

"As soon as I get the rest of my things from the house. Until then, I'll do with what Heather has already moved over. I'm not spending another night without her."

They all walked into the kitchen and sat around the island, their family hub for meetings and planning. Sara poured them each a cup of freshly brewed coffee. She poured milk into Marc's sippy cup while Heather lifted him into his booster seat at the island. Sara liked seeing her family together again. Yes, they were a whole family again. Well, almost. They still had not found Andy.

Before Heather's counseling appointment, she and Sara had been working on finalizing everything before the grand re-opening. Sara was excited to know Ben would be there now to help more. One of the things that needed completion before their opening was the landscaping.

"I'm so glad you're back. We were going over what needed finishing for the soft opening. We have the inside done. It is the outside landscaping that needs a few more personal touches. I was hoping you would be able to make sure it gets done on time. Please?" Sara raised her brow in her flirty way that always helped her win her case. It worked on strangers as well as family.

"I'm here for whatever you need. I'll pull my crew from their current jobs if I need to. I know Donovan will be available to help." Ben held Heather's hand up. "I am here for the long haul. For Heather, for Marc, for all of you and Bella Rose Manor. Just tell me what needs attention."

The three of them sat and discussed the landscaping ideas and the work involved. Construction on the gazebo would finish up that weekend. The crew would start work on the pond the following week. The landscapers would work on the garden areas starting the next day. Sara had been afraid they would have to hire an outside contractor instead of Ben since she was not sure of his family status and desires to be a part of the family when they originated their plans. Knowing he was on board with them now was such a relief.

With all the details finalized and Sara's notes and list completed, they made dinner. The conversation changed to small talk, including what was going on in town, discussing when spring would finally be there and how that affected their lives. After dinner they all cleaned up the kitchen before Heather and Ben said goodnight to take Marc home to put him to bed. Sara said she would lock up and meet them for breakfast in the morning at the manor.

The landline phone rang as Sara was locking the door. The phone had not rung much in the last several weeks. Sara debated letting it go to the answering machine but picked up the receiver.

"Hello. Bella Rose Manor, Sara speaking."

"Yes, this is she," Sara responded after listening to the caller.

"Are you sure? You've seen him? You've talked with him?" Sara pulled a stool from the island over to the counter so she could sit down. She was silent for quite a while as she let the caller speak.

"No, no need to tell him. I am thankful to know he is alive and safe. It's up to him to contact us. If you say he changed his name, are you sure it's him? You said you had not seen him in over ten years."

"Okay. Yes, I'm sure you would know him. Did he talk of coming home anytime soon? Has he mentioned home or us at all?"

"Ah, I see. Well, at least you are there for him. No, don't push him. I know how he gets when he's pushed. He'll disappear again to who knows where."

"Yes, please keep me updated. I agree it's best not to tell him that you have contacted us."

"Thank you so much for the phone call, Larry. Hope to talk to you soon."

Sara hung up the phone and stared at it a moment. She finally knew where her brother was, and that he was doing alright. Now she had a decision to make. She needed to go home where she was sure not to be interrupted so she could think out loud. She did not want to risk being there if Heather or Ben returned to the manor for any reason.

At home, she made herself a cup of tea, then sat down at the window seat in her living room where she could relive the conversation with Larry about her brother.

After much thought, she decided she would not tell Heather about it. Yes, it was exciting that she knew where Andy was. However, Andy had not made the phone call. He did not even know Larry had called. It was evident that Andy wanted to remain hidden. It would do no good to tell Heather. If she did tell her sister, she would have to tell her about being in touch with him the day before the accident. For two reasons she was not ready for that. One, she did not want to remind her sister of that day. It was enough that Heather had reminders of it every day when she looked in the mirror or even walked. To find out that Sara had kept something from her as well? No, now was not the time. She would wait until Andy called on his own. The second reason was that she did not want to raise their hopes that Andy would come home. Even Larry had mentioned that he did not think Andy was ready.

She took her last sip of tea and told herself life was good. It was unfortunate that she had such a big secret to keep from her sister. She knew it would come out someday, just not yet. She would live with the consequences when they came.

Sleep did not come easy for her that night. She kept seeing her brother in her visions. Her dream took her back to when he was a kid, back to when they had happier times.

Chapter Sixteen

The day dawned early at Bella Rose Manor. Marc woke up before anyone else and climbed from his toddler bed into the queen size bed with his mama and Daddy. It was a great way to start the day—family time. Ben got up a few minutes later to get ready for work. He needed to talk to his crew before they headed to their first job of the day. Ben needed them at the manor instead. He wanted them to finish the work there before going to their other jobs. He would call the other customers and reschedule. It was also time to talk with Donovan about him managing the company. Ben knew he would do an excellent job as General Manager. He had been there with Ben from the very beginning; it was time for Donovan to get a good break in life. Not that his other workers did not deserve a good break, but there was something special about Donovan and his wife, Cecelia. They were close to his heart.

Heather took Marc to the manor with her when Ben left for work. They found Sara cooking breakfast for them. She poured herself a cup of fresh coffee and let it sit to cool while she got Marc's breakfast ready. He wandered off to play, pulling the toys out of the toy box and scattered them throughout the great room. She realized she would have to teach him to keep the toys in the small space designated for them. They were also going to have to teach him that the toys were not his alone; they were mainly for the guest's children. She would have to find a different place for him to play on his own.

As the two ladies were finishing breakfast and cleaning up, they heard a knock at the side door. Donovan was there to let her know the crew would be working on the gazebo. As he walked out the side entrance of the kitchen, a knock came at the front door. Sara opened it to find another worker letting her know they would be digging for the pond that morning. Sara thanked him for letting her know, then closed the door and walked back to the kitchen, shaking her head. It was going to be a busy but productive day.

Ben came home at noon to follow up with his promise to supervise the landscaping crews. Between the gazebo, the pond, the garden, and the walkway, the place was overrun with construction workers.

Sara and Heather were inside accepting deliveries for the furnishings for the bedrooms. The babysitter stopped by to see if they could use her help to watch Marc while all the work was going on. She was a lifesaver indeed. Marc was having fun watching all the workers and big machinery, but they knew he would be safer in the hands of the babysitter. He whined and complained about leaving, but finally went with the babysitter. They all could concentrate on their work without worrying that he would be in the way or get hurt.

The doorbell rang amid the chaos of the morning. Sara yelled that it was open, thinking it was one of the delivery people or a crew member. Nicole walked in instead.

"Nicole, Hi! How are you? I've not seen you since the hospital. What brings you around?"

"Joe and I have a reservation for the soft opening, and I wanted to get a sneak peek. I also wanted to see how my patient was doing. I heard she's not been back for her check-ups. I know it's not protocol, but I've been talking with her doctor." She looked around for Heather.

"What do you mean she's not been back? I thought she was there a couple of weeks ago."

"Not according to Dr. George. I was working with her again yesterday when Heather's name came up. Doc mentioned the last she saw Heather was her second appointment when the boot came off. Is she doing okay?"

"She's doing great. The scar is still there on her face, but it always will be, and she still limps, but the doctor said that would be with her for the rest of her life as well. She's fine. At least she seems to be. Do you want me to get her? She should be upstairs."

"Oh, that's okay. It's not my place to say anything. I was just in the area and thought I would stop by."

Sara noticed the concern in Nicole's voice. “Is everything alright?” Sara asked before she even moved to go upstairs.

“Yes, of course,” Nicole said.

Sara went upstairs and told Heather that Nicole was there to see her. Heather looked at Sara with a questioning look. “Why?”

“Not sure. She mentioned that you hadn't kept your appointments with Dr. George? Have you been missing your appointments?”

“I'm doing fine. There was no reason to go back.”

“Please go down and see her. Let her see for herself that you are fine.”

Heather walked down to meet Nicole. Sara followed close behind.

“Hi Heather, it's so good to see you again.” Nicole turned to face her.

“It's good to see you too. How have you been?”

“I'm fine. How have you been? Are you feeling well?”

“I'm doing well. My scar is healing, as you can see. I still limp, but that will always be with me. I'm doing great otherwise. Did Dr. George send you to check on me?”

“Yes, and no. Like I told Sara, Joe and I have reservations here for the soft opening, I wanted to check the place out first. When I was talking with Dr. George at the hospital, I told her I would be here. She asked me to check on you. Says you haven't been in for your follow-up appointments. I will be happy to tell her that you are doing well.”

“Would you like a quick tour since you are here? We're not finished, as you could tell by all the construction workers and trucks outside, but we will be by soft opening.” Heather started to walk so Nicole could follow. Sara told them she wanted to check on the outside crews but would catch up to them.

Nicole stayed for a cup of coffee after the tour before heading back to work. She said that she and Joe would be there for the soft opening to spend the night. She was looking forward to it and seeing it all finished. Adding that it was already looking beautiful.

Chapter Seventeen

Daniel opened his eyes the morning after he had opened up to Larry. He lay in his hotel bed, thinking of what they had talked about, and could not believe he had shared so much information with him. But damn, Daniel thought, Larry was so easy to talk to. He still had not told him everything and was trying not to. He did not think he was ready. It was bad enough that Larry knew who he was. Karen did not know. At least he doubted it. He did not remember her from his childhood, even though she said she had grown up there. Maybe it was time to be honest. Keeping the truth from her could hurt her later. He did not want to ruin their friendship and was hoping their friendship would grow. He was trying to start a new life with a part of that being open and honest.

He peered out the window in hopes of seeing Karen before he headed to work. He was about to close the curtains when he saw her car pull up to the office. Today was the day. He took a deep breath and taking his coffee mug with him, walked out the door to greet Karen before she went into the office.

"Good morning, Sunshine," he said as she was closing her car door.

She smiled as she turned at the sound of his voice. "Good morning yourself."

"I have to get to work in a few minutes, but I'd like to know if you are free this evening for dinner?"

"I am, as a matter of fact. I will be out of the office at six tonight. Are we going somewhere, or are you cooking again?"

It's a surprise. I'll be here right after six to pick you up."

"Sounds like we are going somewhere."

"I could be picking you up to carry you to my room." Daniel winked at her as he turned to leave. "See you tonight." He turned and walked to his car and headed to work.

The truth was he had no idea where he was going to take her for dinner. He would not have time to make a great dinner after he got off work, and he did not want to go to a crowded restaurant. He decided he would ask Larry to recommend a nice place to take Karen. Then he shrugged his shoulders. If he asked Larry about a place to go that was quiet, he would want to know why. Daniel felt torn over what to do and what all to tell Larry and especially Karen. He did want to be honest with Karen. He thought he owed Larry his honesty because of being a family friend for years. He remembered Larry and his wife spending time with his family. He remembered Larry and his Dad going fishing together. He would play it by ear and see how the day went.

Larry greeted him when he arrived at the cove to work. "Good morning. I see I didn't work you too hard yesterday. You came back for more." He laughed as he started down to the water's edge.

"Nope, that was not enough to run me off. Yet. I did bring extra strong coffee with me today to help. What are we working on today?"

"I have a boat dock to repair before we can lower it into the lake. At the end of the season, the rough storms tore some of the boards from the front side. Some areas need sanding to smooth away any danger of getting splinters when people walk on it."

"Let's go then. The day's a wastin'," Daniel began to walk to the truck to get the tools. Larry headed to the dock to examine the total damage and determine how much lumber he would need to purchase for the repairs.

The two of them worked well together throughout the day. They had the pieces replaced on the dock, including sanding off most of the rough areas before lunchtime. They took a break for lunch with plans to finish sanding the dock and then push it into the water anchoring it into position that afternoon. They needed to push it out far enough for guests to dive off for swimming and boats to come in and dock to pick up passengers. Larry always attached a short ladder on the left side of the dock to aid people climbing out of the water. It was a lot different than swimming in a swimming pool. Climbing back onto the dock was not always easy. Having that ladder made it safer.

While they ate lunch at the local sandwich shop, they talked about the upcoming summer season and the returning guests. Daniel knew some stayed for a couple of weeks, some for only a weekend. Larry said he knew most of them as they had been coming for several years. A few who had come as children now were returning grown, married with children of their own.

"You've been rather quiet this morning, young man. What's on your mind?"

Daniel took another bite of his sandwich and a drink of his water, finishing it to give him time before answering.

"You are very observant. I do have a few things on my mind. One is Karen."

"Yes, you told me that you liked her. Has that changed?"

"Oh, no, quite the opposite. I like her a lot. So much so that I want to share with her the things I told you yesterday and even more."

"There's more?"

"Oh, yes, there's more. I have been keeping it inside for a long time. I think it is why I ran. No, I know it's why I ran."

"Care to share?"

"That's just it. I don't know if I am ready. Although holding it all in is about to kill me. I'm not sleeping. I want a drink so bad I can almost taste it. And seeing Karen and knowing how she may feel about me once I tell her has me afraid to open up. Can she, heck, can you handle my secret?"

"Son, I've spent my life listening to people and keeping their secrets. It's not my place to spread rumors, bad news, or someone's life story unless they tell me I can."

"Thanks, Larry. I guess I could practice by telling you. Then if you don't run me off, I know I can tell Karen. It may change her life and not in a good way, depending on how I handle telling her."

"Okay, then spill it. I'm all ears." Larry sat back, raised his arms, and locked his hands at the crown of his head.

"I can't tell you here." He locked around at the lunch crowd, who were still eating. "Can we go back to the cove?"

"Sure. I get it, less corn." Larry motioned for the waitress to bring their check for their meal. He hoped Daniel understood his reference to corn having ears to hear. After he had paid, including a good tip, they drove back to the cove. It was warm enough to enjoy sitting on the large rocks at the edge of the property. The water would submerge these rocks as the lake rose with the dam opening in late spring and with the summer rains. For now, they would enjoy nature's seats.

Once they sat and were as comfortable as they could get on the rock, Larry motioned with his hand palm side up for Daniel to talk.

Daniel sat, leaning his elbows against a separate rock behind him. His legs dangled over the edge of the large rock.

"Okay, here goes. You already know about me, at least as a kid. I get that. Karen doesn't know about me except what she sees of me now and what little I have told her. You also know me by my real name. She does not. That's not the main thing she needs to know about me. You need to know about the real me too. You need to know what I am more than who I seem to be now or who I was. I'm not the same person." Daniel took a deep breath and looked out onto the lake. He thought before he spoke.

This lake had been his safe place as a child. For a few weeks each year, at this lake, was when his father treated him as a father should. His Mama and Daddy got along and were happy. It was a different story at home. It was not horrible, but it was different. His parents did not always get along. For some reason, once he was old enough, he began to run away. He never dealt with the possible reasons; he just always ran.

He turned back to Larry. "I stopped coming here with my parents in my early teens. I know they kept coming for a few years without me, but I never returned, as you know. I was already on the run. They may have shared that with you." He waited a moment for a response; when it did not come, he continued.

"I took off for good as soon as I was old enough and had my diploma. I had left before as a teen, only to have them bring me back. Once I had the diploma, I traveled around the country. I disappeared. My folks did not know where I was. No one knew where I was. I changed my birth name and did not go back to school for a while. I started college but got in with the wrong crowd and started drinking. I dropped out and later went to a trade school instead of college. I'm trained as a chef if you can believe that one." He chuckled. He did his best to pretend he could not cook most of the time. Cooking always brought up more bad memories. Not to mention people expecting more out of him than he was willing to give.

Larry adjusted the way he was sitting to face the young man with him but continued to watch and listen as he released truths about himself.

Daniel continued. "I would return home after a couple of years and then take off again. They never knew what I was doing. All they knew was I would return home at my worst, clean up, get sober, then when something else happened, I would be on the run. The most recent time that I was once again ready to go back home, I even called my sister. I set up a time to meet with her. Unfortunately, my timing could not have been worse; neither were my intentions. That may be why I fell off the wagon and never showed up as I said I would. See, I had heard about the death of my parents. I figured there had to be an inheritance. I wanted to stay sober, go home, claim my inheritance, stay for a while so they would believe I'd stay forever. My plan was always to take off again once I had the money. I planned to spend my life on the run. I thought I'd be set once I had my inheritance. At least for a while. I figured my folks had a lot of money to share with us kids." Daniel stopped and caught his breath. His life story was flowing faster than he thought it would. It was so easy to talk with Larry.

"So what happened this time that you broke your promise? Were you feeling guilty about your motives? Or was it something else? You seem genuinely troubled by this." Larry was sitting up straighter and leaned slightly closer to Daniel. This young man needed him. He needed a father figure to believe in him and to trust him. He could sense there was a lot more to his life story. He would do whatever he could to help him. He had a special spot in his heart for him.

Daniel continued his story. "I had contacted her a few days earlier to set up the time and location, which gave me a free night to waste hanging around. I kept a low profile, hoping no one who knew me would see me. The best place to hide? Inside a dark and nasty bar. I sat in the back, watching people come and go, watching people having a good time, drinking to their heart's content. Even though I had chosen a bar, it was not my goal to get drunk or even to have a drink. I knew better. You know how temptation can get you. It draws you in, especially if you are in the wrong place. That's what happened. I thought I could handle it. I had been sober for over a year." Daniel lowered his eyes in disappointment.

"Then, against my better judgment, I had a drink." He looked up at Larry. "One stinking drink! That led to another, and another, and another. By the time the bar closed, I could barely see straight. Somehow, I did make it to the place I was staying. It was noon the next day before I woke up. I knew I was a goner. I headed back to the bar for another drink. The hair of the dog type thing, you know?" Daniel looked out over the lake. Flashbacks of those days filled his mind.

Larry nodded his head. He understood after witnessing others in the same boat. The area he lived in had plenty of bars. More bars than churches, unfortunately. He had seen his share of drunks on the road and in boats on the lake. People always thought they could drive a car on the road or a boat on the lake while they were drinking. They thought they were fine and that an accident would not happen to them.

"I kept a watch on the time so I could meet with my sister. I had sobered up somewhat because the bartender refused to serve me more than one drink. He knew I was drunk the night before and didn't want to be associated with me if something happened. Well, something did happen." Daniel's eyes drifted into space. He stopped talking. What he had to say next was the hard part. It was the nightmare he had been having for almost a year. It felt like just yesterday each time he recalled the events from that night. He glanced at Larry for a second. He could not maintain eye contact. He set his gaze out across the rippling waters of the lake. He took a deep breath, then spoke again.

"I drove away from the bar. I headed to meet with my sister. I was nervous and excited. I was hoping for a great reunion. She had sounded happy to hear from me, so I hoped all would go great. Oh, I still had my thoughts of claiming my inheritance and then running away again. I was hoping for at least acceptance back into the family. I mean, who avoids going home when one of their parents dies? Who stays away when both parents die? Me! That's who."

Daniel continued to tell Larry all the details that led him to arrive in Pennsylvania, including the part that he would find the most difficult to tell Karen. He explained what happened that night and why he never met with his sister. He included some details of his brief stay in Florida before coming to Pennsylvania. He added that Karen knew some of it, but not all. By the time he finished talking, they both had tears in their eyes.

Larry took his time to respond as he digested Daniel's story. Finally, he spoke. "Daniel, the important part is that you can open up about it, at least to me. I can tell it weighed heavy on your heart. I could tell from watching you over the last few weeks that something was bothering you. Yes, I've been watching. We watch out for each other around here. We know when a stranger comes to town. When that stranger starts spending time with one of our young locals, we pay attention. And when that stranger is not at all a stranger and works for me, well, I'm here for you." He saw Daniel smile slightly.

Larry continued. "You were here about a week when I finally saw you. Karen told me there was a new guest at her place and a little bit about you. I look out for her. Since it was early in the season, I wanted to make sure she was safe. I rarely worry much when there are a lot of people around, but it is slow this time of year. A strange male on his own who isn't just passing through the area? Well, I wanted to see this person. As soon as I saw you, I knew who you were. I relaxed a bit because I knew your parents. I knew what stock you came from. I realized you had changed your name but shrugged it off as just something people do from time to time. I might have gotten in touch sooner if I had known what you have experienced. I was excited to see you again after all these years. Karen told me that you were here to spend some time thinking and figuring out life, which is why I didn't push reconnecting with you. And, to ease your worries, I have not told Karen anything about you."

"Thank you, Larry. I came here to hide out for a while. I was hoping no one would recognize me. Since it's been so long since I've been here, I was hoping none of the people I knew as a child were still here or hoping that my looks had changed enough to be unrecognizable. The area has changed so much I'm still finding my way around. I've already stayed longer than I thought I would. I certainly had no intention of falling in love."

He stopped talking and shot a glance at Larry. "You did not hear that."

"Oh yes, I did, young man, and it is wonderful. However, if you love Karen, you need to tell her. And you need to tell her everything. If she loves you, the two of you will be able to work it out. She's more than you know. She has a big heart." Larry was smiling.

"What are you smiling about over there?"

"Oh, imagining you and Karen getting married and you living here. Then I can hire you full time."

"Wait. What? Married? Live here? Work for you?" Daniel turned to face him with a look of shock. He stood up and stepped to a different rock, scratching his head. "I may not have thought this through as much as I thought I had."

"Sit down, son." Larry motioned for him to sit beside him. "All I'm saying is I'm excited for you. There's no need to rush into marriage, but you do need to be honest with Karen. Now let's get up off our butts. I'm too old to sit on a rock this long," Larry said.

They spent the rest of the afternoon finishing the dock and clearing more brush. Larry wanted to have it all done to push the dock out into the water sometime over the next couple of days.

Larry kept his eye on the young man who had just poured part of his heart out to him. He felt himself smiling. It was so good to have him back in his life. He had grown close to him when he'd come to the lake with his folks. It hurt when he stopped coming, though he would never admit that to him. He needed to let the adult relationship they were forming now be enough. The thought that he may marry and move here? That idea warmed his heart.

Daniel headed into town to pick up something to make for supper after they finished their workday. Finding nothing to suit him, he decided on a pizza that he could pick up after picking Karen up. His thought was a picnic on the dike. There usually were not a lot of people. It was beautiful and with few to no interruptions. He hoped the conditions were right for him to tell her all he wanted to share.

Larry drove home after work. His wife had left him a note that she had a meeting, and his dinner was staying warm in the oven. He was glad he had the house to himself. It was good for the soul to have alone time occasionally. Tonight, that's what he wanted. Alone time with thoughts and fond memories.

Karen was ready when Daniel stopped to pick her up. Daniel had noticed that she was on time for everything and appreciated that about her. Daniel walked her to his car and opened the passenger side door. Karen asked where they were going before getting into the car.

"A pizza picnic on the dike. Complete with blankets and flashlights – in case it gets dark. We have to stop at Geno's for the pizza on the way.

"Sounds romantic." She smiled at him and reached for his hand while he drove.

The sun was beginning to set as Karen and Daniel finished eating. The sunset reflection glistening across the ripples on the lake was a beautiful sight.

They chatted about their day and other small talk while they ate, but Karen could tell there was more Daniel wanted to say.

"What's on your mind? You've looked distant since you picked me up."

Daniel looked away from the lake where he had been watching the beautiful sunset and looked at Karen.

"Oh, Karen, there is so much I want to share with you. So much you should know about me."

"We've not known each other very long. I don't expect to know everything about you."

"True, but there are important things you need to know. Things I want you to know."

"Okay, I'm listening." She turned her full attention to him.

"Here goes nothing, or everything," he mumbled to himself before beginning. "Karen, while it's true we've only known each other for a short time, I already have strong feelings for you. So strong that I have to tell you things about me that few people know or even need to know."

"You've told me about being in Florida before coming here and what took you there. What else is there?"

He jumped right in, "I'm an alcoholic, which I told you. The reason I went to Florida was a small car accident that happened in Tennessee," he hesitated. This part was going to be hard to share. "I hit or was hit by something and never realized it 'til the next day when I was leaving the hotel where I stayed and noticed the damage to my car. Since I could not remember what I hit or hit me, I realized I had hit bottom – drunk – again. I had no idea what had happened. I panicked. I even quit my job. Well, I simply never returned to my job. I got in my car and kept driving."

"Okay." Karen was listening.

"You see, I was supposed to meet my sister that night. Our parents had died within six months of each other, and I figured there had to be an inheritance for me. I planned to go home, claim it, then return to my job. I had been sober for over a year, was doing good at my job, and felt good being sober. I had no desire to permanently be back with my family. I called my sister and told her I was coming home. She asked if I had heard about our parents. I told her that was my reason to be coming home. She accepted that and me. She even sounded excited to meet with me." His story felt like rambling to him, but he continued. Karen was not interrupting him.

"It had been over three years since I had been in touch with my family. I told my sister I wasn't ready to return home to stay. I didn't even want to meet at the house. She told me we could discuss that when we met. We agreed on the time and place to meet. I was looking forward to seeing her. Then I got nervous. I was so nervous that the night before we were to meet, I found a bar. My original plan was to go in, gather my thoughts, and prepare to meet my sister. I went to the bar because I could hide in the back where no one who might know me would see me. While I sat there, I noticed everyone having a good time drinking and told myself I could handle one drink to calm my nerves."

Daniel hesitated as he recalled that day. "Only one. Well, that led to a second and a third. Before I knew it, I was off the wagon. I managed to find my way back to my hotel room. The next day I went back to the bar for another drink to get rid of my hangover. One drink was all the bartender would give me. After that one drink, I was too embarrassed to meet my sister. I got in my car and took off driving. I never even called my sister to tell her I wasn't coming. I knew I had hurt her. I figured my leaving was better for everyone. After all, my family expected me to be running. As far as I knew only Sara knew where I was. At least that's what I told myself. I found a hotel, checked in, and fell asleep. The next morning was when I noticed my damaged car. Karen, I don't remember hitting anything, nor getting hit. I know I didn't stop. If I hit someone or something, I don't remember. I even thought maybe someone had hit my car while it sat outside at the hotel. Until I realized that was impossible because of how I had parked." He was shaking and almost in tears. He hoped he was making sense and knew he was repeating some of his story.

"Oh, Daniel, I'm so sorry." She reached out to hold his forearm.

"There's no reason for you to be sorry. I'm the one who screwed up—all on my own. The thing is, I'm thinking of going home again. It's been almost nine months since that night. I've been sober again for the last six, almost seven months. It should have been eight months, but I've had a few slip-ups in Florida. That is why I came to the lake. I knew it would only get worse again if I stayed there."

"I know you've been sober since being here. I'm proud of you." She was smiling, but her eyes looked away. Her body still faced him; it was her eyes that could not.

"I agree you should go home," she almost whispered.

In truth, she did not want him to leave. Not yet. Not ever. She knew when he arrived to rent a hotel room that he was not going to stay. It thrilled her when he found a job. She selfishly hoped that meant he would stay. Now, here he was telling her he was leaving to go home.

"That's just it. I can't go home. Not yet." Daniel took her hands in his. He looked into her face and then her eyes as she looked at him again. She did not say a word. She couldn't.

"Karen, I have more to tell you," He paused.

What more could there be? Her heart ached as it was. She could not take more, could she? She continued to look at him, trying to imagine what was on his mind. She hoped it was not bad news.

"Karen, I can't leave, not without telling you," he hesitated and swallowed hard. He momentarily lowered his eyes. He continued to hold her hands.

"Karen," he hesitated before saying what was on his heart. His eyes met hers. "I'm in love with you." His eyes and his heart waited. He felt his heart skip a beat or two.

The tears that had been in her throat rose, flooding her eyes. A tear slid down her cheek. Her emotions overtook her ability to speak.

Daniel reached out and wiped the tears from her face. "Why are you crying?"

"Daniel," the voice that spoke was shaky and soft. "I've not been able to get you off my mind since our first serious conversation." She sniffled back her tears and dabbed at her nose with the napkin Daniel handed her.

She looked at his pure blue eyes. Felt his love. Believed she could feel his soul. Finally, the words came. "I never believed in love at first sight, and even though it wasn't exactly at first sight, I easily fell in love with you. I kept it bottled up inside because I was afraid by telling you it would chase you away. I knew you had a history of running, and I could not risk being the reason you would run again."

"Karen, you could never be the reason I run. I want to be with you. I have never felt this way for anyone before. Now I am undecided about what to do."

"What do you mean?" Her tears stopped as her fear of reality crept in.

"I need to go home, at least for a little while. I need to reconnect with my family. And before you ask, yes, part of it is because of the inheritance. My sister assured me there was some inheritance but said that it was too complicated to explain over the phone. She said I needed to come home to find out all the details. I will come back once the inheritance is all straightened out."

"Are you sure? You promise you will come back?"

"Yes." Daniel was still holding her. He had one more thing to ask and was unsure how she would respond to his next statement. "I'd like you to come with me," he blurted out.

"Daniel, I can't. You know I have to be here at the hotel and gift shop. The season starts soon when we will be busy until late fall when it gets too cold for people to camp and enjoy the lake. I have to stay here." She had pulled her hands out from his grasp. She looked out over the lake. She had found her love, yet could not be with him. At least not for a while. Love was cruel.

"I know you do. I know I can't expect you to drop everything and take off with me. Even for a short visit because, in reality, I'm not sure how long I may have to be there. I'm hoping it is a matter of meeting with the lawyer, signing some papers, then leaving."

"And if it's not that simple? Then what? Will you still come back?" The love of her life seemed to be slipping away before they had even kissed! Why did love have to be so complicated?

I will inform them that I have to come here to visit as soon as possible and that they need to meet you. You can come down to meet my family on a weekend or the middle of the week if that would be easier. Have Renee run the place for a few days. Is there anyone else that you normally hire to help during the busy months? Can they do it without you for a few days?"

"I am sure they can. It's just that I've never taken a day off during the summer months." Karen leaned back to think. She loved him, but how were they ever going to work this out so they could be together. What if it did not work out after all. She sighed. "Let's take one day at a time."

"I know, this isn't going to be easy, is it?"

"No."

Daniel wanted to hold her in his arms and tell her everything would be perfect in the end. He couldn't do that. Hold her, yes, if she let him, but tell her it all would be perfect? He doubted life would ever be perfect. He wondered if it ever had been perfect.

Chapter Eighteen

Life settled down at the manor for a few days after the soft opening. It was time to get ready for the official grand re-opening. A few final touches, and they would be ready.

The feedback left by those who visited at the soft opening had come in handy. Some had no suggestions but gave positive feedback. Others offered suggestions. One suggestion was to add coupons for things in town, such as discounts on purchases, a carriage ride through town, and a discount for the local dairy bar. Other suggestions included a copy of the recipes for the food they served. And the best was for their bosses to give them a longer vacation so they could stay longer. Most everyone who had only taken the tour during the soft opening wanted to return for the full experience. Some had already made reservations for future dates. The grand opening weekend was reserved by mostly first-time guests.

Heather had taken Nicole's advice and made an appointment to see Dr. George for a follow up on her healing progress. Her facial scar was less noticeable plus her hair covered it unless she styled it into a ponytail. The only time she noticed it was when she looked in the mirror, which she had learned to avoid. No one in the family mentioned it anymore. She had enough memories of the accident. The metal plate and screws in her leg would always be a reminder. Her limp gave that away. The long sleeves she always wore covered up the scar on her arm. She was grateful to be alive. Her physical scars were healing, and she thought her mental state was intact. She felt blessed that Ben had survived and so very thankful that her little boy was perfect. The bump on his head had not lasted very long. He had no nightmares about it and continued to go with the flow of life through all the changes in his young life. He was still so small he may never remember his grandparents that had died; she hoped he would never remember the accident.

Heather often sat back and just watched Marc play at the manor and their home. She realized that occasionally, she held her stomach while she watched him. Then sadness would try to fill her mind. Though no one talked about it anymore, she would never forget finding out she had lost the baby in the accident. She had not even had a chance to tell anyone that she was pregnant. At the dinner the night of the accident, she and Ben discussed other things. Ben was busy talking about plans for the manor as well as keeping his company going. They discussed selling their house or turning it into a rental. It was not far from the manor, and they could get an excellent rental income from it. They talked a lot that night, but nothing about her.

She never got the opportunity to tell him she had been to the doctor that morning and received the news. She felt slighted that the conversation had been more business than personal that night. She had told herself that there would be another chance and this time she would make a big deal of it with a special dinner for him at home the next week. She was not that far along. Then fate stepped in and took care of that decision for her. There was no baby. Not this time around. And her doctor told her that due to her injuries, she might not be able to get pregnant again. It had taken them a while to accept that. Not that they weren't still practicing.

She loved that they had reconciled. Ben was the love of her life. They were not trying to have another baby; they had even stopped talking about it. She mentally accepted that Marc would be an only child. Ben hated to hear she had been pregnant. She pretended to everyone that found out that she had not known either. It was easier that way. At least she thought it was at the time.

Ben accompanied her to her appointment with Dr. George. It was nice that he now worked at the manor and could get away from time to time for things like this. He always said he was too busy on a job site to get away in the past. He believed his workers could not do any work without him. After the accident, he knew they could. They had done a great job while he had been in the hospital. He was impressed with the way Donovan took charge.

He was a natural at the construction work and the management end of the business.

While they were waiting in the lobby of Dr. George's office, they started to talk about what was coming up next at the Manor and how well the open house had gone. When Ben began to mention the last-minute things they had to do, Heather stopped him. "Ben, why is it that you talk so much about work?

Can we talk about us? About Marc? About our plans? Something other than work?"

Ben turned to face her. "What about our plans? We are bound to the manor at least for the next five years. We can't leave, can't move, can't do anything but help Sara and expand the bed and breakfast business that your grandparents started."

"And what's wrong with that?"

"Nothing. I am stating facts. There isn't much to decide about our future; it has been decided for us."

"Don't you want to go places, do things?"

"Sure, but we can't."

"Yes, we can. There is nothing that says we can't take time off. We will have to talk with Sara about all of our work schedules and about taking time off. I am sure Sara wants some time off to go do something else."

"What else would she want to do? She's been working at the Manor for almost seven years now. It's her life."

"That's exactly what I'm saying. Sara has nothing else besides the manor and us. She hasn't dated since her divorce. She has not traveled anywhere since Mama and Daddy died. I want to avoid getting into that rut. I want time for us to get away and enjoy our little family. I want to handle the manor while she is away doing things and meeting new people. Perhaps even find a new man in her life."

"Ha. I can't see her with a new man. She is so, oh, what is a good word, independent? In control? In charge? Take your pick. Do you know any man who wants that in a woman?"

"Whoa, big boy. I agree most men like to be the strong one in the relationship, but an equal playing field would do her good. She needs someone in her life, someone to take charge of things once in a while. To take her in his arms and calm her concerns. To wipe away the tears she hides from everyone. To take away her loneliness."

"She's lonely?" She has us; she has her guests. She had lots of friends in town."

"It's not the same. I know when we separated after the accident, and you filed for divorce, I was devastated. I didn't know how I was going to make it on my own. I found strength I never knew I had. I realized I was capable to make it on my own, however it was not something I wanted to do. I am thrilled that we have reconciled. I honestly think Sara could use someone in her life, other than us."

On that thought, their conversation ended when the nurse called her back to the exam room. The interruption saved her from discussing further what was on her mind. Ben also was saved from what was on his mind. He shrugged his shoulders as they stood up and followed the nurse to Dr. George's office.

Dr. George had read through Heather's file before she met with them in the exam room. Everything looked good to her. She did want to have a final meeting with them to be sure Heather was mentally adjusting to the changes in her physical appearance and how she would be the rest of her life. And to see if they had any concerns.

"Good morning," she greeted them when she entered the room. "How are you doing today?"

"Fine," they said in unison.

"Cute you two. It's so good to see both of you together. I hear things are coming along well at the manor. When is the opening?"

"It's in three more weeks. We had a soft opening last weekend, and it went very well. Everyone seemed to love it. And we have reservations for the entire first month already," Heather relied.

"That's great! I may have to find a free weekend and reserve a room for my husband and myself."

"That would be wonderful. It's filling up fast, so you may want to make plans soon."

"I'll keep that in mind." Dr. George opened Heather's file. She then checked Heather's vitals. Everything seemed perfect.

"Let's discuss how you are with the scars on your face and your arm. Are you dealing with them okay? Have you given any more thought about having the plastic surgery we discussed?" Dr. George looked at Heather.

Ben looked at Heather inquisitively. He had not even thought about that after the first few weeks. He had gotten used to it and accepted it as part of his beautiful wife. He did not know she had even considered plastic surgery.

"To be honest, I avoid the mirrors for the most part. That way I think about it less often. The scar is fading slowly; it had been much worse. What's your take on plastic surgery? Will it make a big difference?"

"With the way it is fading, since you seem okay with it, I would leave it alone. The surgery will set you back a few weeks during the healing process. I know the manor needs your attention pretty much full time, so if you did want it, I would suggest having it done before you got too busy at work."

"Yes, we are getting ready to open full time soon. And yes, I'm okay with the way it is. Ben, are you alright with it?"

"You are as beautiful to me now as you ever have been," he replied. Playing it safe was a thing he learned a long time ago. It was true though; she was beautiful.

Dr. George was glad they were both comfortable with the scars. She then approached the other touchy subject for any young couple. Pregnancy.

"We do need to touch on the one other concern I have. I want you to understand what could be. I know you wanted to have another child."

"We have discussed it," Ben started, interrupting anything else Dr. George may have said. He reached to hold Heather's hand.

"Yes, we have. And we're fine with whatever happens," Heather added.

"We keep practicing," Ben said with a wink directed at Heather.

"Practicing is fine. I would like to do an exam and order some tests to be sure everything is good inside. The damage was minimal, but I want to be sure it's healed and see if there is the possibility to offer more encouraging news. I'd love to give you good news."

Heather looked at Ben. They both told Dr. George to schedule the tests. The two left the office hopeful and excited about their future.

Sara had been babysitting Marc while Heather and Ben were at the doctor's office. She was enjoying a day off, at least a few hours; spending them with Marc was special. She knew that once the manor opened for business, it would be a long time before she got a moment to herself. She enjoyed being busy, but somehow, she was hoping to find some alone time and even someone special who would spend it with her. She saw how Ben and Heather were so in love. She had watched how Joe and Nicole were when they were together. They were like newlyweds even though they had been married for several years. She knew that most of their guests at the manor would be couples or families. She admitted to herself that she had moments of feeling lonely. It was one thing to be alone; it was another to feel lonely. She did her best not to let others know she felt that way. She was fine at being alone. This feeling of loneliness was something new to her.

She had been married once, but it had turned into a disaster. She was so in love at first. She was so happy to have someone love her. She envisioned her life to be like her parents and her grandparents – a lifetime spent together. Instead, here she was, still young and a divorcee.

Her marriage began declining when her husband's business started failing. Then he started drinking. The more his company failed, the more he drank. When he drank, his whole demeanor changed. He became angry at everything. He started yelling at her for no reason. The yelling gradually became worse until the day he hit her. She continued to stay with him. She put up with it. At least for a while. She convinced herself that she loved him and that he would get better when his business improved. She did her best to make him happy. He kept drinking. His anger continued, as did the assaults on her.

A co-worker noticed her black eye and the way she held her arm one day at work. Then she saw other small changes to Sara. She was quiet. She wore her hair differently. She had stopped going out with the girls after work. The co-worker spoke to her in private and told her of a shelter where she could stay to get away from the abuse. They discussed it at length, with Sara concluding that she did not need that.

Then, one night, it got so bad at home that Sara knew it was time to make her move. She had heard enough horror stories and seen a few shows dealing with spousal abuse.

She realized and accepted that even in her situation, it was only going to worsen. Nothing she did was going to make him change back to the way he had been. She remembered hearing stories of how his father had hit his mother. When she first heard about it, she was already married, and she dismissed it from her mind. She was determined her marriage would not end up in that situation. Her husband had witnessed it. He told her how much he hated it. So how could he turn into his father? Yet, he had.

And so, on a nice warm, sunny day in December after her husband had gone to work, she packed her bags and left. She arrived at the shelter, then spent two weeks settling in. She told one counselor that the last straw for her was when she landed at the wall and slid down to the floor when he hit her. Still, she had not called the police, but she mentally planned her escape.

She spent time talking with the counselors, the staff, and the other victims at the shelter. She learned a lot about a different world than how she had grown up. She had not wanted to be a part of that kind of life. Yet, she had become one of its statistics—a victim of spousal abuse.

The counselors and staff at the shelter suggested she call her parents. It took her several days to get the courage to call. She feared they would tell her to lay in the bed she had made for herself. She never dreamed they would understand. When she finally called them, she broke down and told them everything that had happened in the last several years of her marriage. Her mama cried along with her as she listened. All she wanted to do was hold her daughter.

To Sara's surprise and relief, they invited her to come back home to live with them. They felt hurt that she had not confided in them sooner. They told her they would have done something to help her leave him. No man should treat a woman that way. They thought they had taught their children to come to them if they ever needed anything. Now they wondered what they might have done wrong. Maybe they had taught them too well to look out for themselves and to be strong.

One of the first conversations she had with her parents when she returned home was how she felt she had disappointed them. She told them she wanted the perfect marriage they and her grandparents had. Instead, she ended up abused, alone, feeling like a failure. Her father told her she was not a failure. Her mama told her they would never be disappointed in her. They were proud of her and all she had accomplished, especially with what she had survived. Her mama later told her privately that even the perfect looking relationships – weren't. When Sara questioned her, Susan told her that someday she'd understand.

Chapter Nineteen

Sara had decided to take a few days off before the manor opened. A few days to unwind, refresh and prepare for the 'no time off for a while' that she was facing. She was waiting for Ben and Heather to return from Heather's doctor's appointment. She gave them time to tell her their news without paying attention to the details. Then told them she was leaving in the morning for Gatlinburg, Tennessee, for a short vacation to shop, rest and enjoy some free time. Ben and Heather looked at each other and smiled. They were happy for her and told her it was about time.

They spent the evening discussing the final touches required before the grand opening. They were ahead of schedule; The fresh flowers and chocolates were being delivered the night before opening, and the fresh food was scheduled for pick up the day before opening. Heather and Ben assured Sara they could handle it. They told her she should go and enjoy her time off.

Sara was startled awake from a deep sleep late that night when her phone rang. It immediately caused a headache. She grabbed the phone and said a sleepy, mumbled hello.

"Sara?"

"Yes, who is this? Do you know what time it is?" She asked as she leaned on her elbows and looked at her clock.

"Sara, it's me, Andy."

Sara sat straight up in her bed, her eyes wide open, her headache gone. "Andy! Where are you? How are you? Why are you calling? Are you in town? Are you coming home?" All these questions flew out without a breath.

"I don't know," he began. "Well, first, to answer all your questions. I'm in PA at the lake, I'm fine, and I'm calling to see if I'm even welcome to come home."

"Of course you are! You have always been welcome. We never understood why you left. I never understood why you didn't show up when we were supposed to meet last fall."

"It's all a very long story. I can't tell you over the phone. I may never be able to tell you the complete story. I do know I've reached a time in my life that I want to come home. At least for a little while."

"Are you planning to run off again? Because if you are, I'm not sure you should even come home."

"No, I'm not planning to run away, although I am unsure how long I will stay. That is another long story. I promise not to disappear again. Would it be alright if I come this weekend?"

This weekend. Sara's heart sank a bit. She had her bags packed; she was going away for a few days, including the weekend. But here was her brother asking to come home – this weekend.

"Of course you can!" She said with enthusiasm, while her mind was a whirlwind of things to get done before he arrived. And the realization that her weekend away would never happen.

"Thank you, Sis. I'll see you either Friday night or Saturday morning. I'll call to let you know a more specific time. I have to take care of a few things here first," he sighed. "I love you, Sis."

"I love you too. We'll see you in a few days!"

"See ya soon."

Sara was now wide awake. She looked at her phone to see what time it was. Three AM.! Ouch. She needed to get some sleep. Tomorrow was going to be a long day with a lot to get done. Her plans had changed in an instant. Again her priorities were not of herself. Strange how life kept changing while one just blinked. She lay back down and closed her eyes. Her mind was making lists. That's what she did – make lists.

She met Heather and Ben at the island in the kitchen in the morning. They had slept in, thinking Sara would be gone by the time they got up. They knew something was up when they found her in the kitchen drinking coffee with a pen in her hand and a notepad on the island countertop. The smile on her face was another giveaway. They were curious and concerned.

"Now what's going on, Sis?" Heather asked as she poured herself a cup of coffee then sat down next to Sara.

"You won't believe it! I got a phone call at three this morning."

"Who would call at three in the morning?" Ben asked.

Heather looked from Ben to Sara. Her eyes lit up and a big smile emerged. "Andy. That's who. Did Andy call?" Unable to be still, she stood up and started to pace as she carried her coffee mug with her.

Sara's smile grew. "You guessed it. He's coming home this weekend!"

"Wait, what? Is he finally coming home? Where is he?" Is he alright? Where has he been? Why is he coming home now? How long is he staying?" Her line of questioning was longer and quicker than Sara's had been to Andy. She took a sip of coffee as she sat back down; her shoulders slumped. "No, wait, what does he want?" Heather shook her head as she realized he rarely came home for the sake of coming home. He always wanted something.

"Hold on. Not so fast. Here's the gist of it. Andy is in PA at the lake. Remember where Mama and Daddy used to take him when he was small, but we were older and had to stay with our grandparents?"

"Yeah, I remember. We always wanted to go there, but our parents never took us," Heather added to explain it to Ben briefly.

"Right. Anyway, Andy says he is doing fine. He says he will answer all our other questions when he gets here. Says it's a long story."

"I'd say it's a long story. Almost four years' worth of long story!" Heather sounded a bit bitter. She set her coffee mug down, no longer thirsty for it.

"Why so bitter?" Ben asked. He reached for Heather's hand.

"Why? Why?" Heather spoke in anger. "Because he wasn't here for either of our parent's deaths or funerals. Nor after we had our accident when I almost died. He wasn't here while we did all the remodeling of the manor. And not even during the reading of the will. HA! Now I know why he's coming home! He heard about the will."

"What makes you say that?" Ben asked.

"He's finally heard about our parents' death and thinks he's going to inherit a lot of money, so he wants to come home to claim it. That's it! Isn't it?" She stood and walked to the coffee pot to refresh her cup. Her hands were shaking; her mind was racing. She should be excited, but she was nothing near that. She was near angry.

"I think he is sincere about coming home. That it has nothing to do with the will," Sara said, trying to calm her sister. She knew Andy had known about the will since before their accident. He did not even know about the accident. She had no way of contacting him when it happened. She did not know anyone else who would have told him.

"What makes you say that?"

Sara put her pen down that had been in her hand the whole time they had been talking. She stood up and took a few steps away from them. She faced away from them. "I have a confession to make."

"Say that again. A confession?" Heather looked at her sister in disbelief.

"I've been keeping something from you." She turned back to face them. It was time to share what she had been holding in for all these months.

Ben and Heather were all ears. Ben put his coffee mug down and reached for his wife's hand to steady her. He could feel her anger.

"Okay, spill it," Heather said as she wondered what and why her sister had kept a secret from her. That was not at all like her.

"Remember the night of your accident? When I sent the two of you out on a date, Marc to a babysitter and said I was meeting someone?"

"Yes, and... Go on." Heather leaned in to listen, still confused.

"That someone was Andy. He had called earlier that week to set up a time and place to meet. I asked him on the phone if he had heard that our folks had died. He said he had and that he wanted to come home to be a family again. To be there for us. Said he had been sober for over a year and was ready to deal with life again. So, I went to the restaurant we had agreed on and waited. And waited. And waited. He never showed up. He never called. It was the last I had heard from him or of him. Until a few weeks ago."

Heather stared at her sister. She had not uttered a word while her sister confessed her secret. A brief moment later, it hit her. "WAIT a minute. You heard from him a few weeks ago too?"

"Not exactly." Sara sat back down. "Before you get too excited or mad, madder, at me, let me tell you what I know. I got a call from Larry Carr a few weeks ago. Larry lives and works at the lake in Pennsylvania. He was good friends with Daddy and Mama when they would go on vacation there in the summers. Anyway, Larry called me on the landline phone. He told me that Andy was there living nearby and was working for him. That was the first time he had seen our brother since he was a young teenager. Larry said he was going by a different name, but he knew it was him as soon as he saw him. Larry said he was sober and had begun to talk with him, to open up. I asked Larry if Andy had mentioned coming home, and he told me that Andy was thinking about it but that he was not sure if we would accept him back. Plus, from what Larry said, Andy is seeing someone there. Larry told me he would let me know if he had anything more to tell me. He knew by pushing him, we all may lose him again. He's right, of course."

"So, you're telling me, telling us, that Andy has been fine all along and just ignoring us? Hiding from us? Why would he do that?"

"Well, for one thing, if he is *now* sober, that means that he was a drunk for a while, right?" Ben tried to give excuses knowing they were not good reasons, but ideas of Andy's thought process. "And if he was drinking and drunk, he's most likely an alcoholic. Alcoholics tend to do things out of character, like run from family, hide from the world. A lot of homeless people are alcoholics. There are also a lot of them that maintain normal, successful lives. I'm just saying that maybe he was ashamed to come home. Your parents raised him like they raised both of you. You are both successful women. He may feel like he is a failure, a disappointment."

"You may be right," Heather conceded. Her anger towards Andy was subsiding. She still did not like that Sara had kept a secret from her.

"We won't know until we hear the story straight from Andy. We need to get everything done here before he arrives so we can make him feel welcomed, needed, and most importantly, loved."

"Sounds good to me. First up, who's cooking breakfast?" Ben got up to pour everyone a fresh cup of hot coffee.

"HA. You asked. You cook." Sara said. "I have more things to write on my list." She chuckled as she accepted her fresh cup of coffee and went toward the office. Ben looked at Heather who was shrugging her shoulders. "I'll take my eggs sunny side up with a side of bacon." She then walked out of the room, leaving Ben alone to cook. He wondered if he'd ever learn not to ask stupid questions. Then he pulled out the frying pan to start breakfast.

Sara sat down at the office desk and contemplated how life would change when Andy came back. How long would he stay? Would he honor the will and wait for the five years, or would he get angry and return to his old ways and leave? She did not want that to happen. She wanted him to stay. But would he want to stay if he was seeing someone in PA? Would she want to move to Tennessee? Would she be able to move? So many questions. Only time would tell what the answers were. She wondered if she could override what the will said. Would anyone know? Could she get the inheritance monies from the trust funds and bank accounts early? She may need to call her attorney. Or maybe she'd just let it be and tell Andy that it's the only way it can be. He can stay and earn his share or leave; then, his portion would get divided between her and Heather. She smelled the bacon cooking. All of this would have to wait; breakfast was calling.

While Sara, Ben, Heather, and Marc were eating breakfast at Bella Rose, Andy took his last sip of coffee in Pennsylvania before heading to work. Coffee was the only thing he wanted for breakfast. He had not slept at all the night before. He was excited and a bit nervous after his conversation with Sara. He was anxious because later that day he would be telling the lady who had won his heart one last truth.

Larry greeted him in his usual cheerful way, then noticed how tired Andy looked. His eyes were barely open. His smile was gone. He hung his head when he tried to look at Larry. He looked more than tired.

"Did you not sleep well last night? Please tell me you were not out partying all night?" He asked even though he could tell he had not been drinking. Larry knew the look of drunken and hungover eyes. When you live in a town with more bars than churches, you just know.

"No, no party. And no drinking, not even one, in case that's your next question."

"I never was going to ask that. I can tell it wasn't drinking by looking into your eyes. So what kept you up all night?"

"I called and spoke with my sister, Sara, last night." Andy smiled a small grin. "I'm going home. I only plan to stay for a visit. They may not want me to stay very long, plus I may decide I want to leave soon after getting there."

"It's about time." Larry was thrilled to hear that news but tried not to show his genuine emotions. "Have you told Karen?"

"No, not yet. I avoided her this morning. I wanted to talk with you first. I know this is going to be a hardship on you this time of year."

"Daniel, I mean, Andy, I told you last week that if you wanted to go, you didn't even have to think twice about it. I will be fine. Several young men are able and willing to help me out this spring. And I do have others coming once the season opens and gets busy. No, don't let me or this job stop you from going home. The one to worry about is that young lady you are so fond of. And truth be told, she is quite fond of you. I can see it when the two of you are together."

"That's not going to be the hard part. I've already told Karen about running, about almost going home, and that it was in the plan when I got here. She already told me to go home when we had that conversation."

"Then what is going to be the hard part?"

"Telling her I've been lying about my name. She only knows me as Daniel. How do I tell her that my real name is Andy?"

"Be honest with her. She will respect you for that. And, you know what? Since she has already given you her blessing to go home, I think telling her the whole truth will be easy. Karen is a very caring and understanding young lady. She is respected and loved by everyone in this community because she is so kind and giving."

"Yes, perhaps you are right. Maybe it won't be so bad when I tell her. Wish me luck. I'm here to work today, so let's get busy. And before you tell me to leave, I am not meeting my sister until the weekend. So I have a few days."

"Alright, then let's get to work."

Andy worked the full day. He tried to concentrate on work, but his mind kept wandering. His fear of losing Karen, his anxiety of going home, and worrying if he would be accepted or rejected had him exhausted by the end of the day. And he still had to talk with Karen.

When Andy left the job site Larry wished him luck and added that he knew Karen would accept him whatever his name was. Andy hoped he was right.

Karen looked over toward the hotel before reaching her car after work. She had errands to run before going home. Daniel hadn't called her since the day before. She was starting to worry about him. They had such a great relationship going; she wondered if something had happened. As she turned to open her car door, he pulled into the parking lot. He started to drive towards the hotel when he saw Karen standing there, so he turned his car toward her instead.

"Hi Karen, I'm glad I caught you before you left," he said. He hesitated, but when she did not say anything, he added, "We need to talk."

Oh no, Karen thought, *The talk.* "Okay. When do you want to get together?"

"Do you have time now before you go home?" He hoped she had time before he lost his nerve.

"Sure. I'm in no hurry. Where do you want to talk?"

"In my hotel room, if that is okay with you."

"I'll meet you over there." She closed her car door, locked it, then began to walk the short distance to the hotel room he was renting. She wondered what he had to tell her. She knew he was leaving; maybe he had decided to leave sooner than planned. He drove across the parking lot and parked his car, then waited for her. His thoughts were going a million miles an hour and a dozen different directions. Caught up in what he would tell her, he had not offered to drive her over. He then found it odd that she had chosen to walk. Things were different for them already.

"I'm glad I stayed a bit late at work. Otherwise, you would have missed me," she said, catching up with him at his door.

"I'm glad too. Sorry I didn't call you today." He opened his door and followed her in.

They sat together on the sofa. Andy poured them each some lemon-aid to drink. It was a habit they had gotten in when she came over. It felt natural.

Karen took a sip of her drink and looked at him. "So, what's on your mind? Have you decided when you are going to Tennessee?"

"Yes, that is part of what I want to tell you. However, there is more I need to tell you. Some of the details and then a confession to make. Something more I've kept from you."

"A confession?" She leaned away from him. It was more of an automatic reflex than a conscious move. She immediately leaned forward and hoped he hadn't noticed. "What are you saying? Can you tell me the confession first?"

"No, I want to tell you my plans first. That will lead to the other. Please bear with me on this. This is hard enough to say. Once I do, I hope you will understand and not hold it against me." He reached out to hold her hands in his. It was a way for him to show his love for her and keep her from hitting him when he told her the truth. He had no idea how she was going to react. He was hoping Larry was right, that she would understand.

"I'm listening." She sensed herself putting up a roadblock. She felt a guarded wall go up against her heart. Her heart: broken before, but now in love with this man who sat in front of her. This Daniel, her Daniel. She hoped that he was going to be *her* Daniel. She braced her emotions.

"Okay. Here goes." He took a deep breath. "The easy part we have already discussed. One you encouraged me to do, which is to go home to Tennessee. I wasn't sure when I would go for several reasons, but last night I eliminated one of those reasons. I called my sister. She told me I am welcome to come home. So, I'm going home this weekend before she or I change our minds."

"I'm glad you are going home. You need to make amends and get back with your family." Karen squeezed his hand to show she approved.

"I know I do. I was up all night last night fretting about whether to call or not, then I called her, at three AM!" He shook his head in disbelief that he had called her at that hour.

"You called your sister at three in the morning? Bet she loved that."

"I did get her out of bed, but she sounded excited that I was coming home. So that's a plus. I hope it stays that way. I do have a habit of running away, as you know. Now I have no desire to run anymore. I want to stick with my decisions, get back with my family, hopefully have a good relationship with them, and be honest with everyone. That brings me to the other thing I have to tell you."

"Okay."

"My name," he hesitated. "My real name is not Daniel. It's Andy." He blurted out the rest.

"O…kay," she responded hesitantly, her hand still holding his. "So why does it say Daniel on your driver's license?"

"I had a fake one made several years ago. I kept the real license, but there are times when I'm on the run that I use the fake one. I don't, or didn't, want people to know the real me."

"Why not?"

"Because when I run, I want to disappear from my real life. I don't want people to find me when the media sends out the search stories on the TV or radio or signs. I preferred being anonymous. Then, while I was in Florida, I decided I needed to find the original me. Coming here helped me realize I did not want to run anymore. That led to a lot of truth being revealed."

"So, you're not Daniel. Is the rest of your life story the truth?" She felt the urge inside her to pull away from him. To stop holding his hand. Instead, she remained as she was. She would hear his full story and then decide. She could tell he needed her to at least listen.

"You know the rest of my story, all of it. If you doubt any of it, even who the real me is, feel free to ask Larry. He knows my family and me from when I was a child."

"Larry? Larry knew all along who you were? Is he why you decided to be honest and contact your sister and go back?" She pulled away enough to take a better look at him, letting go of his hand. Not only had Daniel, or Andy, lied, but Larry had also kept a secret from her. Why?

"He is part of it, yes. You are the biggest part. I met you, and once we started to get to know each other I knew if I did not open up and be honest with you, that in time, I would lose you. I may still lose you, but I will take that chance. I will lose you knowing you know the truth."

"Daniel, I mean, Andy, you are not going to lose me." She reached for his hand and held it to her heart. "Your name could be George; it would not matter to me. I only care about you as a person, who you are, and who you are becoming. You've had a rough life that you put onto yourself, but I can see changes in you since you've been here. The changes could be because of me, or because you've had time to think, your time with Larry and talking with him, or some other reason. Whatever it is, I'm glad it has changed you. For the better, by the way." She saw the pain still in his eyes as their eyes met. "Dan... Andy, let the pain go. You're on your way to a new life. A better life. A positive life. Let go of the old."

Andy squeezed her hand tight. No words would come. Knowing that the love of his life was going to stay was overwhelming. He felt a lump in his throat, followed by tears falling down his cheeks. Noticing his tears brought Karen to tears. Sitting together, arms around each other, they cried until there were no more tears.

Chapter Twenty

Andy and Karen joined Larry and Grace for dinner, giving Andy time to say goodbye before leaving for Tennessee. They talked about when Andy used to come there as a child and about his parents. Then the conversation moved on to his plans once he returned to his family. Andy said he was not sure when he would return but to count on it, he would be back. He agreed that he would be in touch. He thanked Larry for being there for him, for listening, and for all the fatherly advice. Larry said that his door was always open, as was his phone line.

Karen and Andy returned to his room after dinner. Karen helped him pack all his belongings from inside the hotel suite so it would be vacant for her to rent to a new guest. He told her he would call when he got to Tennessee, if not before. He assured his love that he would let her know as soon as he knew what was going on and the plans. He promised her that he would be back. He was not going to run away again. Especially not from her.

When everything was in his car, except for the last-minute things he would need in the morning, they walked down to the lake to watch the final moments of the sunset. They wrapped their arms around each other as they stood watching the sky darken. The water displayed gentle rippling waves to the shore. A slight breeze began to blow, causing Karen to shiver. Andy took her face in his hands and gently kissed her. She wrapped her arms around his neck and drew him into her. She did not want him to leave. They held each other as the last of the sunset disappeared, replaced by the moon casting its glow across the water.

They strolled hand in hand away from the lake. It would have been easy to fall into each other's embrace and spend the night together, but they had agreed that their love was strong, and they could wait. Instead, Andy walked her to her home. They kissed each other good night, and Andy walked back to the hotel. Karen watched him until she could no longer see him in the darkness.

She was up early the next morning to meet him at the hotel to say goodbye. They shared a kiss with tears in their eyes before he got into his car. They waved goodbye, then Karen watched his car disappear around the corner, listening until she could no longer hear the sound of the engine. He was gone. She hoped and prayed he would be true to his word to come back.

Andy headed south to a life unknown. He thought about the unknown and the known during the long trip. The few things he knew were that his parents had both died while he was not around. He knew he was mentioned in the will, along with conditions that Sara said she would explain. He knew his oldest sister was excited to have him come home. Andy did not know what his other sister thought. Little did he know what other surprises were in store for him when he got there. The long and lonely road was full of daydreams, anxious thoughts, speculations, and wishing Karen was with him. Thinking positive was difficult when so much of his life had seemed negative.

Sara could not sleep the night before Andy was due home. Thoughts of the manor, her family, and the past year kept her mind full. She got up early, anticipating his arrival. It was going to be great to have her whole family under one roof. Or at least all living on the same property. She poured herself a mug of coffee as she thought about the upcoming day.

Heather and Ben joined her in the manor's kitchen a couple of hours after they had eaten breakfast in their home.

"So, are you ready for our little brother to be here?" Sara asked as they all sat down.

"I hope he doesn't have ideas that he's going to grab his portion of the inheritance and run."

"I told him on the phone there were conditions in the will for all of us. We'll see what he does once he finds out what they are."

"I realized this morning when we were getting Marc up and dressed that Andy has never met Marc. Does he even know I have a child?"

"You're right. I don't know if he does or not. Andy said he had heard about our parents' deaths, but we never talked about anything else. We'll find out soon. By the way, how did things go with your doctor on your last visit? Everything going according to plan and the way you hoped?"

Heather looked at her before she answered. She had already told her sister what the doctor had said. She repeated most of the details anyway, realizing that a lot had happened since their previous conversation, and maybe Sara had forgotten.

"Yes, I'm healing well. The scar will always be there on my face, and I will always have the limp, which I knew. I could opt for plastic surgery on my face, but the doctor feels there is no need for it if we are comfortable with how the scar looks. Besides, it is fading, so it won't be that noticeable after a while. Plus, if I wear my hair so it covers part of my face, no one can see it. And with a little touch of makeup, it doesn't show much anymore. I'm so glad the accident wasn't worse."

"Me too. Did I tell you I spoke with one of the officers who responded that night?"

"No, I thought the investigation was closed. What did he say?"

"Yes, the investigation is officially closed since there is no evidence of another vehicle involved and no other witnesses. However, the officer told me the county is discussing putting up a slower speed limit through there and installing better guard rails. That is a bad section of the highway. Yours wasn't the first one to happen along that stretch of road. He also told me that he goes to the site from time to time to look for more evidence even though so much time has passed."

"What else could they find now? I do hope they make it safer. I'm so glad we don't have to drive that road very often. It still makes me nervous."

"I hate thinking it was my fault. I almost killed my family," Ben said. He hung his head and looked at his son, Marc, playing with a stuffed bear on the floor.

"Ben, it wasn't your fault. I don't blame you for any of it. It was simply an accident." Heather reached to touch his arm. She did not blame him for any of it. She believed things happen for reasons people may never know. She knew she was unusual in her way of thinking, especially about things that could have been a tragedy. But, she tended to take things as they happened and could accept them without question. She didn't like some things, such as losing the baby and when Ben wanted a divorce, but they had worked through them. She was a fighter when she needed to be.

"I know, but I will always wonder if there was anything I could have done differently. I still don't remember what happened in the split second before we went off the road. I know I was suddenly waking up over the embankment, and you were--"

"Let's not talk about it, shall we? What's done is done. Time to talk about better and happier things. So, is everything ready for the manor to open in two weeks?" Heather turned her attention to Sara.

Sara smiled. "We are all set. We are getting calls for bookings into the late summer!"

"That's fantastic!" She swallowed the rest of her coffee. "What's on the agenda for today?"

"We need to make sure the one guest room is ready for Andy. I know we have that small guest house down the lane, but we haven't finished the remodeling on it. It has been set aside for Andy, and since we didn't know where Andy was, when he may show up if ever, I wasn't concerned about redoing it until this summer after we opened. I figured if Andy did show up and stayed, he could help with the remodel and do it his way. Later we can design it to be a rental for couples who want to stay in a larger space if Andy decides to leave. It would work great for those with small families. We could make it an option for people.

"That sounds good to me. I had not given it much thought while we were remodeling the manor. It is hidden by the trees and landscaping, so it is easy to forget about it being there.

Ben stood up and gathered the coffee cups from the island to put them inside the dishwasher. Heather slid off the bar stool and picked Marc up. "Time to get you ready to meet your uncle."

Sara went back to the office. She looked around to make sure it was clean, organized and that things she did not want Andy to see yet were in the desk drawers or behind the hidden opening. No one knew about the secret space except her and her late mama. The papers inside there were now her responsibility to reveal when the time was right. She walked to the door when everything seemed to be in order, turned off the light, and closed the door. Today was another day of change for her family. She had no idea how it was going to go when Andy arrived. She hoped that it would be an easy transition and all would go well. But she suspected there would be bumps along the way. Andy could be one of those bumps.

They had done all they could in the guest room on the first floor for Andy before noon. Clean sheets, a new quilt, new curtains, fresh new towels in the private bathroom. Ben had gone to the florist to get fresh flowers for that room, the living room, and dining room table. They were using Andy as their first guest after their soft opening was an advantage. It allowed them to experience last-minute preparations in real-time. Andy was to arrive later in the afternoon, which was later than most guests would be arriving. They had timed their work to be completed by noon when most guests would arrive. Everything so far was on schedule.

Sara walked outside to do a run through that started at the front steps. She was getting nervous. True, it was only her baby brother coming, but it was her long-lost baby brother. She wanted to make a good impression so he would decide to stay.

Everything looked good to her. The entrance was clean; everything on the wrap around porch was in place. The great room layout was inviting. It was free of clutter and Marc's toys. Sara made a mental note to talk with Heather and Ben about Marc's toys in the great room. Once they were officially open, that area was for the guests. She continued walking through the manor. The dining room and kitchen were spotless. Andy's room was perfect.

The day seemed to drag on after lunch. They were all anxious to see Andy. As the day wore on and it got closer to dinner time, they began to worry. Sara was starting to feel disappointed. Had he stood them up again? Heather tried to stay busy with Marc. Ben wandered around the property, anticipating the next project while ensuring everything was ready for the guests coming in two weeks. He wanted to avoid any last-minute surprises. Depending on how things went when Andy arrived, they may not have much time to work on projects. Or it was possible that Andy would jump right in and give a helping hand to get the work done.

No one was very hungry when dinner time rolled around, so they each munched on whatever they found in the refrigerator or pantry. The meal Sara had planned sat waiting to go into the oven. Andy hadn't called since the day before. They had no idea when he would be there.

After eating, they gathered in the living room to wait. Ben started a fire in the fireplace. He and Heather were busy watching Marc play with the few toys Heather allowed him to have in there. Sara kept pacing from the front door to the sofa, to the front door, to the fireplace.

Finally, they heard a car approaching. They all looked at each other, then nearly knocking each other over, they rushed to the door. They stopped and stood on the front porch. Andy was finally home!

Andy had driven slowly up the lane. He was nervous. When he looked up at the manor, he saw his family waiting for him. A smile crossed his face. His family. He was home. Wait, who was that little person? His smile grew. More family than he expected. Nice.

He parked his car and looked up at the front of the house as his sisters raced down the steps to greet him. Sara was the first to reach the vehicle. He opened his door to have Sara almost drag him out of his seat.

"Hey, little brother! Get out here! I need a hug! I need to look at you. I'm so glad you are here," Sara's words came out all in one breath. She could not decide if she wanted to look at him, hug him, punch him, or something else. All she knew was that her baby brother was finally home!

"Okay, let me get out." Andy stood up and wrapped his arms around his oldest sister. He smiled as Heather was right behind Sara and wrapped her arms around him as well. Ben and Marc stood back as the family connected for the first time in about four years.

They had a lot to catch up on. First was an introduction to his nephew, Marc, who had been watching and wondering who this person was. Marc looked up at him as Heather introduced them to each other. Marc reached out his little hand to shake his Uncle Andy's hand. Andy squatted down and gave him a short hug.

"Hello Marc, it is good to meet you." Marc smiled and rushed back to his mother.

They all helped Andy carry his luggage from the car. Even Marc carried a small bag. Andy was looking around at everything as he walked with them to the front door. There was so much to take in. So much had changed since he was there the last time, he was in awe. When they walked inside, he was blown away.

"Wow! What a difference! It's beautiful! You all did a great job!" He held his oldest sister's hand. She had not let go of it since they started walking towards the house. “So, where am I staying? Out back, as in the doghouse??” He hoped everyone would take his comment as a joke.

“Of course not. We have given you the best of the guest rooms. It will eventually be for other guests, but you can stay there while we get your house remodeled the way you want it.”

“Wait, what? I have a house?” He let go of Sara's hand and looked at her in disbelief.

“It's a long, long story. We can discuss it over the next several days. First, let's get you and your belongings to your room. Are you hungry? I have dinner in the oven.” She had put it in the oven about a half-hour earlier. She knew they could eat whenever he arrived. If he never showed up, they would have leftovers tomorrow. She remembered when Andy was home from time to time that he had loved to cook. She wondered if he still did. She also hoped her cooking was good enough.

“Yes, I'm starved. It was a long trip. I haven't eaten since lunchtime. I got stuck in a few traffic jams, road construction, and passed two accidents along the way. Not a fun trip, that's for sure. But I was determined to get here.

“Why didn't you call?”

“I didn't want to get your hopes up. I was so nervous, and to be honest, I was not sure I would go through with coming here. I felt that if I called and then changed my mind, it would be worse than if I didn't call at all. I have disappointed you all so much in the past. I am so sorry, but I'm here now. I'm home,” he said then, silently added, “for now.”

“I'll forgive you – this time. And all those other times as well. You are here, and we are about to have a fresh start. So let's get your things into your room and then eat! Come help, everyone.”

They placed his things into his room and left him alone to freshen up. He looked around the room. There was a flower arrangement with roses on the dresser that brought a smile. Adding to the room beauty was the Log Cabin patterned quilt with matching wall hanging. He looked inside the private bathroom that coordinated with the bedroom. What was he expecting? Certainly not this. Not for him. He had expected them to put him in the doghouse. Instead, the girls and Ben had welcomed him home and given him one of the beautiful new rooms. He was impressed with the remodeling they had done. Country modern, if there was such a thing.

Andy met up with his family in the kitchen after taking a few moments to unpack some of his clothes and wash up from his long trip.

"What do you think of the room?" Sara asked as he entered the kitchen.

"It's perfect. You all did a great job. I can't wait to see what you have done with the rest of the place.

"There is plenty of time for that later and tomorrow. For now, let's eat. I hope you like it. It's not fancy, and I'm sure you could do it better."

"I'll take it, whatever it is. We'll talk about my cooking later."

Sitting down to eat dinner was something Sara had been looking forward to ever since she learned what was in the will. She looked around the table at each one of her family members as they ate. They were finally all home. The way their mama had requested it. Sad that her death was what brought them all together, Sara hid her deep thoughts with a smile.

"Welcome home, everyone." She raised her glass of water with everyone joining her. Even Marc raised his sippy cup of milk.

Their conversation during dinner centered around his trip, the weather, and general topics. Andy was enjoying the meal his sisters had made. He held up his fork with a bite of food, ready to eat.

"Do you remember how I used to like to cook when I was little and home?" He did not wait for an answer. "Well, I am now a certified chef." He took a bite then, with a mouth full, asked, "Does the manor have a chef yet?"

"Oh, my God, yes, we need a chef! Are you willing to be the chef at Bella Rose Manor? Or are you saying that because my cooking is so bad?"

"I do love to cook," was his only response.

In unison, Sara, Heather, and Ben said, "You are hired."

Andy made no further comment. He was unsure how long he was staying, so he could not commit to anything so permanent.

After their late dinner, Andy said he was tired from the ride, and as much as he wanted a tour of the manor, he needed a good night's sleep. He also needed to call Karen, but he did not tell them that.

Andy had called Karen when he arrived at the manor so she would not worry. He knew she would be concerned. He had also called her a few times along his trip to let her know he was doing okay. Odd, he thought, or maybe not so odd, that he had called her, but not his family.

After agreeing to an eight o'clock breakfast with everyone, Heather, Ben, and Marc said their good-nights and headed to their home. Sara stayed behind for a few extra moments to chat with Andy and give him another hug.

"I'm so glad you are home. If you need anything, I'm in Mama and Daddy's old house by the gazebo. You have my cell phone number if you need to call. You know where the kitchen is when you get up in the morning. You're welcome to start cooking," she winked as she walked to the door in the kitchen that led outside and to her home. "We'll see you tomorrow. Love you, little brother."

"Love you too, big Sis. I'm glad I'm finally home." Andy turned and walked down the hall to his room. Yes, he was finally here. He lay down across the bed and called Karen.

Andy was busy in the kitchen searching cabinets, drawers, and pantry as dawn was sending a dim light through the windows. The coffee was brewing. He thought back to his conversation with Karen the night before. She was glad he had made it there, wishing him the best. She also told him that she missed him. He missed her more than he thought he would.

Sara came into the house as the coffee finished brewing. "Perfect timing!" she said as she reached for her initialed coffee mug and filled it to the rim.

"Not perfect. Breakfast is not ready yet," Andy said as he reached out and hugged her. I'm going to make a quiche for everyone. Is that alright?"

"It's perfect. Everyone will love it." Sara sat at the island. "I think after breakfast, we will give you a tour and let you see everything we have done around here. I am unsure what you remember about this place. We've changed so much; it may not matter what you recall."

"I can tell by the little I've seen that you've changed a lot. So glad you kept all the roses that lead up to the house. Granddaddy planted most of those, didn't he?"

"Yes, most are the same ones that have been here for over 30 years. We added other plants. We now have two more garden areas for more roses, other flowers, and other greenery. Another smaller garden outside the kitchen area will be for some vegetables and herbs that will produce some fresh food for our guests."

"Good thinking. I love working with fresh foods, and spices taste so much better when they are fresh."

"While we are taking the tour today, will there be time to talk about the will?" He asked as he stirred the mixture for the quiche. He did not look at her when he asked. He was afraid she would think he was only there for the money.

"You waste no time, do you?" Sara sat back, slightly taken aback by his rush into the legal things. She shouldn't have been surprised. After all, that was the one thing he had mentioned when he called the first time. The time he chickened out of their meeting and ran away.

"Yes, we can go over the will, but that will have to be on Monday. I wanted us all to go over it again at the attorney's office."

"Why at the attorney's office?" I'm not planning to fight it."

"No, that's not the reason. I have a couple of questions for him about it, and I'm sure you and Heather may as well. We can discuss the details and any questions we may have in his office since he will be right there to answer us. Remember, I told you that there are conditions to it that we've had to follow. One of those conditions was completing the remodeling and opening the manor again. That is about complete. We are opening our doors in two weeks. We have a full house registered for the first eight weeks!"

She changed her concerns to excitement when she talked of having full occupancy to her manor. Yes, she still thought of it as solely hers. That would have to change. She knew she was not in this alone. She had grown accustomed to Heather and Ben being there to help. Now Andy was home. She silently wondered how long he would stay or what he hoped to get from them. She loved him, but she was not sure how much she could count on him. He had disappointed the family so much in his life. Oh, how she wanted to be more positive, to be sure there was no reason to worry. She knew time would tell. She watched Andy cook as she sipped her coffee. He looked content in the kitchen.

Heather and Ben came into the kitchen with Marc in tow. He ran up to Andy and hugged him. So young, so innocent, so loving. He did not know his uncle yet, no knowledge of his history, no idea of the bad things in his uncle's life. All he knew was he was already someone to love.

Breakfast finished, the kitchen cleaned up, and everyone full of energy, Sara announced it was time to give Andy a tour of the manor and the land around it. Everyone was welcomed to join in, or she would take him on her own. Ben announced that he had work to do by the pond. Heather said she had to take care of some last-minute delivery schedules. Her absence left Sara and Andy on their own to get to know each other again as they walked.

They started the tour with the guest rooms. Andy's room was the Log Cabin room with a log cabin patterned quilt and matching wall hanging. The other guest rooms on the first floor included the Grandmother's Garden room that faced the manor's front and the Carpenter's Star room facing the back. The last one on the first floor was the Tennessee with the Tennessee Waltz Quilt and wall hanging.

Andy liked what he saw. "You have done a magnificent job on these guest rooms. Whose idea were the quilts, and who made them?"

"They were all made by local ladies in town. Several quilt guilds meet about once a month or so, and they all volunteered to make them. We offered to pay them, but they all refused and said they did it in appreciation for all that our parents and grandparents had done for the community over the years."

"That is amazing. Are the guest rooms upstairs the same way?"

"You will see, but yes, each has a different quilt theme."

They continued their tour of the first floor through the great room, office, and library. Sara filled him in on the details of the rooms as Andy took it all in. His siblings had been busy in his absence. Why did they need him?

They finished touring the second floor, where the bedroom themes included Bear Paw, Friendship Star, Double Wedding Ring, and Around the World. Andy then asked about the third floor.

"Did you make any changes on the third floor? I remember going up there as a kid. Mama would always chase me back downstairs when I would interrupt her work when she was in that one room."

"You remember her being on the third floor?" Sara asked. She was surprised by him remembering.

"We still do not have permission to get into that room. The other room across the hall we use for seasonal storage. Heather has it all organized so she can change décor to the manor at any time."

"If she is the one in charge of the decorations, she has done an amazing job. But why can't we get into the other room?" He couldn't figure out why that would be an issue. "Are you telling me that room is still locked as Mama had it?"

"That, little Brother, is part of the will that we will get to discuss tomorrow at the attorney's office. Until then, accept that we can't get in there yet."

"Alright then, I'll consider that a mystery of Bella Rose Estate."

"We all are," Sara said as she led him back downstairs to the first floor. "Shall we go outside and look around?"

"Sure. I'd love to see the garden areas you mentioned. If I'm going to be doing the cooking ....," Andy cut himself off from saying more.

"We all have been taking turns doing the cooking, but now that you are here, I'd love for you to take over. Once we deal with the will's conditions, we can all sit down and discuss our roles at the manor. Heather, Ben, and I have worked it out among the three of us, but now that you are home, we can make some amazing changes. We each have special talents which will help to decide who will be doing what. Of course, we will also help each other in any way we can."

They went outside and visited the gardens, the gazebo, the unfinished pond, and the walkway between the two guest houses. They then went to the third guest house that would be Andy's if he agreed to stay. Sara had not told him any of what was in the will, so she was not sure he'd stay long enough to make that his home. She was afraid once he knew all the details, he would run. So even though it was great to have him home, she held back her emotions. She was not ready for another heartbreak, and if he left again, she knew that would be her reaction.

Heather and Ben joined them later in the day for lunch. "You all have done an amazing job with this place," Andy told them while they prepared lunch. "I know that Mama and Daddy would be proud of you. Not proud of me, but all three of you."

"Andy, you mentioned you were seeing someone in Pennsylvania. Are you going to tell us about her?" Sara was curious. She wanted to know how serious it was, if she'd be willing to move here and, well, she wanted to know all there was to know about her.

Andy's face lit up. "Karen. Her name is Karen Brooks. She owns a small resort with cabins, a small hotel, a gift store, land with lake frontage where the guests can swim, go boating, and enjoy time on the lake. She's single, never married; no kids, in case you're wondering. She is in her late twenties. And yes, I love her."

Sara saw the gleam in his eyes as well as a tinge of red embarrassment on his face.

"Is she coming to see you here?"

"I don't know. We've not discussed it. Karen's busy season matches the busy season here. So getting away right now is difficult for her."

"She is welcome here, any time. When you talk to her next time, tell her she can come for a visit."

"I'll do that, thank you. That means a lot, Sis."

They spent the rest of the day in small talk and catching up on minor things, nothing about where he had been or why he was on the run. Sara feared if she pushed for explanations, it might push him away. Andy did not volunteer any information. He was impressed that no one asked where he had been or why he had disappeared for over three years. He wondered why they did not ask. Most people would have drilled him for answers.

Heather was busy putting dishes away after dinner and moved her hair away from her face when she stood up. Andy noticed her scar.

"What happened to your face, Sis?" The words were out before he could stop them.

"Oh, this?" she asked as she touched her face. She had been doing her best to forget about it when she was not looking at the mirror. She did her best to cover it in public. She was more relaxed about it at home because everyone knew the reason for her scar. In fact, it rarely got mentioned.

"Yes, that. What happened? Did you have a bad fall?"

"You could say that. In a car, over an embankment."

"Ouch. When was this? You should have gotten in touch with me to let me know."

"Andy, you didn't show up for either of our parents' funerals. What makes you think if we had contacted you somehow that you would have shown up? We didn't know where you were at the time."

"I deserve that." He was not going to pry. If she wanted to talk, he would listen.

"Did you notice my limp? I have a metal plate and a few screws holding it together. I broke my leg in the same accident."

"Oh, Heather, I am so sorry."

“Why are you sorry? You weren't anywhere around. It wasn't your fault. I don't blame Ben, and he was driving. Accidents happen. We heal, then we move on. There is no evidence to indicate the involvement of another vehicle. A policeman keeps looking into the case during his off-hours even though the case is closed. The witnesses saw no other car at the time, so it's pretty much over and ruled an accident.”

“You're taking it quite well.”

“There is no other way to take it. My family is fine. I may limp, have a scar on my face, oh, and one on my arm.” She pulled her sleeve up to show him the one she kept hidden by her long sleeves. "But I still have my husband and my son. And the doctor says the internal injuries weren't so bad that we can't have more kids. All in all, I'm happy.”

“Any other news I should know about?”

“Not that I know of,” Heather yawned. It was getting close to supper time, and she was also tired. “I think it's either nap time or dinner time. What do you think? Are you ready to cook for us?”

“Always. Let's go; you can help.” They both let the subject of the accident drop.

After dinner, more family time and a good night’s rest, the siblings headed to their early morning meeting with the attorney. Ben stayed with Marc, who always loved to help as much as an almost-three-year-old could help at the manor. That was one advantage to working from home; he had a lot more time with his son. Ben felt blessed that his secretary and Donovan were handling the business so well. He would need to go down to the office soon to say hello and address any issues. He wanted to discuss selling the business to Donovan. It was time. Donovan had proven himself more than once that he could oversee the company.

At the attorney's office, Sara introduced Andy and Mr. Williams. They each took a seat in his office and wasted no time getting to the matter at hand, reading the will for Andy's benefit. Once read, Andy sat there in silence. How was he supposed to stay at the manor for five years? And what was it about the attic? He was perplexed. Something did not make sense to him. Was it because he had spent so many years away from home that his mama was doing her best to make him stay home? But she had made the same demands to his sisters.

"So, are there any questions?" Attorney Williams asked while looking from one to the other of the siblings sitting in his office. It certainly was one of the oddest wills he had ever dealt with in his nearly eighteen years as a lawyer.

Andy raised his hand slightly, as kids do when they are in school. "I have plenty. Where to start." Andy took a deep breath and leaned forward in his chair. "Okay, first, do we have to follow what the will says, or can we do our own thing? I know my sisters have already followed through with remodeling the manor, and it is going to open soon, but is there a way we could change that five-year stipulation that is in there? Not only for me but for each of us? I can't believe our parents, especially Mama, would write it that way. She knows how we are."

"Which could be why she wrote it that way," Sara interjected before Mr. Williams had time to answer. "Mama understood you might not stay. You were already gone when she wrote it. She didn't know if you'd come back at all. And she didn't want you to show up merely to take whatever money she had set aside for you and run off again. She wanted us to become the family she always wanted, even if she couldn't be here to see it."

Sara was shocked at how angry she sounded. "Sorry, I don't mean to sound angry, but it's true. I agree with Andy. Is there a way for all of us to get around her five-year requirement?"

"The only way to do that, and you are welcome to try, is not to honor her wishes. The bank has instructions to hold and invest each of your inheritances for five years. You would have to fight them over it."

"Okay. We'll talk about that one after we get home," Heather chimed in. "Now, about that attic. When can we get the key?"

"You can have that after you open the manor for business. The soft opening you had does not count. But a few weeks after you open permanently, you can come back for instructions for the key."

"Instructions? You mean we can't just have the key?"

"Nope, sorry. I have a copy of instructions for how you are to get the key, and those I cannot share until it's time."

Andy looked at his siblings one at a time. "That is unbelievable!"

"That's for sure. Now that you know what the will says, you have some thinking to do, Andy. Are you going to be able to stay with us for five years?"

"I am going to have to think about it. We can talk at home. I also want to talk with Karen. Maybe even Larry about it."

Andy stood to leave. He reached out and shook Attorney Williams's hand and thanked him for taking the time to reread the will for them. Sara and Heather also stood to leave. Sara told Attorney Williams they would be in touch.

Andy was quiet on the ride home. He was in his own little world. He certainly hadn't planned to stay around for five years. He wasn't exactly going to run and hide, but he wasn't planning to stay at the manor. He wanted to be with Karen. He missed her so much.

When he got back to his room, he took his cell phone out of his jeans pocket and called Karen. He told her about the will and its conditions. He told her that he wanted to stay for the money and help his siblings out, but he also wanted to be with her.

Karen told him to think about it over the next few days. She told him that she missed him and asked when the best time would be to visit him if he stayed there. He was amazed that she wanted to visit, especially since this was almost her busy season. He knew in his heart that their friendship was more than casual friends. Her desire to visit left him with a smile as they finished their conversation and said good night.

They sounded like teenagers – "you hang up," "no, you hang up." Finally, he said good night and that he would call her sometime over the next few days after he'd had a chance to talk with his sisters and think things through.

Chapter Twenty-One

Opening day had finally arrived at Bella Rose. Andy had little time to talk to his sisters while they rushed to prepare for their guests, but in the back of his mind, as much as he hated to admit it, he wanted to stay – for the money. He loved his sisters, but it was the money speaking louder than family. He was conflicted. He wanted Karen to be with him but could not envision her giving up her life and career in Pennsylvania to join him in Tennessee. There was too much going on to make his final decision, so instead of deciding, he concentrated on helping his sisters and Ben prepare for their first guests. He had agreed to do all the cooking, including baked goods that they could offer their guests later in the day. Baking was his specialty.

Nicole and Joe were the first people to arrive for the weekend. They had spent the soft opening at the manor and offered to assist with the grand opening any way they could. Sara had welcomed their help.

Sara scheduled a time for the guests to meet in the living room on their first evening. This would give everyone a chance to get to know her and each other. Other than breakfast time, the meeting was the only thing scheduled for the guests. The rest of their stay was up to them to plan and enjoy the area.

Sara began by welcoming everyone and introducing herself. Then she invited each person to introduce themselves. She followed that by giving a brief history of the manor and a few recent remodeling details. She mentioned a few things to do in the area and within a short drive. She concluded with the breakfast schedule and asked if they had any questions.

One guest asked about the notebooks that were in the room. She explained that they were there for them to write in before they left. When there were no more questions, she introduced Andy.

Andy came in and invited them to the dining room for a special treat. The special treat was Southern Banana Pudding. He served it with homemade whipped cream topped with a swirl of warm dark chocolate sauce. He served it in elegant wine glasses that had the Bella Rose Manor Logo etched on them. The logo was an open rose, monogrammed with 'BRM' in the middle of the rose. Everyone loved the dessert. The ladies wanted the recipe. The ladies also wanted to know if the wine glasses were available to purchase. Andy told them they would look into it, but currently they did not have them for sale.

Sara made a note to call her supplier about increasing her order for the glasses and to inquire about a wholesale price. She would sell the ones they had on hand if she could get new ones in time for the next group of guests. They did have a couple dozen on hand, but she wanted to make sure she could get more before selling those.

Andy posted the morning menu in the kitchen. A copy was also placed in each room so the guests would know what was being served. Guests were asked about any special food issues when they made their reservations. Many people were on special diets or had food allergies, and they wanted to accommodate everyone the best they could. Andy was lucky with this group of guests. No one had any special needs. They were willing to try anything, which thrilled Andy, as it made his life so much easier.

The next morning the guests gathered around the dining room table for coffee and breakfast. Chatter filled the air as the guests shared their plans for the day. Two couples were going for a drive into the mountains. One couple was going to visit the antique shops and see the historical sites in town. Another couple was going to visit their daughter and grandchildren living in the area. Nicole and Joe planned to relax outside at the pond, enjoy the gazebo and walk the trail with Ben as their guide. They did not need to go sightseeing since they lived close. They were using this time to relax.

Sara and Heather were busy after everyone left for the day; cleaning, changing sheets, switching out the bath towels, and laundry. Andy was busy cleaning the kitchen and making snacks and a dessert for that evening. He was also compiling the recipes for the ladies who wanted to take them home. Their request had planted the idea to create a recipe book guests could buy during their visit or online. This would require him to give away some family secrets and some secret things he had created recently. He would have to create new items to keep the guests returning for new experiences in his kitchen. Ahhh, *his* kitchen. He smiled. That was the first time he had thought of staying for the five years – it felt good – *The Chef of Bella Rose Mano*r. What a title. Well, it would be if the place became famous. If they did it right and word got out with positive feedback and recommendations... he could see them being well known. He would have to talk with his sisters. He was beginning to feel part of the family. But what about Karen? He looked around and could envision her there. Standing by his side, helping in the kitchen. Or out helping his sisters. He was sure there would be a place for her here.

The guests spent the early evening relaxing near the fireplace and socializing in the great room. Andy brought out some snacks and drinks for everyone. There was no alcohol available, but there was coffee, sweet tea, and sodas. The guests invited Sara, Andy, Heather, and her family to join them for a while.

The conversations ranged from the sights seen, items bought, and more personal sharing. This group loved to talk and share. The oldest couple there was James and Helen. They had booked their stay even before the remodel was complete. Helen had contacted Sara when Glen and Susan had died, to send their condolences. She then requested notification and a room when the manor reopened. Sara had called her a week before the soft opening to let her know the opening date and that a room would await them. James and Helen had been friends with their grandparents. James had met Robert while serving together in the Army and had stayed friends over the years. Listening to James and Helen talking of days gone by had everyone listening. It seemed everyone loved stories of the past.

After most of the guests had gone to their rooms for the evening, the siblings sat at the kitchen island discussing their successful first official opening day. Nicole and Joe came in and asked if they could join them. Sara welcomed them to join. Andy asked how they had liked the first day compared to their visit a few weeks earlier. They said it was wonderful to get away both times. Joe added how glad they were to have met the family, even though their initial meeting was not the best experience. Andy looked confused. Sara explained how Joe and Nicole had been the ones who had rescued Heather, Ben, and Marc after the accident last fall. Heather added Nicole was the reason she was still alive. Andy listened intently. He was so glad that Heather's injuries had not been worse, and that Ben and Marc were not seriously injured.

Joe added details of the accident, including the accident's date and that the weather had not caused the accident, but that as soon as the ambulance and Medivac left, it started to pour. He said the rain fell so hard it washed away any tire marks or other evidence. He said that there was no indication of another vehicle, thanks to the hard rains. Andy listened to the story.

Later that evening, before returning to his room, Andy opened the calendar app on his phone. His heart sank when he scrolled back to the date Joe mentioned. It was the same day that he had taken off to Florida to spend a few months. The time he found his car damaged at the hotel. The time when he did not remember anything because he had been too drunk. He looked again and thought back. It was the same night he was supposed to meet his oldest sister.

He called Karen when he got back to his room. He paced while they spoke. They discussed how he felt at home with his family. Keeping it positive, he told her he was the official chef at Bella Rose and enjoyed the title and the work. She told him she was happy for him. Andy picked up on the sadness in her voice.

“Karen, what's wrong? You sound sad or depressed. Is everything alright there?” He sat on his bed to listen to the woman he loved. He sensed her need for him.

“Yes Andy, everything is fine here. I miss you, that's all.”

“I miss you too.”

There was a moment of silence between them. “Andy, are you coming back?”

“Yes, of course I am. However, I have no idea when," Andy's shoulders sank as he continued. "I know I told you I'd be back soon, but my sisters need me here, and we have been so busy. I've not even had time to deal with what the will says and means. Part of it states something about me needing to stay here for five years, and I doubt I can stay that long and not see you. I want to be with you. We've got to figure something out.” He hesitated before continuing. “Karen, have you given any thought to coming here?”

"Yes, I have, but the summer season is starting, and it's hard to get away."

"Not just for a visit; I mean to stay – with me."

"Is that what you want?"

"I want to be with you. I miss being with you. But Karen," he took a breath. "I may have figured something out tonight that I need to deal with or keep quiet about."

"What was that?"

"I can't talk about it. Not yet. I hate keeping secrets from you, but I also don't want you involved if I can help it. You deserve the best of me."

"Okay. I trust you. I'll let you fill me in when you're ready. How are things going otherwise?"

"Things are going great. The guests love it here so far. I'm busy in the kitchen most of the time, creating some amazing desserts and breakfasts. The guests even want some of the recipes. I'm thinking of writing a small recipe book to sell." There was excitement in his voice as he spoke.

"That's a great idea! I may want a copy."

"I may be able to arrange that," he said. He wondered why Karen would want them; she could have the chef who would make them all for her. It was still too soon in their relationship for him to mention those thoughts out loud. After she got to know him better and more of the truth came out, she may not be interested in him, let alone the recipes.

She had been sitting on the sofa in her living room, looking out her window. As she listened to how excited Andy sounded, she missed him even more. She felt a tear run down her cheek.

It was late when they ended their conversation. It had been a busy day for her. Things were not going well at the lake, but she was not about to tell Andy. He had enough on his plate. She could handle her situation. The early spring rains had flooded a couple of the cabins when high winds had damaged sections of the roofs. She had to get those repaired before her renters arrived. She had two roofs to repair, flooring to replace, and one cabin needed new furniture due to the water damaged. She had consulted with Larry, who recommended contractors who he trusted. Grace had gone with her to pick out new furniture. Karen was grateful for their help.

For some reason, Karen's thoughts turned to when she was a little girl beginning to learn how to swim. She had swam out to the boats anchored to buoys and got her foot caught in a rope. There is no lifeguard at the lake, and her screams were hard to hear, but Larry heard. He had been working on his dock at the shore. He saw her out by the boat and took off from his dock on his jet ski. He got to her as she was running out of energy to stay afloat. She was only nine at the time. She promised him she would not do that again. She kept her promise but continued to swim, being sure to stay away from boats anchored to buoys. Larry was glad the incident had not deterred her from her love to swim. It would be difficult to live on a lake and not be a swimmer.

Swimming had not been on her mind when she got off the phone with Andy. She was tired and confused. Her heart was torn. Her responsibilities were here, as the owner of her rustic resort, but she wanted to be with Andy. She fought with her thoughts. She was glad he was back with his family, but she was jealous that he had a family to go to. She wanted to be a part of what he had. What if she did not like them? What if, in the end, she lost him? So many thoughts and questions. Now was not the time to deal with them. Yet, he was always on her mind.

Karen had a hard road to climb, as the saying goes. First, she had to take care of all the repairs in the cabins. Then she needed to talk with Renee and Larry to ask them if they could handle the resort for a few days without her. Her summer help would be arriving in a few days, which would help ease the burden on them. She had no trouble trusting them all, but it would be her first time to take a vacation in the summer since she became the owner. She lifted her head high and smiled to herself.

Yes, she had a plan. She would head to a state she had never visited, meet a family she knew little about, try to win the heart of the man she had fallen in love with after only a few months, and convince him to move to Pennsylvania and the lake area.

Her thoughts were scrambling. "When did I get so brave and aggressive? My mind and heart are fighting. Which will win? How realistic am I being? How can I expect Andy to leave his family for me? He did keep running from them. Would he now run from me?" She shook her head to get back to her here and now. She had things to take care of before dealing with what may end up being a fantasy. Love had a way of making risks worth taking. She needed some sleep before she acted on anything.

The last night of the grand opening weekend had arrived. Andy had compiled the last few pages of recipes he had used to give the guests a sample of what would be in a future book. He included a link to the Manor's website where people could order the recipe book upon its publication.

Before Sara went to bed, she went to each guest's room and placed a note under the door. Guests had gotten accustomed to finding different special touches each morning. The first morning it was coupons from a couple of the businesses downtown. The second morning it was a fresh rose and a handwritten note outside their door. The last day it was a thank you note for choosing to stay at the Manor, wishing them well on their trip home and inviting them back again. It included a reminder to write comments in the notebooks. The custom-designed notebooks matched the individual rooms. The name of the specific room with a photo of the matching quilt adorned each cover. Sara had written on the first page of each one. It was a welcoming and informative message about the Manor, with each one ending with a different positive, uplifting quote and her signature.

The last morning's breakfast was French Toast, fruit compote, and bacon. Drinks included fresh coffee, orange juice, and apple juice. Real Maple Syrup and homemade whipped cream also waited for the guests. Fresh flowers adorned the table, and a piece of dark chocolate in the shape of a rose lay on top of each place setting. The extra touches of elegance made Bella Rose stand out from other country manors. No one could be sad or depressed when a dark chocolate rose rested on your morning breakfast plate.

One couple left immediately after breakfast since they had a long trip home. Another couple went back to their guest room to finish writing in the notebook. James and Helen made themselves at home and continued sitting at the dining table. Sara asked if they were alright. They said they were but wanted some alone time to enjoy Bella Rose one last time. When everyone else had left the dining room, they stood up and walked hand in hand down to the pond. After staying there a few minutes, they made their way to the gazebo, where they sat for almost an hour.

Sara was about to go out and make sure they were alright when they at least moved. Sara stepped back. She did not want to intrude. James stood up and reached for his wife's hand to help her up. They put their arms around each other and slowly made their way through the garden and back to the manor. Sara smiled as she watched them from her office. They seemed like newlyweds even though they were slow, and she knew they had said their I Do's almost seventy years before.

She thought back to when James told them about how things used to be at the manor. The property that had begun as one building, adding a second, and third building soon after it opened. A small place overall, but it was a beautiful getaway. A nice change from what life had been for him and Robert. WWII had brought them together. Helen had talked of how things used to be in town. The streets were all cobblestones. The shops closed on Sunday so that everyone could attend church and then enjoy a Sunday meal with family. More often than not, the meal was at the grandparent's house. Then folks would either go for a walk or sit back and talk for the rest of the afternoon.

Sara was still in the office when they came inside. They knocked on her door even though it was open. She called for them to come in. Helen started a conversation, but James walked away.

“Sara, dear.”

“Yes, Helen, how are you? I hope you and James have enjoyed your stay with us. It has been so nice to have you here this weekend. I know you wanted to have your last look around the manor, but I hope you can make it back soon.”

“I wish we could too, but at our age, I doubt that will be possible. We are old. We love being active and traveling, but those days are coming to an end.” She reached inside her jacket and pulled out an envelope.

“My dear, sweet Sara. We have written you a check...”

“You've already paid me Helen. James took care of that when you first arrived.”

“No, this is separate from the payment to stay here. This check is for you and your siblings. You see, we never had any children of our own, and we wanted to give you something in memory of your parents and grandparents. And instead of waiting for *that time* and a will,” she made the air quotes when she said *that time*, "we wanted to give it to you now. You are free to use it any way you see fit. We know that the remodel has set you back some financially. We also know that your mother, God rest her soul, put some restrictions on that will of hers. We want to give you something to hold you over or help out with some remodeling you may not have done yet. Or you can save it for a rainy day when you have repairs to do. As I said, it's yours to do with what you want." Helen stepped away as Sara took the envelope.

"Now," Helen smiled and continued, "This too has conditions, to a certain degree. This evening, after you all have had your dinner and your family gathers in the great room enjoying the fireplace and the peacefulness of the day, you may open it. Not beforehand." Helen shook her bony finger at Sara and stepped aside. "I want you to have a special family time tonight. You all have done a wonderful job with the manor. Your folks and grandparents would be proud of you." She turned away from Sara. She was shedding a tear and did not even know why.

She left the office and met James in the hallway, where their luggage was waiting for them. James picked up the suitcase, then set it down again. He saw Helen's eyes. He reached for Helen's hand as they walked to the fireplace. While still holding hands, they reached up to the mantle with their free hands and rested them there. Their hands lingered there a moment, then they turned, picked up their suitcases, and walked out the door to their car.

Sara watched her favorite couple leave. She wiped a tear from her eye as she watched them pull away, then returned to the office to place the envelope, unopened, into the safe in the office.

She had to wait several more hours to open it and wanted it safe so no one would find it and where she would not lose it.

Chapter Twenty-Two

Once again, the manor was temporarily vacant. Sara and Heather were busy cleaning and doing the laundry in preparation for the new guests arriving in a few days. Sara liked to get things done as soon as possible so they could relax before new guests arrived. That way, if something unexpected came up, they'd have time to deal with it. She was not a type-A person, but she liked to get things done, just as she liked to arrive places early.

Ben was busy planting some early flower bulbs and making some changes in the gardens. He was enjoying his new role and work. Gardening was becoming his passion. A chance to get away, think, plan, and relax while still working. It was a far cry from his contractor days. He maintained ownership of his business but had put Donovan in charge.

Andy was already working on the menus for upcoming guests. He was also preparing dinner for the family, making something new and unique while using up all the leftovers. When he announced dinner was ready, everyone stopped what they were doing to enjoy family time.

As they sat around the table, they noticed that Sara had a funny look on her face. Everyone wondered what she had on her mind. She was hiding something; they could tell. They waited for her to speak, but when she did not, it was Andy who asked.

"Okay Sis, spill it. What is that look about? Care to share?"

"I'd love to share, but I can't."

"Not another clause from Mama's will, is it?" Heather asked.

"No, not the will. But I am not permitted to share 'til after dinner and clean up when we gather in the living room by the fireplace."

Everyone looked at her with curiosity showing in their eyes and through their facial expressions. Could they take another surprise? They could not tell by her face if it was something good or bad.

Andy moved to the stove. "Okay people, grab your plates, let's inhale, I mean, let's eat."

They all did as he told them. As much as they wanted to take their time and savor what he had made, they all found themselves eating faster than usual. They all wanted to know what Sara had up her sleeve.

Sara was as anxious as everyone else. Although she knew there was a check inside the envelope, she had no indication of the amount. She could not imagine it was much, but Helen had been a bit mysterious about it. And how did Helen know about the conditions in her mom's will? Had someone told her? Or did she know how Susan was – sneaky and a bit mischievous. Whatever it was, Sara pushed the questions aside. They all would know soon. No one knew how their lives would change once they opened it.

After they had finished dinner, cleaned the kitchen counters, and put the dishes in the dishwasher they retreated to the living room. Ben started a fire in the fireplace while Sara went to the office to retrieve the envelope. Marc made himself comfortable on the floor with his toys. He was so easy-going and went along with the flow of people and ever-changing things. It didn't matter what was happening around him when his family were around. He had no interest in this mysterious envelope.

Sara returned to the living room with the envelope in her hand and joined her family near the fireplace. Then she proceeded to relay the conversation she had had with Helen. Sara reminded them that James and Helen had known their grandparents and had stayed at the manor during those early years. Sara told her family she had learned that they had never had any children of their own and wanted to give them this. She held up the envelope. She told her family what Helen had told her. That instead of going through a will when they passed, they wanted them to have it now.

"So, what is it?" Andy voiced what they all were thinking. Sara looked at each one of them and noticed they were all leaning forward in anticipation as kids do at Christmas. As much as her curiosity was getting to her, she snickered at what she saw. None of them knew that much about James and Helen except what they had learned over the weekend. They were an older couple, truly in love with each other, who had worked hard most of their lives and did some traveling. They had not been close to the family. Not that they could remember.

Finally, when Sara finished telling them the backstory, she held up the envelope again. She took a deep breath. Why were she and her siblings so anxious? So curious? Secrets. That is what it was. The way Susan had written her will had them all suspicious of the unknown. The possibilities followed by disappointments. They had felt it all when they had read their mama's will. Now, this. Something James and Helen wanted them to have now, and not through a will.

"Okay, here goes." Sara took the antique letter opener she had brought along. The envelope, a five by seven manila envelope that she had hidden in her secret safe, was about to reveal a surprise they could never have imagined. Sara knew it was a check but thought there might be more. She had not revealed what she knew. Sara could feel the presence of James and Helen watching her. It was a chilling feeling, but then a warm, almost realistic sense of a hug. She opened the envelope and set the letter opener on the coffee table. She pulled out a letter that was folded in half.

"It's a letter?" Heather asked. "Only a letter?"

"So far," Sara said before opening the folds of the pages. It was a couple of pages, handwritten by Helen, but from them both. She unfolded it and began to read.

"*Dear Sara, Heather, and Andy,*

James and I have been a part of your family for many years. As we told you before, James met your grandfather while they served together in the Army during WWII. Your grandmother and I met after the war ended when we each got married. Our friendship was immediate and lifelong. We had many things in common. The men had even more in common through their military journey. They had a bond that neither your grandmother nor I could even begin to understand. We quit trying after a few years.

It is because of that friendship that James and I feel so close to your family. We did our best to stay in touch and to come to visit at least once a year. After your grandparents passed away, we still came to visit. We watched as your mother grew from a child to a beautiful woman, marry your father, and take ownership and expand Bella Rose. We watched the struggles and hardships. We had several years where our health kept us from visiting, so you may not remember much about us. Then we heard about your parents passing and that you had taken ownership of the manor. When we learned some of what your Mama and Daddy did and what you have done to remodel and expand it, we had to come for one last visit.

Yes, this visit was our last. We are in ill health and need to stay close to home and with our medical contacts who know how to treat us. James has cancer. The doctors say it won't be much longer. I have my own issues that I won't expand on. We put on a good 'healthy' front, don't we?

Anyway, we wanted to let you know how much we appreciate your family and loved knowing each of you. This tribute to your family is a piece of what we want to give you.

Sara, Heather, Andy, your families, spouses, children, we want to give your family a small token of our love. I know sharing our stories will help you learn more about your legacy and those you will find in time, I'm sure. They are in writing, somewhere. From us, now, please accept this check that we have enclosed. Along with the check, there are papers that will tell you more.

Please accept them and all our love.
James and Helen"

She picked the envelope up and took another look inside. She pulled out a smaller envelope and opened it. She gasped when she saw the check.

"What?" the others said in unison.

Sara turned the check so they all could see what had made her gasp. Heather gulped. Andy fell silent and stared. Ben's eyes opened wide.

"Oh my. What a generous gift," Heather said.

"What are we supposed to do with that? Two hundred fifty thousand dollars is a lot of money," Ben added.

"There's more," Sara said as she reached inside for yet another envelope. She opened it and found a document for a trust fund for Marc. There was also another letter inside. Sara opened it and began to read while everyone sat listening, wondering what more there could be from this couple they hardly knew. What they were about to hear would change their lives like they could never have imagined.

"Dear Sara, Heather, and Andy,

The check you have found is only the beginning. The bank has an account set up for you, more specifically for the Manor. There is a million dollars allocated to that account. We have set it up to use any way you need for Bella Rose Manor and Estate. If you have repairs, upgrades, additions, other monies running low, and debts to pay, please use it.

We do have one request for the use of part of it. We would like to see a small chapel built by the pond. You do not have to build it very large, but we hope it is big enough to hold about 45 - 50 people. That way, all your guests can be comfortable being in there at one time.

Love you all,
James and Helen"

When Sara finished reading the letter, there was silence in the room. The only sounds were the crackling of the fire, Marc playing with a dump truck. No one knew what to say.

Sara was so taken by it. She was shaking with tears flowing down her face. She was not the only one with tears falling.

You never know how your kindness will affect others even years later. A friendship made generations before touched their lives in ways they never expected.

Sara said a silent prayer for James and Helen. She hoped somehow, they would be able to come for another visit; she would make sure it was a free visit. It was the least she could do.

Chapter Twenty-Three

Life was settling down to a new routine for Sara. She sat in her office and leaned back in her desk chair. The same chair her father and mother had sat in for so many years. Her thoughts were of everything that was going on with her siblings, her nephew, and herself. From her perspective, they all were doing well.

Marc was growing and had adjusted to the move, having a new uncle, and the guests being around. He was an easy-going child. He would be going to preschool in the fall, and she knew he'd make new friends, learn a lot, and have fun. He was a smart little boy.

Ben continued to maintain the manor, houses, gazebo, and all the landscaping. He had soon realized that overseeing the maintenance and grounds was a full-time job. His contracting business was thriving under Donovan's management. He had talked of selling it to Donovan, but that had not transpired yet.

Heather was busy being Mama to Marc while she helped Sara clean, decorate, and give personal touches for their guests at the manor. She also helped Ben out when she could.

Andy was continuing his recipe book endeavor. He continued to talk with Karen almost every night. She had finally told him that she had suffered some damage to the cabins but had assured him that all the repairs were completed, and she was doing well. Andy had been giving out hints that he wanted her to at least visit. She said she wanted nothing better but did not know when she would be able to get away. She would have to talk with Renee and Larry. Although Larry owned the neighboring property, he often helped Karen when she needed something. She had been planning to surprise Andy and show up unannounced one day soon, but he made it hard to keep her secret.

The guests were keeping them busy. Some guests liked to mingle and associate with the siblings and family for a while. Others wanted to go exploring the area downtown and on into the mountains. The Smokies were not that far away. The mountains were impressive; the shopping was good too.

Cades Cove offered an incredible slow drive with a chance to see wildlife, including deer and bear. And it was a favorite day trip for many guests. Guests could go antique shopping and learn the area's history within a few miles of the manor. The only time everyone was together was for breakfast. Andy was an excellent chef, and a request for the recipes always followed his meals.

Sara and Heather made sure that each guest felt at home the moment they arrived. After they registered at the office, they could take their suitcases to their rooms and return to the office for a complete tour. If they had other plans, they could take a tour later. Sara conducted the inside tour, and Ben led the outside tour. The guests' rooms were always spotless. They were complete with fresh flowers, brochures from several local places, and of course, the notebook. Guests were enjoying what previous guests wrote and adding their own comments and stories.

The notebooks were a success from the beginning. Sara and Heather took turns reading them out loud once the guests left. They were learning a lot about their guests, as they wrote their reasons for being there, their expectations, and their experiences during their visit. So far, everyone had complimented the hosts and had remembered to sign and date their entries.

A few days after they received the check from James and Helen, Sara went to the bank and deposited it. She had made an appointment to discuss the trust and the other monies that sat waiting for them. It was still such a shock, a welcomed shock, but a surprise, nonetheless. She wished she had gotten to know them better while they were guests. They were such a sweet couple. All the other guests enjoyed getting to know them.

Two weeks later, Sara finally received a call from the bank telling her there was an open slot in the banker's schedule and asked if she wanted to come in. She eagerly agreed and rushed home to gather papers and notepad.

She wanted to take notes so she could share the information later. Taking notes was the only way she knew to help her remember.

She locked up the documents when she returned home and sat down at the desk. She opened the top drawer to put her notepad away. It had been on top of her desk when she grabbed it, but it belonged inside the drawer. She heard the movement of metal as she placed it inside. She looked and noticed the skeleton key she had forgotten. Her thoughts went back to several months earlier; her mama's death, the will, its conditions, and finding the keys. She wondered again if they had anything to do with the attic; the mysterious, off-limits attic.

She was lost in thought when her phone rang. She tossed the keys back in the drawer, closed it, and answered the phone.

All she heard at first was someone crying. Then she realized it was Helen. Sara asked her what was wrong. Between quiet sobs, Helen told her that James had died during the night. Helen continued to cry on the phone to Sara while she told of his last few days with her. Sara sat, listened, cried, and offered condolences from the family. She told Helen if there was anything they could do for her, to let her know. Helen thanked her and said all she wanted was for James to be remembered.

Sara sat and looked out through the window when her conversation had ended. She could see the pond and the vacant land next to it; the spot where James and Helen wanted the chapel. There was plenty of room for it, and the view was amazing. She smiled as she envisioned a small white chapel with a lawn in the back, with benches for people to sit and enjoy the view. It would be a great way to remember James and Helen. Building it now needed to be a top priority. She would speak with Ben about all the details. He was the expert and the one to get the job done.

Other things needed attention soon as well. Andy needed to make his decision. Was he going to agree to stay for the five years, or would he head back to Pennsylvania to be with Karen? They had not even met her yet, and Sara was already worried about how she would fit into the family. She worried that Karen would pull him away from them after they had finally gotten him back. What were the chances of her moving here? Only time would tell. Time was what they had now. Bella Rose Manor was up and running. There were already no vacancies until mid-summer, and those of fall were filling up fast. It was time for the next chapter in their lives and the life of the manor. New beginnings. New growth. The future. She smiled when she thought of how far her family had come in a relatively short amount of time. They had survived everything so far.

She walked into the great room, and the future came running up to her wrapping his arms around her legs. Little Marc. He was growing so fast. She smiled, picked him up, and walked into the kitchen to get a snack for the two of them. A snack would hold them over for dinner. She could already smell something cooking and knew Andy was not too far away.

He had prepared a new dish for everyone to try. They had gotten used to breakfast foods for dinner when he worked on new recipes for the menu and his book. They were willing guinea pigs in his world of creating fantastic food dishes. Most of what he made was amazing.

Later, while they all gathered to eat his latest creation for the breakfast menu, Sara was unusually quiet. She was usually talkative about what was going on, something about the guests, news from town. She had a knack for keeping a conversation going. For her to be so quiet was unusual, but no one said anything about it. They knew that she had something bothering her or something heavy on her heart when she got that way.

It was not until after dinner that she opened up and said she had some news to share. They all turned toward her and listened. She told them that Helen had called, and that James had passed away the night before. She told them that she had sent along their condolences and told Helen to let them know if she needed anything. She looked up through her tears and saw Heather wiping her eyes. They were all saddened by the news. They had not gotten to know them very well in the short time they were there, but their love had touched their hearts.

Sara did her best to lighten the mood. She sat up, wiped the last of her tears. "I know we have a lot going on, but we need to make building the chapel a priority. In memory of James.

Ben agreed. He said he would get with his crew and draw up some plan ideas. He was glad he had such a good crew of men working for him. They would do almost anything for him.

They started discussing a few ideas, including the chapel, landscaping along the driveway, the color scheme, and some inside decorations. When they finished, Heather said that she and Ben had some news to share.

A hush fell over the room as Heather and Ben stood up at the head of the kitchen island. They lifted their glasses of sweet tea. They looked at each other and smiled larger than anyone had in a very long time.

Sara and Andy's eyes grew big.

"Sara, Andy, we are pregnant!" Heather and Ben were smiling from ear to ear. Sara stood up and hugged her baby sister. Andy reached over and shook hands with his brother-in-law.

"Congratulations! I'm so excited! When is the baby due? When did you find out? How could you keep this from me?" Sara rambled off question after question.

"We are due in January. We found out for sure this morning. And, before you ask why we didn't tell you sooner, Sis. Because even though the home pregnancy test was positive, given my history of losing the baby during the accident, and the chance that I would not be able to carry to full term, let alone get pregnant, we wanted to wait before we got everyone's hopes up. So, yes, it is only seven months, but we have plenty of time to prepare," Heather took a breath after saying everything she needed to in one breath to avoid interruption.

"I understand your reasons. I still wish you would have told me sooner, but you do know me. I wouldn't have been able to keep it quiet," Sara said. Then her smile faded.

"What's wrong, Sis?"

She gently shook her head. She did not want to spoil the mood. But she said it anyway. "Mama and Daddy won't get to meet this new little one."

"I know, I thought about that. Somehow they know, and they will be here with us. I feel the same way about Grandma and Granddaddy. They will be here."

"You're right. Our parents and grandparents will always be in our hearts. Plus, we will tell this little one all about his family. The same way we will tell Marc. They come from an amazing family, including their aunt and uncle."

"This calls for a special dessert!" Andy said as he went around to the kitchen. He opened the refrigerator and pulled out an elegant dessert of chilled chocolate raspberry mousse. Andy topped each one with a large dollop of fresh whipped cream and a fresh raspberry, then carried them on a tray to the island. He had made one for each of them, including a small one he had made specifically for Marc.

It was a night of celebrations. One for the new life that was growing inside Heather to become part of their family. Another in celebration and mourning James's life. He had had a wonderful and blessed life. And for Sara, it was a celebration of family, accomplishments, and love.

Chapter Twenty-Four

Andy had been busy, working on new recipes for the cookbook to sell and helping as much as he could around the manor. No matter how busy he was, he called Karen every single day. Some days more than once. He missed her. Their long talks over the phone helped some. It also made him want to see her even more. The timing never seemed to work out for her to make the trip South or for him to head North again. They lived over 500 miles apart. How was it ever going to work? Her business was seasonal. His was the year around. He tried to figure it out every night while he was in his own house at the manor. The guest house that he had tried to make his own, did not yet feel like home. It was missing something. Or someone. He had family all around him, but he was lonely. Late one night, unable to sleep, he called Karen. He knew there was a chance that she was asleep, but he needed to hear her voice.

"Hello." A sleepy voice answered.

"Karen? So sorry if I woke you, but I need to hear your voice again."

"Andy?"

"Yes, it's me. I know we talked this afternoon, but I miss you."

"I miss you too." Karen sat up in her bed as she woke up. She looked at the clock. It was 3 AM. Why was he up? Was something else going on?

"Andy, is something wrong? Are you okay?"

"I'm fine. I have been thinking about us and could not go to sleep until I called you. I'm so sorry it is so late, or early, depending on how you look at it. Karen, is there anyway, anyway at all you can come to Tennessee to visit? Please?" He hated to beg, but he would beg if that is what it took to get her by his side.

"Andy, I've been thinking about you as well and missing you. I, well, I've talked with Renee and with Larry. I wanted to surprise you with this, but seeing how you can't sleep and all, I guess I will let the secret out."

"What secret?"

"I'm planning a trip to see you this weekend."

"For real? You're coming here?" He felt like a kid again. He may have felt tired and lonely when he made the phone call, but he was awake now.

"Yes, I will see you Friday sometime."

"Oh Karen, you don't know how happy that makes me! I know we had talked about me coming back there to see you, but I'd love for you to meet my family and see this place. It is amazing."

"I know. I thought about it long and hard and realized that I do need to meet your family if we are going to have any type of relationship, even if it is long distant for a while. Getting to know your family seems like the right thing to do. Have you told them that you have invited me?"

"Of course I have. They keep asking about you and want to meet you."

"I'm glad. I am so excited! But Andy, I do have to get some sleep now. I'll see you in a few days."

"I can't wait! Good night Karen." As he went to disconnect, he whispered, "I love you." All he heard was a click. She had disconnected. He did not know if she had heard him or not. He hung up his phone and waited. There was no call back from her, so he assumed she had not heard his closing words. That was okay. He'd tell her again when she came for the weekend.

Andy finally fell asleep moments before his alarm went off. He was still sleepy and felt like he was in a dream state until he was in the shower. He woke up enough to know that he had not been dreaming. Karen was coming to visit him and meet his family! He could not wait to tell his family. He knew Sara would want to do something special. She always did.

His sisters noticed he was smiling more prominently than usual at breakfast.

"Hey little brother, I guess you slept well last night; your smile is bigger, and there is a gleam in your eyes."

"Oh, I didn't sleep much at all last night."

"Then how do you look so awake and full of energy? What's your secret?"

"I called Karen late last night. Some would say early this morning, but who cares. Anyway, long story short, Karen will be here on Friday!"

His sisters screamed like teens who found out a famous star was coming to town. They would finally get to meet this Karen person. They each gave Andy a big hug as they jumped up and down.

"It's about time," Ben said. She's all you ever talk about. I was beginning to think she was an imaginary friend."

"Oh, she's real. You get to find out in a few days!"

"We have got to get busy! We have a special guest coming. Time for more fresh flowers, extra spotless cleaning of the manor, and the grounds," Sara was babbling in her attempt to organize and make everything special for Karen.

"Sis, there is no need to do anything special for her. She runs her own resort. She knows it's not always clean and perfect. She is a normal person."

"No, she is not a normal person. She is the love of your life. She is special and a bit crazy for loving you."

"Who said she was crazy?"

"She must be if she's with you," Ben answered for them all.

Everyone laughed. Andy felt good to know his family could laugh at him. He took it as being part of them instead of having a desire to run. This is what family was all about. He hoped things would be better once Karen arrived.

Friday arrived with everyone on their toes. Ben did his usual property check. Sara made sure everything was in its place. Heather made sure Karen's room was ready. Andy, well, Andy was a basket case. He had not seen Karen in several months. He was already pacing the floor. They started watching for her as soon as breakfast was over. They knew it was a long trip and that she may not arrive until late afternoon, but that did not stop them from glancing out the window.

Marc was the first person to notice a car pull up. He ran to the door squealing. His loud squeal got everyone's attention. They all scrambled to the door. Each was trying to be first. Marc was accustomed to people arriving, but they had told him that this person was special to his Uncle Andy.

Andy pushed between everyone. He turned to them all and shook his head.

"Do you think you all could back up a few yards? I don't want you to scare her away before she makes it through the door." Andy motioned for them to back up as he went out the front door to greet the love of his life.

Karen parked her car and immediately saw Andy running down the steps to her. Her exhaustion from the trip disappeared as her heart melted when she saw Andy. She smiled as she opened her door and stepped out. Andy reached in to pull her into his arms. His hug was so tight she almost lost her breath. Her grip was as tight as his. She never wanted to let go. This welcome felt like home.

"I am so glad to see you! You are even more beautiful than I remember!" He kissed her and held her as she returned his kiss. A long, few moments later they walked arm in arm up to the front door. Andy warned her of an impending ambush he knew was coming, even though he had warned his family to chill out.

"Welcome to Bella Rose Manor," Sara announced as the door opened. She stepped aside so they could come in. Ben and Heather rose from the sofa as if they had simply been relaxing, pretending to be calm and nonchalant about their new guest.

Marc ran up to Karen and held up his hand for her to shake. "Welcome," he said. "Glad to meet you, I am Marc."

Marc. I'm glad to meet you too."

Andy introduced everyone to Karen, adding that there would be a quiz later. She snickered. His family was small enough that she knew she could remember their names. Plus, Andy had told her a lot about them in their phone conversations. The reception that they gave her made her feel right at home.

"Would you like something to drink? To use the restroom? Something to eat before dinner?"

"No, thank you. I'm fine. I would like to get my things out of the car if you can lead me to my room."

"I have the Log Cabin room all set for you on the first floor. Ben can help you and Andy carry your things in," Sara answered. "Andy can show you where the room is. Once you get freshened up, we would love to show you the place."

"Dinner tonight is in about an hour. We are going downtown to our favorite place, since Andy didn't want to cook tonight, though I don't know why not?" Heather added with a wink toward her brother.

"Thank you all. I will only be a few minutes once I get my things. I'd love to see this place. It's beautiful, and it is almost all Andy talks about when he calls." Karen had been looking around to capture all the beauty since she arrived at the bottom of the driveway. It was beautiful from the moment she turned onto the lane.

Andy walked her to her room as he helped carry her luggage inside. He was hopeful that the amount of luggage meant that she planned to stay awhile. It was more than a weekend's worth of clothes. He realized most women packed a lot, but Karen did not impress him that way. She was not into material things like some people. She did not wear a lot of makeup nor fancy clothes. She was a country gal, raised to enjoy life and people, and to make the most out of what she had. He loved her for the way she was.

He kissed her again before giving her time to freshen up and unpack if she wanted to. He told her she could meet them in the kitchen. He had a broad smile on his face when he entered the kitchen. One that looked like it would never leave.

"Look at that smile," Sara said as she winked at him and gently punched his arm. Her baby brother had a glow of love on his face.

"Sorry, but I'm happy."

"You don't say. We would never have guessed," Heather said. "I hope she fits in with the rest of us. You know she has to pass the sister test," She said as she winked at Sara.

"What the heck is the sister test," he asked. He looked at Ben, who shrugged his shoulders in response.

"Don't ask me; I didn't have to pass that. You all just took me in."

"Believe me, you did have to pass a test or two before we would let Heather marry you," Sara said. She looked at Heather. "Of course, she would not have accepted it if we had said no."

"You got that right," Heather said. "I would have married this guy no matter what. It's the best thing I've ever done. Oh, except for being a Mom to Marc. And now this little one," she smiled as she patted her growing belly.

Karen took her time to unpack and freshen up. She had been nervous about meeting Andy's family, worried that they would not like her. Then stressed that things would go wrong between her and Andy. She was doing her best not to worry about her resort at home, even though she had left it in the competent hands of Renee and Larry. She knew they could handle it all, but it was still her baby.

About twenty minutes after she arrived, she walked into the kitchen. She expected them to all be waiting for her. Instead, Andy was the only one there. He told her the rest of them had gone to get ready for dinner, leaving him in charge of giving her a quick tour before they left. She was relieved it was just the two of them. They had not seen each other in so long; it felt great to be alone with him.

Karen could not get over how beautiful the manor was. The attention to detail in the guest rooms with their own personality was impressive. Details that she hoped their guests appreciated. She knew she did. It also gave her new ideas for her resort. Maybe she could get some tips from Sara and Heather. They finished the tour with Karen mentioning that she would love to adopt some of their ideas for her place. Andy told her that he was sure the girls would love to share what they knew with her.

Everyone met in the great room to head downtown. They had to take two vehicles, but that was perfect. Andy and Karen rode with Sara. Heather, Ben, and Marc rode in their own vehicle since it had Marc's car seat inside.

Marge, who had known the family for years, greeted them at the restaurant when they arrived.

"We have a guest?"

"Yes, this is Karen. She is from Pennsylvania, and a good friend of Andy's," Sara said as Marge walked them to the tables that had been pushed together to accommodate their large family. Marge handed out the menus and took their drink order. She left to get their drinks and give them time to chat and decide what they wanted to eat. Karen leaned into Andy and asked him what was good on the menu. He told her that everything was delicious. Not as good as he could make it, he added, but very tasteful. Karen smiled and chose the eggplant Parmesan and a house salad. Andy told her that it was a good choice.

Their drinks arrived, and Karen took a sip of her iced tea. She made a face and set her glass down on the table, pushing it away from her. "Oh, that's sweet!" Her eyebrows raised as she looked from the glass to Andy.

Andy chuckled. "Now you know what I had been trying to tell you in Pennsylvania. Sweet tea is a southern thing and loved by everyone here. It's a staple."

"If you plan to be here for very long, you need to get used to it. It grows on you." Ben took a big swig of his. He handed Marc his sippy cup and added, you must be a certain age to drink it though due to the sugar content. Marc here is too young. He prefers milk, apple juice or even water."

She took another sip and shook her head. "I'm not sure about this, but I'll try." She took another sip and hoped their meals would arrive soon so she could dilute the sweetness.

After dinner and dessert, followed by coffee, they drove back to the manor. Karen was ready to sit and relax. It had been a long trip. She had learned a lot more about the family during dinner. So many stories had them close to tears from laughing. She felt at home with them. She had also shared some details about her life.

Ben automatically made a fire in the fireplace of the great room when they returned to the manor. He had taken on that responsibility, and it was now second nature to him. Karen and Andy sat side by side on the love seat facing the fireplace. She leaned her head on his shoulder and closed her eyes. She was asleep within a few minutes. Andy pulled the hand crocheted afghan from the back of the love seat and placed it over her, being careful not to wake her.

Everyone was discussing the plans for the next day. They wanted to make a good impression on Karen. So far, they liked her. They told Andy that he had done well in finding her and falling in love with her. Andy smiled and looked down at the woman he loved. He had not told his family how he felt about Karen but realized they knew.

He was not yet willing to ask Karen if she would consider moving to Tennessee. He thought that time might come before she returned to Pennsylvania. Once she got used to the place and the people. And of course, the sweet tea.

About an hour later, everyone started to get up and head to their homes. Andy eased the afghan off Karen and nudged her to wake up. She barely opened her eyes but woke up enough that she walked to her room with Andy's help. Andy helped her lie down and put a cover over her. She was too tired, even to change clothes. She may regret it in the morning, but Andy could not bring himself to wake her enough to change. It did not matter to him.

As soon as Andy left the room and closed the door, Karen woke up. She got up, changed into her nightclothes, and went back to bed. Karen fell asleep with a smile on her face. She had looked asleep to everyone while they chatted, but she had heard almost every word. Unbeknownst to them, she had found out how they felt about her and was glad it was positive.

The truth was she liked them too. She was also in love with Andy but thought it was not time to tell him. She was still unsure of what she would do if he wanted her to move to Tennessee. Could she leave the lake? Leave what she had built up over the years? Could she just up and leave it? That was something she would have to think about later. Or would he possibly be willing to move to the lake with her? Her eyes closed, and she fell asleep with a smile on her face, thinking of what her future might hold.

The next morning Karen awoke to the wonderful aroma of fresh coffee. She also could smell breakfast cooking. She got up and took a quick shower before wandering out to the kitchen. The only one there was Andy.

"Good morning, sleepyhead," Andy said to her when he saw her. "Did you sleep well? You certainly fell asleep early last night."

"I slept well, thank you." Karen grabbed an empty coffee mug that was on the counter and held it out to Andy. He poured her a cup. He knew better than to make her wait. She held it up to her face to capture its wonderful aroma. As much as she liked coffee, it was the aroma that smelled a lot better than the actual drink. She peered over Andy's shoulder to see what he was cooking.

"Hey, you can't peek at what I'm making. It's a surprise." He reached out and kissed her, trying to distract her.

"Looks like an omelet in the making to me."

"Alright, it's not such a surprise, but it is made especially for you," Andy added cheese to the center and flipped one side over the other, then added even more cheese to the top. He took it off the burner and placed a lid on top to keep the heat in and melt all the cheese.

"Would you like toast with your omelet?" he asked as he reached for the loaf of homemade bread.

"That would be wonderful Sir." She took a seat at the island and waited for her breakfast. She was already feeling at home.

Andy turned from the stove and caught her turning her head from watching him. She looked natural sitting there. He wondered if she would ever be able to call this home. He served her breakfast when her toast was ready and poured himself a cup of coffee. Then he sat with her while she ate.

"Aren't you eating?" she asked as she took her first bite.

"No, I ate earlier. You were a sleepyhead, and I was getting hungry."

"So sorry. I guess the trip wore me out more than I realized. And sorry, I didn't mean to fall asleep on the sofa last night either. I know I must have made a 'wonderful' impression on your family."

"You have made quite an impression. Seriously, my family likes you."

"They don't know me that well. How could they like me?"

"Believe me; I've not stopped talking about you since I came home. They know a lot about you."

Karen was enjoying her breakfast. She was eating faster than she planned. Andy asked if she wanted anything else to eat, she honestly said, 'No. I am full. You know this is the best breakfast I've had since you left Pennsylvania."

Andy picked up her dishes and placed them in the dishwasher. He wanted so badly to ask her what her thoughts were about moving here and giving up on Pennsylvania and the lake. He knew it was too soon. She had not been to town, had not traveled around the area, had not even been on all their property.

"Shall we go for a tour of the grounds today? Then we can drive downtown so you can shop at the antique shops and see what our little town has to offer."

"Sounds like a good plan to me. Can we go to, what did you tell me, Cades Landing, while I am here?"

Andy chuckled. "You mean Cades Cove?"

"Yes, there. Is it a lake like our coves at home?"

"Far from it. It is a beautiful place in the mountains, but without a lake. There are deer, bear, and other wildlife along the drive. It takes a couple of hours to get there and a while to drive through it. I'd suggest we do that in a couple of days. It's best to get there early in the morning or early evening to see the most wildlife. That is if you are staying that long."

"That's fine with me. I spoke with Renee as soon as I got here yesterday. Between her, Larry, and the summer help, they are doing fine without me. I was informed to stay as long as I want. I won't stay too long as it leaves a burden on them once the summer season is in full swing, but it is nice to know they can function without me. At least I think that's a good thing to know." She tilted her head. Maybe it wasn't a good thing.

"I understand that. Here the summer is a busy time, also a time in April and again in August when the Bristol NASCAR race is in town. Plus, we are busy the first week in October when we have the National Storytelling Festival in our town and Apple Festival in another nearby town that same weekend. We also have a busy 4th of July week when we have a festival downtown complete with a parade, floats, vendors, food, and fun."

"Wow, you have a longer season than we do." We just have a few months in the summer."

"Our area has a few things going on. I will say that for a small town, we are active. The things that go on in the surrounding areas help bring guests our way."

Andy reached for her hand and walked her out the side door to begin the property tour. They walked through the garden that led to the gazebo, then down the path to the pond. Andy explained to her the new construction that was going to take place to build a chapel. He told her how James and Helen had left them money for the manor and the request for the chapel.

Karen was taking everything in. She saw how much he loved his home as he talked about the area. She knew that there was no way he would feel at home if he moved to the lake with her. She, if he wanted her, would have to move here. She sighed.

"Are you alright?" Andy asked when he felt her sigh.

"I'm fine. I had a few things on my mind, but nothing to worry about." She followed Andy past the pond to where the construction was starting for the chapel. They walked hand in hand while they viewed it from all angles to see the building's layout. She could sense something while they were there but could not put a name to it. It was just a feeling.

They finished their walk and returned to the manor. Sara was busy in the office when she heard them walk in. She was checking the reservations and activities for the week of the festival coming up.

Antique Days was a significant event in town, and she was planning a special evening at the manor for their guests during that week. Most folks spent most of their time downtown during the event, but she planned things at the manor if it rained, causing them to spend more time there. Sara motioned for them to come into the office when she saw them at her door.

"Good morning Karen. I trust you slept well, and that Andy made you one of his fantastic breakfasts?"

"Good morning, Sara. Yes, I slept well, and you are right; breakfast was fantastic. Andy is an excellent cook. He'll make someone a great wife one day." She chuckled and hoped they would appreciate the joke.

Sara chuckled. Andy just gave her an odd look. Where did this gal get her comments? Quick-witted and beautiful, what more could he want?

Andy told his sister they were heading to town to show Karen the area and the local shops. He asked her if there was anything she needed. She said she had given Ben her list. "You two go and have a good time."

He drove under the speed limit on the way downtown so she could take in the beauty. She was in awe of the countryside with all the mountains around them. She was so used to flat lands, small hills, the lake, and its islands, that to see the amazing view from wherever they were in the mountains took her breath away. It was a beautiful area. Andy parked his car behind the courthouse. Karen looked nearly straight up to see the clock tower on top of the courthouse. She had not spoken since they left the manor. This place was so different from her home area. He took her hand and walked her to the bridge that led over the small creek where two mallard ducks were swimming.

They continued their walk to the main street where old buildings, two and three stories tall stood, with businesses on the first floors and housing on the second and third floors. Andy started to explain the history of the town and the buildings. Andy described The Front Porch restaurant as having fabulous Sunday brunches and being everyone's favorite for many in the area. Unfortunately, the owners had divorced, forcing the business closed. He told her that he had thought about buying it and reopening it at one point in his life.

As they walked, she noticed a few shops were empty and for lease or sale. She asked why. Andy told her he was not sure, but he suspected the rental fees, taxes, and seasonal business played a factor. He continued talking about the historic town. He mentioned that improvements had to follow the rules to maintain the historic look. Andy told her how one family had to find old bricks to replace their chimney to stay within the town's restrictions. Karen liked the idea of reviving the old and found herself liking this little town.

They reached the small park and sat on one of the benches. She kept looking around, almost daydreaming as she compared his hometown with hers. There was no lake close by here, although there were some in the surrounding areas. There were no mountains at home. Here they jetted up in the distance everywhere you looked. She looked forward to their trip to the Smoky Mountains to see what he had talked about when he was in Pennsylvania at the lake. He said they were breathtaking. She would wait to make that determination once she got there.

Andy stood and reached for her hand to help her up after sitting for a while in silence. He knew she was deep in thought and hoped she saw what a great place this area was. He wanted her to love the area first before he asked her to move.

She took his hand and kept holding it as they walked back to the other end of town to his car.

“This town is so quaint and cute. I'd love to spend more time here and learn more. Do you think we can come back in a few days?” Karen asked, still taking in her surroundings.

“Anytime you want except tomorrow. Tomorrow we are going to one of the most beautiful places in the world. Since summer is not officially here, it won't be as crowded as it is in the middle of summer, giving us an advantage. I suggest you take a sweater or light jacket. The mountains tend to be a bit cooler due to the higher elevation. It is even cooler if there is any breeze."

“I will. I'm looking forward to it. I've seen pictures, but I'm sure it's much better in person. What time are we leaving?”

“Early. How's seven AM sound?”

“Early,” she said with a smile. She squeezed his hand. “I'll be ready. Are you cooking breakfast first, or are we going out to eat on the way?”

"I'll be making breakfast. There aren't any places to stop to eat until we get there. There is this wonderful pancake place in Gatlinburg. If you want to leave just a bit earlier, we can eat there before heading to Cades Cove. We will need to leave by 6 to get there when they open. Any later, and there is a line to get in."

"Let's leave early and eat there if you say it's that good. Oh, should I bring my camera?"

"Most definitely. You never know when you may see a bear, deer, turkeys or just the beauty of the mountains. None of which you want to miss!"

"A bear? Are you kidding me?" she shot Andy a look of disbelief. She did not want a close encounter with a bear.

"No, I told you that you could see bears and deer and other wildlife in the park. You have nothing to worry about, we will be in the car the whole time, unless you want to stop to look and take pictures. Lots of people stop along the way to photograph the bears. They are usually up in the trees beyond the fencing or at least some distance away. We will stay safe, trust me."

"Okay, if you say so. I do trust you. We have bears around the lake from time to time, you know. I look forward to seeing them here."

They had been driving while they were planning their trip. Before Karen knew it, they were back at the lane leading to the manor.

"Who planted all these trees and rose bushes along here?" Karen was looking from side to side as Andy inched along. She admired their beauty. They were almost in full bloom. A few more weeks would be simply perfect for a photo opportunity. She appreciated his slow driving so she could see all the beauty.

"My grandparents planted them when they first moved here. Over time they planted other plants and flowers. When they first settled here, they started with one small house. That is the house where Sara lives now. Soon after, they built the other two. The one where Heather lives and then where I live, both used to be rentals. Several years later they added the manor. My mother inherited it when her parents passed. And now Sara owns it as she is the eldest in the family. Tradition. That's one of the drawbacks of being the baby of the family."

"Oh, being the baby of the family isn't that bad. At least you had siblings."

"True. I can't imagine being an only child. How did you do it?"

"It is the only way I know. It was easy for me. I had lots of friends at school, a few that lived close, and remember I had lots of friends in the summers. Each summer brought new people and some of the old. I made new friends each year."

"Very true. I didn't have many friends here but did have several while I was at the lake. It's a wonder that you and I didn't meet back then."

"I was thinking the same thing. The years you were there we were little. By the time we were older and more likely to pay attention to remember things, you never came back. Memories of the kids I met when I was small are long gone. Most of my memories of the lake are from my teen years and older."

"This is true. I also hung with the guys back then. Girls never held my interest until I hit those teen years," Andy laughed.

"I'm sure. And then none of the females were safe," Karen smiled at him.

When they reached the manor, Andy parked the car, and they went inside. No one was home. It was odd that it was so quiet, but not concerning. There were no guests due until the end of the weekend. True to Sara's work ethic, everything was ready and waiting.

Karen went to her room while Andy went to the kitchen. They did not notice everyone down near the pond watching the contractors as they made progress on the chapel. The first of the walls were going up.

Karen joined Andy in the kitchen about a half-hour after they had gotten home. Before she had time to say hello, the side door opened, and Marc ran in before everyone else. He looked at his Uncle Andy but went immediately to Karen and reached up for her to hold him. She saw the mud on his shoes as she lifted him and instantly sat him on the edge of the kitchen island. She took his shoes off so he wouldn't drag the mud any further than the kitchen. Andy watched how natural she was with Marc and smiled. Another reason to love her.

Sara walked in behind Marc and told them they had been at the chapel talking with the construction workers and watching the first wall go up. She added that it should be complete in about two months, which would be great for the end of the season and fall guests.

Heather asked Karen how she liked their little town? She said she loved it and wanted to spend more time exploring. Andy chimed in and said that would have to be delayed as they would leave before dawn the next day and head to Gatlinburg and Cades Cove. He said he would show off the mountains and the wildlife at the cove, followed by the shops in the area. It would be a long day, but he hoped she would enjoy it.

"Breakfast at the Pancake Pantry?" Sara asked as she poured herself a glass of water.

"Of course. I offered to make Karen breakfast, but then mentioned those great pancakes, and she changed our minds. Pancakes won."

"Karen, you are going to love it. Take your camera and a sweater."

"Andy has already told me."

Chapter Twenty-Five

Getting up and on the road at dawn was difficult, but they made it. Andy had made them each a travel cup of coffee to take along, for which Karen was grateful. She could wait to eat, but coffee was a must first thing in the morning. Especially that early.

Andy took an extra step to rewash the windows and windshield even though he had washed the car a few days before. He wanted Karen to be able to take pictures while they drove without opening the windows. Especially if a bear got close, he knew she would not want to open the window, let alone get out of the car.

Karen grew up living in the country, seeing the countryside, with woods and space between homes. In that way, this area was the same as at home. In another way, it was so different and so much more beautiful. Andy crested the hill along I-26, revealing the view of fog lifting over the mountains in the distance. As he continued the drive into the mountains, Karen became mesmerized. The sight of them and the valleys were breathtaking. The fog continued to lift as the day dawned. The mountains and farms took her breath away. She had never seen such beauty. She did her best to capture it with her camera, although she knew the photos would not do it justice. She was in love with the area. How could anyone not like this part of the country?

Andy had taken the back way so she could enjoy the ride. He would take the interstate on the way home. Going down a hill and around a curve, Andy announced that Gatlinburg was less than a mile ahead. He had not filled her in much on what to expect. Most of what she knew about it was what she had briefly researched on the internet. Since the mountains were so much better in person, she knew that the town would be too. She put her camera down but continued to watch as he drove. She watched as the three-lane road turned into two lanes. At the first traffic light, she was face to face with Hard Rock Cafe. They turned left, and she saw stores, sidewalks, the Aquarium, and a hotel. There was a lot to take in. Her head was on a swivel.

Andy parked his car near a sign that said, *Parking only 'til 9 AM.*

"Why only 9 AM?"

"Oh wait, you'll see by the time we get finished with our tour and start to head back. This town gets crowded even this early in the season. In the middle of summer, it is crazy. So crazy that we try not to come again until fall."

The Pancake Pantry proved a success. They enjoyed some of the best pancakes Karen had ever eaten. She understood why Andy's family recommended it. To work off some of what they ate and because Karen was curious about the town, they walked a few blocks looking in a few shop windows. Most had not opened for the day yet, but Karen was impressed. She hoped they would have time to shop a bit after Cades Cove and before heading home.

The scenery along the way to their destination was beautiful. Karen was busy taking pictures while Andy talked and drove. He was doing his best to sell her on the area, but after one look at her face as she snapped photos and looked around, he knew she loved it.

At the entrance of the cove, Andy told her to keep a watchful eye. This time of year was when the bears were out of hibernation and when cubs were small. Mama bear would be on alert protecting her babies. If there were cubs around, their mama would be nearby.

A half-mile into the thirteen-mile loop, cars were slowing down, and some had pulled over and parked. Andy knew what it meant. He joined them and parked his car.

"There must be a bear close," he said as they looked around. They stayed in the car until they spotted the bears. A mama bear and two cups were up in a tree about 100 yards beyond the fencing. Karen had her camera ready with the telephoto lens. She opened her car door and got out. She walked up to get closer to the fence. Andy was right by her side. He smiled as he watched her. So much for her being afraid of a bear.

She took several pictures as the bears climbed down the tree. She loved to watch them, but as the bears moved away from the tree and walked toward the fence, she said it was enough. She told Andy it was time to move along. She wanted to be safe.

Andy continued along the single-lane dirt road loop where he saw several herds of deer, a fox, and another bear. The mountain views were captivating. Karen had to admit, the lake had nothing on this.

As they finished the trip through the cove, Andy looked over at Karen. Her smile alone made him happy. She glanced at her watch, not realizing how late it had become.

Andy drove them back into Gatlinburg and parked in a public parking lot at the edge of town so they could walk the full length of the town. It was late afternoon by then, and an early dinner was in order. Andy stopped at the steakhouse at the end of town. They had decided to eat and then walk it off.

He knew Karen would enjoy the history of how the owner had built the place with large logs purchased from out West. Karen was not only impressed with the place, the service, but the steak she ordered was the best she had eaten in a long time. They were both too full to indulge in any of the dessert choices and agreed a walk was definitely in order.

"This place is amazing," Karen said as they left the restaurant.

"This whole day has been amazing." Andy took her hand as they walked. They took their time and went inside several of the shops. He was surprised when she did not buy anything. He never heard of females who did not buy a lot when they went shopping.

"I'm saving my money to buy something in your hometown," was her reasoning when he asked why she had not bought anything. He just shrugged his shoulders. He paid attention to what seemed to most impress her. His thought was to come back on his own and buy her what she would not buy herself.

The day was ending, and it would be getting dark soon. As they went to the end of town, Andy spotted an ice cream shop where he remembered having excellent ice cream. He still had Karen's hand in his, and without bothering to ask if she wanted any, he pulled her into the shop with him. She laughed when he told her that he wouldn't take a chance to say she did not want any ice cream.

That's one thing you'll rarely hear me say. There is always room for ice cream. Oh, and chocolate chip cookies – homemade, of course."

They ordered a mixture of flavors in waffle cones and sat down outside to enjoy them while watching the crowds of people pass by. Karen always liked to make up her own stories about the people she watched. She shared a few of her thoughts as they ate their ice cream, then they slowly continued their walk.

On their way back to their car, parked at the other end of town, Karen realized why the parking sign she had questioned earlier was there. The little town was full of people. Everywhere! So much to do, so much to see, so little time. Karen made a mental note that she would have to come back. She wanted to experience what else this town had to offer. Nothing close to her home provided this. In a way, she was glad. Her home was a quieter, peaceful place, except for the crowds of people in the lake region in the middle of summer. And yet, she was drawn to this new adventure. She wanted to learn more. When she thought about it a bit, she realized that the manor was peaceful, quiet with a nearby quaint town.

Different from home, but she was already fond of it. She was also very fond of the people. Especially Andy.

"So what do you think? Pretty neat town, huh?"

"This place is like no other place I've ever visited. Look at all the people. Is it always like this?"

"No, sometimes it's busier, then you have to elbow your way through. It slows down in the winter. There are some events we like to attend here in town or the next town. We are local enough that we have the opportunity to stay away from the crowds when it gets too crowded."

When they reached the car, she stopped and looked around. Almost like it was going to be her last time being there. She realized this and shook her head to clear those thoughts out. She wanted to stay. She wanted to stay with Andy. Now, if only he would ask me, she thought.

It was slow-moving through town. Traffic was bumper to bumper. They didn't talk much, allowing Andy to pay attention to the road and other vehicles. He told Karen that the next town was Pigeon Forge, followed by Sevierville, adding that he planned to drive through due to the time, but if she saw anywhere she wanted to stop, he would. Her head looked from side to side, observing the shops, hotels, and entertainment attractions, and all the people in Pigeon Forge, as Andy drove. While the shops were not as close to each other, nor the road a two-lane road like in Gatlinburg, it was still a busy area.

"So much to see. How can I take it all in?" she commented, realizing there was no way to see every building.

"That's part of the charm, or problem, with this area, depending on how you look at it. There were so many places to see as well as the traffic to endure. It makes it hard to drive and look. And this traffic is nothing compared to how it gets in the middle of the summer. The best thing to do is know ahead of time where you want to shop and book your hotel well in advance. I recommend spending at least a couple of days here until you get used to the area. Although as soon as you think you know everything that is here, you return to visit in six months and find something new," he pointed to a new construction off to the left.

They had come to the end of Pigeon Forge, giving Andy a break in the chaotic traffic. "Next is Sevierville. A lot less populated and a lot fewer stores, but a few interesting places."

"Is there someplace you want to stop? You've asked me, but I'm not familiar with the area. Where do you like to shop?"

"Well, one of the places is up the road a ways. It's a Knife shop. I've not been there for several years. I hope it's still there."

"I'm not into knives, but if you want to stop, you may. I could use a restroom."

"Oh, it is a lot more than knives. I pay more attention to their section of kitchen wares. From kitchen knives to pots and pans, dishes, food, and tons of gadgets."

"That is right up your alley and sounds interesting. The stop will give us a chance to stretch our legs and relax as well. And remember – I need a restroom."

"Well, that does it, we're stopping. Can't leave a lady needing a restroom," Andy laughed as he looked at Karen. It was a wonderful day so far. He knew it was a lot for her to absorb, but he wanted to share it with her to help her like Tennessee.

Karen was overwhelmed when they walked into the knife shop. She had never seen such a place. She learned that it was the only one like it and that people drove hundreds of miles to shop there.

They walked around to see everything, then landed in the kitchen supplies area. What a vast array of items! She watched Andy's eyes get big as he went from one section to another. He was in his element, and she felt a touch of pride. She was proud to be with him. He made her happy.

She was having a great time getting to know him and his family. She wondered what would be next before she had to head back to Pennsylvania and her everyday life. Being in Tennessee was feeling like a dream, a wonderful, happy dream.

It was dark by the time Andy turned onto the lane that led to the manor. He glanced over at Karen, who had fallen asleep. He smiled as he drove the last few hundred feet home. Life was good, made even better with Karen by his side.

Chapter Twenty-Six

Life at Bella Rose had already reached a routine. Guests were arriving at regular intervals, weekends were always full, and entire weeks were filling up. Sara was pleased that everything was working well with the manor and her siblings. Everyone had chipped in where needed and were finding where their specialties were. Ben had excelled at his work doing the maintenance, grounds upkeep, and expansion. Heather's interior decorating looked like the work of a professional. She was also doing her best to stay healthy and strong as her pregnancy progressed. Heather was taking no chances of losing this baby after losing her last one during the car accident. All her doctor appointments had been positive. She was waiting now to find out if they were going to have a boy or a girl. They had the opportunity to know sooner but had said they did not want to know. Since then, they changed their minds. She had ideas for decorating the nursery for either sex so was anxious to know which she was having.

Andy had settled into his routine as Chef at Bella Rose Manor. His menu continued to expand as he learned what their guests liked the best. He was finishing the cookbook they would offer for sale to their guests and the general public. The book was a great marketing tool for them.

Ben mentioned the accident at breakfast one morning and how he felt so blessed to have another chance at being a father again. Heather reached for his hand and nodded. Sara agreed and then changed the subject and asked Andy about Karen. Karen had returned to Pennsylvania two weeks earlier, and Sara had not heard any updates about their relationship. Andy said between phone calls and chats on the internet, he and Karen talked often. He told them that he would love for her to move to Tennessee.

"Have you asked her?" Sara asked. She sometimes felt like his mother rather than his oldest sister. He had been a rebel most of his young life, running away for years on end, trouble in school. But this was the first time that she was the 'mother' figure in the family. Before now, their parents were the ones who did all the worrying and wondering.

"No, not yet. I keep waiting for the right time and have come to realize there may not be a *right* time." He hesitated before his next statement. "I would like to take a quick trip to Pennsylvania to see her."

"Of course you can. I only ask that you leave all your recipes here and all the instructions while you are gone. Better yet, make them ahead of time and freeze them. You know we can't cook. When did you want to go?" Sara was excited for Andy.

"Soon. I will have to look at my calendar and see when would be best for Karen as well. She has been very busy with the resort. Her cabins have been full of guests already, like we are here. I plan to stay for only a few days. Long enough to see her, take her someplace special and ask her that all-important question." He stopped talking.

"*THE* question?" Heather gulped her coffee and almost spat it out. "It's about time!"

"I'm not sure if it will be *THE* question, but I plan to ask her to consider moving here. To move in with me."

"Does that mean you are staying?" They had not discussed the will in a while. With all that had been happening at the manor, it was no longer the main conversation topic.

"Yes, I'm staying. I'm not sure what I'll do if Karen doesn't want to move here, but we will work that out. I can't imagine life without her. I'm praying she will join me here."

"Well, look at your schedule and let me know. If need be, I can get some help here while you are gone. I'm sure Cecelia can give us a hand."

Andy cleaned up the kitchen after breakfast; then went to the office to check the calendar for upcoming events. That would determine when he would have free time to take a few days off. That is when he noticed the newspaper article hanging on the bulletin board; the article about the car accident that had injured his sister and taken his niece or nephew. It had been too early in her pregnancy to know the baby's sex. They only knew that she had been pregnant. He felt terrible that she had lost the baby. He was excited now, knowing he would be an uncle again. He hoped all was going well for her and Ben.

Andy noticed the date of the accident as he reread the article. He pulled the thumbtack out and held the article in his hands as he mindlessly sat into the desk chair. He stared at the date. He had seen it several times before, and the family had talked about it from time to time. This time he felt his heart starting to beat faster. He blinked his eyes, trying to hold back the tears; his hands shook. He remembered what that date was. He had realized it before but was in denial and blocked it from his mind. There was no denying it now. He was about to ask Karen to uproot her life and move here with him. Did he have the right to do that? He could not hold in what was now going through his mind.

Sara had been cleaning the great room when she took a break and headed to the office. It was not only her workplace for the bed and breakfast business; it was her get away without going to her home. She loved being in that little room. She felt close to her parents when she was there. It had been their office as well. It was full of memories.

When she opened the door to her office, she was surprised to see Andy sitting there. She noticed that he had been crying and was now staring into space.

"Andy? Are you alright? What's wrong?" Sara went to him and put her hand on his arm.

"Sara." Was all he could say. He lifted the newspaper article towards her. She did not understand. She took the paper from him and set it down on the desk. She had read it so often she had it memorized.

"What is it?"

"Sara, we need to talk." His look was nothing she had ever seen in him before.

"Okay." She went around to the front of the desk, reached to close and lock the door. She did not know why she locked it, but she did. She pulled the guest's chair around by his side, facing him. She knew this was serious. I'm here for you. Talk to me."

"Sara," he hesitated. "I caused that," He pointed to the paper.

"What do you mean you caused it? You were nowhere around there."

"Yes, yes, I was. Remember? We were supposed to meet that day. When I called you to meet me at the restaurant and then never showed. I never called back. I just disappeared for several more months. Remember?"

"Yes, I remember. I thought you stood me up because you were strung out or drunk, scared, or even ashamed. I'm not sure what I was thinking at the time, except that you stood me up. You stood the family up again." She was doing her best not to get angry at him for what was well in the past.

"Yes, but there was more. I stood you up originally because I was drunk. I had been sober for a while and was ready to come home. I didn't know if you all would take me back into the family fold and was so excited that you agreed to meet. I had a free night and went out, to sit and relax. For some reason, I chose to go to a bar. I did not want to drink. I then told myself that one little drink would be fine. That led to more drinks, and before I knew it, I was drunk. And yes, I was ashamed. I was ashamed because I had fallen off the wagon. I knew what that would do to me. I had to leave again to get sober. I couldn't do that to my family again. I couldn't come home as a drunk. I thought it was better to disappear than to bring my drunk-self home."

"We would have taken you back no matter what. But what does your running away again have to do with their accident?"

Sara was intent on listening to her baby brother and letting him know how loved he was and always had been. Yes, he had put the family through a lot over the years, but they always wished he would come home. No matter what.

"Sara. After I decided to run away instead of meeting with you, I drove away on that road. I was drunk. It was not until the next day that I noticed the damage to my car. I could not remember how the car had gotten damaged. I assumed someone had hit me while it sat in the parking lot at the hotel that night. It never dawned on me that I may have hit someone since I didn't remember any accident. Eventually, I did remember hitting something and that I simply kept going, although I did not remember where it happened."

Andy stood up and looked out the window a moment before continuing. Sara stayed silent as she waited. Her brother needed her to just listen, not to judge or make light of what he was confessing. Andy leaned his back against the wall and continued to talk to his sister.

"Several months ago, when Joe and Nicole were here at the soft opening, Joe talked of how they met you all. He mentioned the date when he talked about the accident. It took me a little time, but the date registered a memory. Then it hit me. I was there. The timing was right that it was me. We were so busy that I shoved it out of my mind. Until now." Andy sighed and looked at the paper on the desk and then to his sister. "Sara, I hit a car that night on that road. I caused their accident. I caused Heather to lose her baby." He was in tears again.

"You can't be sure. There were no witnesses that saw it happen except Nicole and Joe right afterward. And they both say there was no other car when they came upon the scene."

"That's because it was a hit and run Sara. Don't you see? I was drunk. I have no memory of it. I was out of it. When I hit them I thought I ran over an animal or bumped something in the road. I remember it started to rain when I got further down the road and that it had rained some earlier."

"Yes, you are right about all the rain. They are blaming the accident on the road conditions because of the rain. And then it started to rain harder after everyone had gone to the hospital, hindering their investigation. The investigators found no evidence of anyone hitting them. And the insurance company totaled the SUV. Ben's car had dents on it from other smaller incidents over the years. It was an older car with several previous dents and scratches, so those they did find they assumed had been there. The main damage they attributed to rolling over the embankment."

"I know all that. But I'm telling you, I hit them. I'm the reason they lost their baby. It was my fault! What am I going to do? What am I going to tell them? Do I tell them? Do I tell the police?"

Sara was silent. She walked over to Andy and put her arm around her little brother. She honestly did not know what he, and now she, was going to do.

They heard a knock on the office door. Looking at each other, silently debating to open the door or not, Andy shrugged his shoulders. They knew it was either Ben or Heather. Sara went to answer the door. As she did, Andy sat at the desk and looked busy so he would not have to look at whoever was there. He was not ready to face anyone, especially his sister or brother-in-law. He was unsure when he would be. Never, was his guess.

"I wanted to let you know we are going to the doctor," Heather said when Sara opened the door."

"Okay, good luck! Let us know when you find out. I can't wait to start buying new baby stuff!"

"You will be the first person I call. See you later."

Sara closed the door and turned to Andy. "We are not telling them anything!" she said in a whispered, yet stern voice of authority. "Everything is going great for them. She's going to have a baby, and I will not do anything to jeopardize that. Furthermore, neither are you."

Andy stood back up. He took a deep breath as he watched his oldest sister. He did not say a word for several minutes. His sister said what he was thinking. There was no need for him to say anything.

"Families always have secrets somewhere along the line. This secret will be ours. If you ever tell anyone else, I insist you tell me first." She picked up the newspaper article, removed the photo of the wreck from the bulletin board, and placed them in a file folder in the back of the desk's file drawer. "Do you understand?"

"Yes, I understand. We will tell no one." Andy breathed a sigh of relief but realized this was something that would plague him for the rest of his life.

"I love you Andy. I will do anything for you—even this. Now I think it would be best to go to Pennsylvania as soon as you can, so you do not see Ben and Heather for a few days. Can you do that?"

"I'm sure I can. Let me call Karen and let her know that I'm coming to visit. I'll at least wait until we find out if it's a boy or a girl. She may not understand my leaving if I am gone before they return from the doctor."

"You're right. But tomorrow, you are out of here."

"Yes Ma'am." He walked towards the door to leave. Sara stood with him and hugged him. He returned the hug. "Thanks Sis." They held onto each other for a few moments. Both had tears in their eyes.

"Don't thank me. I'm still not sure how to handle it once it does come out. If we tell the cops, you will end up in jail." She held him by his shoulders. "Either way, I'm here for you. Now, go call Karen."

Heather and Ben waited patiently in the doctor's office. Several other couples and moms with their babies sat in the waiting room with them. Heather was busy watching the other babies and rubbing her belly. She was not showing a lot yet as she had several months to go, but she knew there was a little tiny life in there. Today they would find out the sex. She knew many people who still did not want to know ahead of time, but she did. And she knew Ben did as well. She hoped that all the other tests and exams would tell them that it was healthy and going as expected.

By the time they were in the exam room, they were both a little nervous. When the doctor asked how she was, Heather said she was anxious to know if it was a boy or girl, but otherwise, she felt great.

Set up with the ultrasound, listening for the heartbeat, the doctor was pointing out the head, hands, feet, and...

"Okay Doc, what is it? Can you tell?" Heather shocked herself with her tone of voice. "Sorry, I'm a little excited."

"Well, let's get a better view. Yep, there it is. You are going to have another--"

"BOY!" Ben said with a big smile on his face while Heather said it along with him, but as a question.

They left the office. Ben's excitement diminished when he realized that his wife had wanted a girl. They had never discussed what they wanted beyond that it be healthy. He never dreamed she would be disappointed. "Maybe next time," he said, trying to cheer her up.

"Not sure I want a next time. Let's see how this one goes. And dealing with three boys may wear me out enough that I do not want another one."

"Wait. What? Three?"

"Yes, three. Marc, this new one," she pointed to her belly, "and you," she managed to smile and almost laughed.

"Very funny."

"Doc did say everything was going well. You are not to overdo anything. So, young lady, no rock climbing, no house building, no running marathons. He did say that exercise was good, especially walking. I would say a few walks up and down the lane at the manor would take care of the walking."

"Are you going to join me in those walks?"

"If you want me to. You know I'd do anything for you."

"I know, now."

"Don't go there. I wasn't myself after the accident. I learned my lesson. You are my life. You, Marc, and this little guy. Which brings up the next question, what are we going to name him? It would be nice to be calling him by his name instead of *the baby* or *him.*

Heather was ready for this. She had been thinking of this for a while but had not shared it with anyone. She hadn't wanted to go through everyone adding their ideas of what to name it if it is a girl or what other names if it was a boy. Too much drama for her. “Maddex”

“Maddex? That's a new one.”

“I know, but it means good and generous. I like it. Plus, we already have Marc, so we could keep with the 'M' theme. We do need to come up with a middle name for him. What do you think goes with Maddex?”

“Maddex Allen, Maddex Glen after your father?” I don't know. Remember, you have this thing of checking what a person's initials spell. Nothing that will cause teasing or jokes as he grows. Something positive or non-threatening.”

"True. So MUK would not work, MAK would work, MGK would work, although it reminds me of MGM. One thing about having a boy instead of a girl, we don't have to fret about what her last name might be when she gets married. Girls always need to think about what their initials will be when they get married.”

“See, it's a good thing to have a boy.”

He can go by his middle name if he wishes when he gets older; after his grandfather that he never got to meet.” Remembering her father made her sad. Marc had gotten to meet his grandfather, but he was so young he would not remember him either. She would have to make it a point to tell both her children about their grandparents on both sides. Ben's parents were also deceased.

As they reached the bottom of the lane to the manor and their home, Ben stopped the car. Heather asked why he was stopping. He said because there was no time like the present to start her walking. He was laughing as she hauled off and hit his shoulder. “Very funny. Now, drive.” He drove.

Sara was waiting for them when they walked into the manor.

“So, are we having a boy or a girl?”

“*We* aren't having anything. *I* am having a ….” She looked at Ben; together, they said, “BOY!”

Sara reached and gave her little sister a big hug. “Congratulations! I'm so happy! Is everything looking good?”

"Yes, I'm healthy, and so is Maddex."

"Maddex? Who is Maddex?"

Heather took Sara's hand and placed it on her belly. "Sara, meet your nephew, Maddex Glen."

Sara felt a tear forming in her eye. "You're naming him after Daddy?"

"Yep. The name Maddex fits both our parents since one meaning is good and generous, and they certainly were that to everyone."

"Perfect."

"Andy is at his place but will be here in a few minutes. You can introduce him to his nephew as well. I will warn you, he called Karen while you were gone. It seems he is taking a few days off to go see her and pop a question."

He's decided to pop *the* question after all?"

"No, not *the* question, but a big one, nonetheless. He is going to ask her to move here."

"Wow, that's a big step. Karen owns that resort. She'd be giving up a lot," Ben chimed in.

"Yes, she does. I agree it's a lot for her to consider. People do all kinds of things for love. We will see. I know if she says no we have a chance of losing our little brother to her, as he may move there. Trouble is then he would also lose out on his inheritance. He and I have discussed that. He didn't have an answer except to say he would wait and see what Karen said."

"I hope she moves here. I like her. She was not here long, but she fit right in with us like she belonged."

"I agree. I felt that Karen was one of us when she was here. She has a lot to learn about being southern, but she'll catch on."

"True, us southern girls are a bit different. Our way of life and living is different as well."

Andy came through the kitchen door and greeted everyone. They introduced him to his nephew, Maddex Glen. After he questioned the name, he agreed the meaning fit the family. Heather sensed Andy's mind was on other things, so she did not continue their conversation about the baby.

"I guess Sara told you I'm going to Pennsylvania for a few days?"

"Yes, she did. "I agree with her, it's a great idea. I hope Karen agrees to move here. It'll be a big change for her, but we can help her feel at home," Heather said

"We will welcome her as family," Ben added.

"I'm not ready to ask her to marry me, but by the time I get there, by the end of tomorrow, I may have made that decision as well."

"Oh, this is news to me," Sara said.

"Well, I've been thinking. Why would any woman just pack up, sell all she has worked her whole life to build, and move to another state if there's no promise of a future for her? I'm not sure I'd do it. But, if it's more than just moving her to be with me, us, that may work better. Besides the fact that I am so in love with her."

"What if she doesn't want to move?"

"I'll cross that bridge when I get there, if I have to."

Andy excused himself saying he had to go pack and was going to go to bed early as he planned to leave before dawn.

No one questioned him. Sara knew the main reason was so he could avoid making eye contact with Heather and Ben for the time being.

Chapter Twenty-Seven

Karen had been busy ever since Andy had called to say he was coming to visit for a few days. She was excited and a bit nervous. She anticipated that he had more on his mind than a simple visit to say hello. It was not what he said, it was more what he did not say. She sensed something was up. Her levelheadedness was telling her not to overthink things. She knew how her heart felt and had already gone to Larry for his opinion. He had always been there for her, especially since her parents had died. He was a friend of her family when she was a child. He had owned his marina forever. Their families had always worked well together. He recommended their resort to his customers to stay; they recommended his marina for boat rentals in return. Now she wanted to talk to him about expanding his business by buying hers.

Larry and his wife, Grace, accepted Karen's invitation to dinner when she called. Grace commented to Larry that she felt something important was going on. He agreed, but neither one could pinpoint what it might be. As far as they knew, everything was going well for her now that the cabins were repaired.

Karen had prepared her favorite dish for her guests. Lasagna. Straight from the store's freezer to her oven. She would be the first to admit she was not the best cook. But she could dress up a meal and was a good baker. But cook the main meal? Not so much. She was accustomed to cooking herself; she was not all that picky about what she ate. She knew she could be better if she practiced or had more than herself to impress. Andy could provide that. She smiled at no one other than her thoughts of the man she loved.

Yes, Andy could teach her to cook. They could be a good team at the manor. If only that were why he was coming for a visit. She could not imagine it being anything else. Her thoughts transitioned to realize that might not be why he was making the trip. She was sad when she thought he might want to break up and was being polite to do it in person. She immediately shook that thought out of her head.

Her guests arrived as she was pulling the garlic bread out of the oven. Grace helped her finish putting the food on the table while Larry poured wine from the bottle they had brought, into Karen's etched wine glasses. Their conversation ranged from the first guests to the resort at the lake, the upcoming events around the lake area, and how busy it would be in a few weeks. They also talked about the construction of new buildings near town and new businesses coming in. The area was growing. They were all afraid that they would not recognize their quiet little getaway in a few years where guests came to relax and enjoy time away from the cities. Too many people from New York and New Jersey were moving in and making changes. The old country feeling was still there but getting more crowded. They all agreed it was a sign of the times. One they did not want to accept.

As soon as dinner was over and the dishes were in the dishwasher, Karen invited them into the living room for coffee. She told them she had something to discuss with them. Something serious.

Larry and Grace sat on the love seat that looked out over the parking lot facing the lake. The growth of trees over the last thirty years hindered the view, but knowing the lake was beyond them was a nice feeling—another sign of the times. Even the trees were taking over what used to be picturesque.

"Okay. This isn't easy to say," Karen started. "I've got something serious to tell you, ask you, talk over with you, however you want to define it. I've put it off, but now the time has come. I hope." She added the last words because, in reality she did not know what her future held. "As you know, Andy has been a big part of my life for a while now. I was attracted to him as soon as I saw him standing at the hotel desk asking to rent a room. Getting to know him has only increased my feelings for him." She hesitated a moment when she noticed Larry and Grace look at each other and nod their heads.

"Andy will be here the day after tomorrow for a visit. He's only going to be here a few days, but I think I know why he is coming. Even before I went to Tennessee, I wanted to spend time with him and get to know his family. You know how I feel about them. They are wonderful. I felt so at home the moment I got there. We never talked about it when we were together, but the little phrases he has been saying have me thinking. He always tells me he wishes I were there, that he misses me and wouldn't it be great to be together—little comments like that. I feel the same way about being with him. I do wish we were together. I have thought about the chance of him moving here; however, there is a long story as to why he can't leave there for at least five years. So I am thinking he is coming here to ask me to move there with him."

Grace gasped. Larry smiled. He had a feeling Andy would want her to move to Tennessee. He was all for it. He had a special attachment to Andy. To see the two of them happy and together would be perfect. Neither one had time to say anything before Karen continued.

"I have given it a lot of thought. If he does ask me, I'm willing to move. Which is why I've asked both of you here." She sat up straighter as she spoke what was on her heart. "I am going to put this place on the market; if he asks me to move. I want the two of you to have the first choice at buying it directly from me before I list it for sale with a Realtor. I would much rather you have it than some stranger. I know you would take care of it, even improve it, yet leave its charm in tack. What do you think?" She took a sip of her coffee and waited for their reaction.

"I think." Grace stopped and looked at Larry for the words. She was in shock that Karen would want to sell. Move yes, but sell? She could still own it and hire people to run it.

Grace continued, "I think this is something we all need to discuss. Why not keep the ownership of it and hire someone or a company to run it for you? That way, if things don't work out with you and Andy, you have someplace to return." Larry sat in silence, listening to his wife speak.

"That thought has crossed my mind. I know I could still own it, hire others to run it, make trips here from time to time to make sure it was all going well. Truth is, I'm ready for a break, ready for a change in my life. This life is all I've known since, well, I was born here. I took some time away to attend college and do some traveling, but I've not known any other life than this. I'm still young. I am ready for more. Don't get me wrong; I love this place, the people, the area, the work. But I think I'm ready for a new adventure. And I think, I hope, it is with Andy." Karen looked from Grace to Larry and hoped they understood.

"But is moving to Tennessee the right place to go? The right time? Is Andy the right person?" Grace was doing her best to help Karen see with an open mind and not the blind eye of a young lady in love. She knew that look. She had it once. Still had it, most of the time. Larry was the love of her life.

Larry stood up, interrupting the ladies' conversation. He took a few steps then turned to face them. Using his hands to help make a point, he spoke. "I see it this way. How about if we all sleep on it? Grace and I will discuss your proposal. You can think about all your options. We may come up with a different option for you. We are grateful that you think enough of us to offer us first dibs to buy it. It would be a great addition to what we already own, but it would also be a lot more work for us and a lot more expense. As I said, let's all sleep on it. It's a lot to think about and consider."

"Okay, we will all sleep on it. Let's meet back tomorrow evening or late afternoon?" Karen hoped to have some answers before Andy arrived. She wanted to share that she had been thinking about moving and was serious about it. That was, of course, if he was coming to ask her to move. She still heard a tiny voice interjecting her hopes with the possibility that he was coming to break up with her.

Larry had his mind made up before they left. He wanted to buy it. It would be great to have the expansion to his business. He could reconfigure the landscape between the two properties and make one large area for all the guests. Owning it would also allow him to return it to Karen if things did not work out for her and Andy. Of course, he would first give Andy a good talking to if he broke Karen's heart, then he'd give her property back. He had talked all this over with Grace on their way home. She agreed. It was an easy decision.

Karen went to bed early that night, but sleep was far from her mind. She spent half the night thinking of how life would be with Andy, and the other half worried about giving up what had been her life. When dawn finally arrived, she could only hope the day would provide some answers.

Before noon her phone rang. Larry called to inquire about her asking price before they went to the bank to ask about a loan. He gave her no promises but assured her that they were very interested in buying it from her if that was what she wanted.

Her smile and positive energy kept her going for the rest of the day. Now all she needed was Andy to be there. One more moonlit night before he would be.

Andy was nervous as he prepared to visit Karen and ask her to move. He was asking a lady he had met by chance to give up the only life she had ever known, to move to a state she had only been to once in her life, with a family she had only recently met. He knew he was asking a lot. His personal history was not the best, but she knew about that. He had been open and honest with her when they first got to know each other. Opening up to her had not been easy for him to do. He had wondered why he had been so honest with her. This may be why. Maybe she was the one for him. His heart was telling him he should ask her to marry him.

Would she be more willing to move if it were for marriage, or would she be willing to move with no promise of commitment? He had one sister who was happily married, another divorced after an awful experience that left her alone. He knew she was comfortable being alone. At least he assumed she was. What would Karen prefer? He decided he needed to go to a local jeweler. Then he pushed that out of his mind since he did not know her ring size, and he did not want to make a fool of himself. Then a thought hit him. Larry. He would call Larry.

Grace answered the phone when it rang right after Larry walked away from his phone conversation with Karen. Andy asked to speak with Larry without giving away the reason for his call.

“Hi Andy. What's up? It's been a while.” Larry spoke with innocence.

“I wanted to let you know that I was coming to visit Karen and hoped I'd get a chance to spend some time with you as well. I know the season is starting to pick up, and you may be busy, so I'd understand if you don't have time.”

“Are you kidding? I will always have time to spend with you. You are welcome here at any time. Even if we are busy, I'll just put you to work if I have to.”

"Thanks. I'm glad to know that. There is something I need to discuss with you. As much as it would be better to do it in person, I need to do it over the phone as I won't have time before seeing Karen."

"Yes, what is it?" Larry sat down. He had a serious look on his face. Grace noticed and came to sit by him. She wanted to know what was going on. Was he backing out of his visit? Was he having second thoughts? Was it what Karen was hoping? Was he not going to ask Karen to move? Her look to Larry told him he better let her listen in. So, without letting Andy know, he put him on speakerphone.

"Larry, I want to ask Karen to move here with me." There, he had said it out loud to someone other than his siblings. "I have no idea what she will say, and I know that I'm asking her to give up the only way of life she's known. But Larry, I love her. You know I do."

"Yes, I know you love her. And yes, this is the only life she's ever known. I can't speak for her, so I can only guess what she will say. I also know that you will never know if you never ask her."

"I know. I'm also torn about something else. My heart is telling me I should be asking Karen to marry me, and that part scares me."

"Why does it scare you?"

"It's a big step. I've seen many marriages that work and a few that fail. When you think about it, I guess I'm one of the lucky ones to see so many that have worked."

"Yes, you are one of the lucky ones. All I can say is Andy, if you feel like you *need* to ask her, it may not be the right time. If you love her and she's the only one for you, if you can't see your life without her in it, by your side through thick and thin, then you know you have to ask her. How do you feel? What does your heart tell you?"

"My heart tells me I love her. I can't see my life without her in it. I see her as part of the manor and being by my side. I see her by my side in all my dreams. It was so beautiful to watch her play with my nephew. I could see her as the mother of my children." Andy took a breath. He could feel his stress and anxiety leave. He knew what he was going to do. He was going to propose. And he knew the best place to do it.

"Andy, you know the answer."

"Yes, I do. Now I need your help. I don't have a lot of time. Is Grace still there?"

"Yes, she's been listening in on our conversation. Sorry I didn't tell you before I put you on speaker."

"Perfect. Grace, you might know this answer. Do you happen to know what size ring she wears?"

Grace's eyes opened wide. A smile went from ear to ear. And to both men she said. "As a matter of fact, I do. She wears a size 5." Larry looked at her, wondering how she knew that. "Hey, when she owns a gift shop where part of the inventory are rings, you try a few on from time to time. A girl's got to do what a girl's got to do." She chuckled when she saw Larry shake his head.

"Thanks. Now one more thing, or two." Andy told them what his plans were and asked for their help to pull it off. Of course they agreed to help.

Andy headed out the door when they hung up. Then he stopped. What style ring? How big of a diamond? He could not do this on his own.

"Sara!" he called as he entered the manor. She could have been anywhere there or even at her own house, but he hoped she would answer.

"Yes?" Sara walked out of the office. She had never heard him talk in such a tone. Something was up. "What is it?" She was expecting him to be getting ready to leave in the morning.

"Do you have a spare couple of hours? I need your help in town."

"Why? Is something wrong?"

"Far from it. I'm going to buy Karen a ring."

"A ring? What for?" She caught herself. He was grabbing her arm and pulling her as a child tugs at his mother. His eyes were wide; his smile was a mix of happiness and playful sneakiness. "Oh, a RING! Of course I have a couple of hours. Let me lock up, and let's go." She closed the office door. They were almost at a runner's pace to get to his car.

"You can slow down, little brother. A ring takes time. Do you even know what size she wears?"

"I sure do. And it's all planned out for when I get to Pennsylvania. Larry and Grace are helping me surprise her."

"When did all this happen?" Sara was excited! Her little brother was getting married – if Karen said yes.

"After we found out Heather was having a boy, I went home to call Larry about me coming there tomorrow. I made the final decision while talking with Larry. He has been like a father to me in so many ways these last several months. I hope you don't mind me talking with him first. He knows Karen more than anyone I know, and I needed his input. And Grace knew Karen's ring size."

"Not a problem. I am glad you have Larry in your life. I can tell you two have a special bond."

They talked about what style of ring and size diamond he wanted on their way to the jeweler. They had to go to the next town as their little one had no jeweler. They went to three different stores where Sara tried several rings on to see how they looked until he found one that spoke to him as the perfect one for his future wife. When he thought about it that way, he gave himself goosebumps. Yep, he was in love.

Andy had Sara call Heather and Ben over to the manor so he could share his news. They had thought he had gone home to get some rest before his trip, but soon found out differently. Andy shared his news with everyone when they got there. It called for a toast of non-alcoholic sparkling wine. They realized Karen might reject his proposal, the big move, and even end the relationship, but no one wanted to mention it. As soon as they had toasted him, he said he was going home to rest as he had originally planned.

Andy, unable to sleep, wrote a note to his siblings, which he left on the island in the kitchen. He then tossed his suitcase in his car and headed North on the interstate. Nine hours later Karen opened her door before he had a chance to knock. She threw her arms around him, kissing him like a long-lost lover. He held her close, refusing to let go. It felt so good to be in her arms. He almost popped the question before they went inside her house.

Karen pulled away from his hold and pulled him inside her house. They talked small talk for a little bit to catch up on the latest developments around the lake and the manor. Andy found a lull in their conversation and asked her to go to the Dike with him. In response, she asked him if he was hungry and wanted to get something to eat first. He said that he was fine, then suggested they could stop somewhere after walking the Dike.

"Let me go change, and then I'll be ready. By the way, where are you staying? I know you aren't staying in one of my rentals."

"No, I talked with Larry and Grace, and they invited me to stay a couple of nights at their place."

"Perfect. Larry thinks the world of you. They both like you a lot and talk about you often."

"I'm kind of fond of him too. We bonded as soon as I got here. I knew him when I was younger, but now both being adults, we have bonded differently."

Karen went to change. Andy used his phone to call Larry to make sure that everything was set up. Larry told him it was. He noticed his hands were starting to shake. He checked his pocket. Yep, it was still there.

While they drove, she updated him on local news, including that her father's classmate organized a group to help preserve the lake area and the town. He was already collecting memorabilia while looking for a place to have made into a museum. She added that she had found some treasures to have included. Andy was only half listening.

He parked the car, got out, then walked around to open her door. They casually walked to the Dike holding hands. His eyes glanced around and saw what he was looking for, the bench in the center. It was empty. Or so it appeared. As they walked, he did his best to keep Karen's eyes focused on the lake and the beautiful sunset. It cast a golden glow across the rippling waters as a gentle breeze moved across the lake. The trees were swaying on one of the distant islands. One of the seven that were part of the man-made lake. A few flowers were in bloom along the pathway.

As they reached the middle bench Karen noticed the red roses and pedals from pink and white roses covering it. She looked at Andy and started to pull him away, not realizing they were for her. Andy shook his head while resisting her tug. He reached to hold her other hand and guided her to sit down. Karen watched Andy as he got down on one knee in front of her. She was speechless, staring at him with her eyes wide open. She could feel her heart beating faster.

"Karen, you are the love of my life. The only woman I have ever loved. I have loved you since the first time I set my eyes on you. You changed my life. You accept me for who I am. You showed me how my heart could love. You are on my mind and in my heart every moment of every day. Karen, I know I am asking a lot by asking but, Karen, will you marry me?" He held out the ring for her to see. He waited.

There were tears in her eyes as she stared at him. A thousand thoughts ran through her mind at the same time. He had picked the perfect location to ask, in the most romantic way. It was her favorite spot on the lake, the lake that was her home. If she said yes, she would have to move. Her life as she knew it would become a part of her past. How could she say yes? She smiled. How could she say no? She would have to leave the family she knew. She'd have to give up the only life and way of living she had known. Her eyes glanced out at the lake as the sun was setting lower. A sign to her that some things must end, yet there is always a new sunrise, a new beginning. She looked back into Andy's eyes.

"YES! Of course I will marry you!" She held out her finger long enough for him to put the ring on. Then she pulled him up off his knees. They were wrapped in an embrace, kissing, when they heard applause and bells ringing. Larry and Grace were walking towards them, clapping their hands, with broad smiles on their faces. Grace had captured the moment with her camera using her zoom lens.

"Congratulations you two! We are so happy for you! Now pose for the camera." Andy and Karen posed for the camera, holding up her hand against his chest to show off the ring. She had looked at it while he proposed and loved it. She wondered how he knew. The ring had red rubies on either side of the round diamond setting. It was on a simple smooth silver band. Rubies were her mother's favorite gem, her own birthstone, and her favorite color. And silver was her metal of choice, unlike most who like gold. It was perfect.

Larry turned the couple around so they could look at the bench. He pointed to where their names and the date they met were now etched along the front side of the bench back, facing the lake. Andy tilted his head as he looked at Larry, who just smiled and winked. It was Larry's gift to them.

The four of them stood as they continued to watch the sunset over the lake and beyond the horizon. "A perfect ending to a perfect day," Grace said as the sun gave its final farewell for the night.

Chapter Twenty-Eight

Sara was doing her best to keep her mind and body busy. The manor had never looked so clean and organized. Even her office was reorganized. She was like a mother when waiting to hear from her child. She had waited before for her brother, but this was a much happier occasion – she hoped. She jumped when her phone rang. She answered with anticipation, but it was not Andy. It was the attorney.

"Hi Sara," he began. "Are Ben and Heather there with you?"

"No, they will be at their house later if you want to call them there. Or call their cell phone. You have their numbers?"

"I do but let me tell you what I found out. I received a notice about a vehicle recall on the car they wrecked. That make and model was recalled for potential power steering failure. That may have caused Ben to run off the road."

Sara felt her tears well up. "Are you sure? The recall is on their particular car?"

"According to the report, yes. When I saw what vehicles were included in the recall, I realized the one matched Ben's. That would explain their accident."

"Thank you for letting me know. You are right. That would explain it. They are out shopping for baby stuff, but I will let them know when they get back. I'll have them give you a call." She hung up the phone, barely saying goodbye. She let the tears fall. The news was shocking. It revealed that the accident was due to the car's defect! It should not have happened. She was also crying because she knew the truth and knew now that it would be easier to keep the truth from coming out. She was still wiping her tears when Ben and Heather came in from shopping.

"What's wrong?" Heather asked when she and Ben walked in. Noticing the evidence of tears and her sister's pale look, she reached out to hug Sara.

Sara relayed the message about the vehicle recall and told them they might want to investigate a lawsuit involved in the recall case. Ben immediately voiced his opinion to sue. He knew something had caused the accident, and if at all possible, he would get the manufacture for all he could. Heather quickly agreed. They were going to fight. Then she rubbed her belly as she felt the baby starting to kick. Maybe it would be a better idea for her health to hold off if they could. Ben nodded in understanding but said he would call the attorney to discuss their options and if there was a deadline to sue. Or even if they could sue anyone.

Evening crept in with no word from Andy. Sara kept watching the clock. She had gone back home after dinner and waited. It was after dark when the phone rang. She answered it, hoping it was good news this time. She heard laughter and then Andy's voice on the other end. "She said..."

Karen finished the sentence, "YES!"

Sara congratulated them and began to cry. Andy told her it was good news and not to cry. "I know. Happy news makes me cry. Have you picked out a date yet?" She wiped her tears.

"No date set yet. She has a lot to deal with here first. I will be home in a few days. We will work on the wedding details later. I wanted to let you know so you could get some sleep and be happy."

"I am thrilled. You just don't know." Now was not the time to tell him the other good news she had received earlier. He had even more to be happy for – he was free and clear. After they said their goodbyes, Sara could not stop smiling.

Andy returned home, leaving Karen in Pennsylvania while she dealt with selling the resort to Larry and Grace. Then she had to pack up everything to move, plan a wedding, and say goodbye to her life as she knew it.

Sara took Andy aside soon after he got home and told him the good, yet bad news about the car. She told him that Ben would join in suing the manufacturer along with several thousands of other car owners who had suffered. Andy agreed it was a relief and that he nor Sara should ever bring up what they knew. Their secret was safe. There was no need to mention it again.

Sara was thankful for her time to relax after the guests had left for the day. She spent her time in the office doing the paperwork, registering guests, updating their website, writing her new blog; it never seemed to end. Her life was anything but dull and boring. It was her work that kept her going. She was not married or getting married; she did not have children, nor was she pregnant. She sat alone and suddenly felt lonely. She took a deep breath, mentally kicked herself in the butt, then went back to work. There was no time for feeling sorry for herself. Karen was moving down soon, there was a wedding to plan, and a baby was on its way. Life at Bella Rose Manor was about to change – again.

Karen moved to Tennessee a month after Andy had proposed. She hated to leave the lake; however, she was in love, which changed everything that mattered. The lake would always be there. She promised herself to visit as she knew she could never totally leave the lake. There was no way ever to forget it. It was in her blood. The change from lake to mountains would take some adjustments. She could be taken away from the lake, but no one would ever take the lake away from her. It would always be a part of her.

A late fall wedding gave them little time to plan the details — a small wedding at the manor. The gazebo was the perfect spot. If it was too cold or bad weather, they could have it inside the chapel, which should be finished by that time. They could have the reception outside or inside the dining room. There was enough parking. Heather's baby would already be born, so they would not have to compete with her due date. That would have been interesting. A baby and a wedding on the same day? Larry was honored when Karen asked him to walk her down the aisle. Nothing was going to keep them away on her and Andy's wedding day.

Summer went by quickly. Heather was preparing to have her baby and had cut back on her work at the manor. With one less person to help, it put extra pressure on Sara, but Karen had stepped in and proved to be a fantastic help. Karen was also helping Sara with the website and blog. They made a good team.

Heather awoke early on a Friday morning at the end of September to pain like she had only had one other time in her life. It was too early! She was not due yet! But she knew it was time, time for baby Maddex to show his little face and to change the world. She shook Ben awake, and he bolted from the bed when he realized the urgency.

Sara was always on call for the manor, so when her phone rang, she thought something was up there. She nearly jumped out of bed when she realized it was Ben calling about Heather. Heather had called her doctor while Ben spoke to Sara. Sara went over to their house to be there when Marc woke up. She said she would bring him to the hospital later. At least that was the plan.

Marc heard the commotion and wanted to be with his mama. They tried to tell him he had to wait, but Heather gave in and said he could come with Sara in her car. Sara called Andy and Karen to let them know. Andy said they would stay at the manor and take care of everything with the guests and not to worry.

Heather was admitted to the hospital as soon as they entered the emergency department. They were going to try to slow her contractions and hope the baby would stay put for as long as possible. Sara and Marc joined her and Ben in the room once she was in a private room and stable. It could be a long wait. That was what they were hoping and praying for. The baby needed to grow as much as possible. Marc was still too sleepy to understand what was going on. He curled up in Sara's lap while Heather rested, and Ben paced.

An hour later, her contractions started up again, with a vengeance. Then her water broke. The nurse called for the doctor. After a quick check of Heather's vitals and the baby's heartbeat, she was rushed to the OR for an emergency c-section. The baby was in trouble. Sara took Marc for a walk down the hallway to see the other babies through the nursery's glass. She felt concerned for her little sister but had to put up a calm front for Marc. He did not need to see his mommy in pain. He was fascinated by the babies in clear beds and told his Aunt Sara he wanted a see-through bed too. Sara laughed and told him they only made those for the tiny babies, and he was a big boy now. He was going to be a big brother!

Heather had opted for natural childbirth with no pain medication, but that was out of her hands now. She was upset that she needed a c-section. She knew it was what God wanted, even if she did not. The nurses worked with her doctor to prep her for the procedure. In no time, she was prepped and draped so she couldn't see what was happening but was awake to hear everything. Ben was by her side, holding her hand and stroking her hair. He was positioned to see what was happening and hoped he would not faint. Their baby boy was born in less than ten minutes. There was no immediate sound from him, no cry, no whimper, but a few pats on his back, and he started to cry — a tiny squeak of a sound.

Heather smiled as she looked up at her husband. He bent and kissed her forehead. The nurse placed the baby on Heather's chest when they had cleaned him and checked all his vitals. His dark brown hair showed from under the cap. His face was beautiful. Together Ben and Heather stared at this little person God had given them. The nurse told them that he had ten cute little toes and long fingers. He only weighed five pounds, but he was perfect and healthy. He would need to stay in the hospital for at least a few days for observation to ensure his lungs were good.

A nurse wheeled Heather back to her private room. A few minutes later the nurse wheeled Maddex in his bassinet to her. Sara and Marc had come back from the nursery as the nurse was bringing in his little brother. Sara lifted Marc so he could see. The nurse picked Maddex up and placed him in Heather's arms as she lay propped up in bed. She could not stop looking at her little miracle.

Sara sat Marc down gently near Heather so he could see his baby brother. He reached over and touched his little head. “Hi little brother, I'm Marc,” he said. Sara bent and gave Heather a gentle hug at her shoulders. She said she would call Andy and let him, and Karen know that everything was fine, and they had a cute little nephew. No one was paying attention to her as she left the room. Heather, Ben, and Marc were in love as they watched Maddex sleep.

It was less than six weeks until the wedding. Heather was taking time off to be with Maddex. Ben was staying home as well but said he would help if they needed him. Although it was a simple wedding, there were a lot of details to make it a perfect day.

Karen planned errands and learned her way around her new home. The more she wandered around and shopped, the more she liked the area. She even enjoyed it when people would hear her talk and comment, “You're not from around here, are ya?” She replied the way she had learned to answer, “No, but I got here as fast as I could.” Oh, the joys of living in Tennessee. Karen was enjoying her new home state.

The time went by quickly. Maddex was growing and doing well. Marc was being a great big brother but did not understand having to wait to play with him. He loved to help bathe him, to hold him, and to give him little kisses. He tried to share his stuffed animals with him, and they had to watch that the animals stayed away from Maddex's face. Everyone was commenting on what a great little family they were.

Sara was alone in her office a few days before the wedding. She looked around at the family photos on the walls. There were pictures of all of them when they were kids. Her parents, her grandparents, the manor in its initial phase, and the most recent remodeled version, completed the array. She had done some rearranging of the family wall to include baby Maddex and Karen with Andy. It always brought fond memories and smiles to her. She had gone in to clean up her desk and go through some old files. After the wedding and honeymoon, the plan was for Karen to join Sara in the office. It would be nice to have the extra help.

Sara opened the top desk drawer and pulled everything out. She had wanted to organize it for months and always seemed to get interrupted. She was determined to get it done. She already had little divider baskets for her small office supplies. She wanted them to be easy to find instead of wasting time moving things around all the time, searching for what she needed. She kept a lot of what she used on the top of the desk to easily find whatever she needed most. She was not usually so disorganized, but then again, it was the typical top drawer. Was there such a thing as *top-drawer syndrome*?

As she began sorting the odd pieces of paper and filing them where they belonged, she also tossed out things she no longer needed. She found the skeleton keys at the bottom of the pile and picked them up. She had forgotten about them. With all that had happened in the last few months, no one had mentioned the will, no one had thought about the attic. And she had not thought about the keys.

She leaned back on her office chair. Holding the one key up, she asked it what it opened. She waited. Willing it to talk to her, she knew she was asking a lot from an inanimate object. She had the urge to take the key to the attic and try it on the door. Then she remembered that the attorney had told them that the key to the attic was in the bank vault.

According to the will, the bank had to be the one to give them the key at the appropriate time. She sighed a deep sigh and placed the key in one of the organizing baskets and placed it on top of the desk. She was not ready to put it inside the desk yet.

She finished filing all the other papers in file folders or file 13 -- the trash. When she finished, she picked the key back up. Maybe it was time to get her siblings together to attempt to unlock the door. Then she realized the timing was still wrong. The wedding was too close. Andy needed to be with them when they went to the attic. As she was discussing this with herself, she was surprised when the office door opened. Looking up, she saw a man and a woman standing in her doorway. She placed the keys back on her desk.

"Hello, may I help you?"

"Hi, you must be Sara? We're Larry and Grace from Pennsylvania." Larry was extending his hand to shake hers as he spoke.

"Oh, of course." Sara stood and shook his hand, then reached to shake Grace's hand as well.

"Welcome to Bella Rose Manor. I wasn't expecting you for a few more hours."

"We got an early start and only stopped a few times along the way for short breaks. It took us less time to get here than we had estimated."

"Come in, come in. Let me get you registered in your guest room; then we can give you the tour. I'll let Andy and Karen know you are here."

"Thank you. I called and left Karen a message when we were almost here. I'm sure they are busy."

"Yes, they are." Sara reached for the form for them to read and sign. Larry was looking around the room; his eyes landed on the family wall. Grace followed his eyes when she noticed his gaze and expression.

"Is this your family?" Grace asked as she pointed to all the photos.

"Yes, that is my grandparents, my parents, us kids over the years. These are photos of the manor over the years. It began as a single dwelling and expanded over the generations. I live in the original building now, Heather and her family live in the second one, Andy and Karen live in the third one." She talked and pointed to the framed photos explaining each one.

Larry's eyes stayed on the photo of her parents. "I sure miss those two. We were great friends back in the day."

"Yes, Andy talks about those days. Mama and Daddy enjoyed their vacations there. I was away at school when they started going there with Andy, so I have never been there.

"You should come to visit sometime. It's beautiful. It is a bit crowded during the summer, and each year it seems to worsen, but we're dealing with it. More people mean more business. I prefer the quiet of the late fall and winter. A bit colder than I'd like, but it is quieter." Grace loved to talk about the lake.

Larry reached on the desk for a pen to sign the papers for renting the guest room. The total cost for the room was all zeros. He was about to ask why when he noticed one of the skeleton keys on top of some papers.

"Wow, that's an old key. What does it go to?"

"Oh, that. I'm not sure yet. I found it inside this desk when we first took over this place after Susan passed. We've not had a chance to check it out. Do you have any idea what it may go to?"

"I'd say it went to a special door or a cabinet of some sort. I've not seen one like that since, well, probably since Andy was a little boy. We had one like that for a while. Do you know if we still have it?" He looked at Grace to see if she remembered.

"I don't even remember us having one." Larry shrugged his shoulders when his wife replied.

Sara let the subject drop. "Let me show you to your guest room. Then I can give you a quick tour before Andy and Karen get back. Or would you like to freshen up a bit?"

"I'd like to freshen up a bit. It's been a long day."

"That's fine. I'll walk you to your room. Do you need help with your luggage?"

"No, we have it. It's all in the front room."

Sara walked them to their room, pointed out a few things about the room, then invited them to join her in the great room when they were ready. She then left them to settle in.

Back at the office, she put the key away inside the top drawer. Something about how Larry looked at the key, yet Grace did not remember one, got her thinking. He knew something. Or she could be imagining it. He was older and said he had one like it at one time.

Chapter Twenty-Nine

The big day had arrived. Both the bride and groom had a restless night's sleep. Andy had spent his last night alone in what he referred to as his 'too large for one person house'. After today he would have the utmost pleasure of sharing it with the love of his life for the rest of his life. That thought brought a smile to his face as he headed to the kitchen for coffee and a quick breakfast. He would change later for the wedding and then meet with the minister, his best man, and the ring bearer. He hoped that Karen, Larry, and Grace were enjoying time together.

After breakfast at the manor, Grace was going to help Karen get ready for her special day. Sara, Heather, and Cecelia were going to finish decorating the chapel, manor, and gazebo for the wedding and reception.

Andy chuckled, thinking of his oldest sister. He knew she would be checking on him throughout the day as well. She might be afraid he would run away again. He knew in his heart that he was not running away. This time he was in it for life.

Karen had slept in the manager's suite to adhere to the tradition and not see Andy before the ceremony. She woke to the early sunrise shedding a dim light through the window. She sat up in bed and smiled. Today was the day her life would change for the better. Yes, she had loved her life so far. It had been good to her for the most part. She wished her parents were still alive so they could see her get married. She had always wanted her father to walk her down the aisle, but she had Larry and Grace to stand in for them. She was grateful to have them in her life. Larry felt honored when she asked him to walk her down the aisle. She was meeting them for breakfast before getting pampered and ready for the ceremony. She was so blessed to have Sara and Heather stand up with her as Maid of honor and bride's maid.

Andy and Karen had planned a simple wedding. Karen, with the assistance of Sara and Heather, had chosen a simple but elegant gown. An overlay of white rose-printed lace adorned the plain satin, sleeveless, heart-shaped neckline bodice. The floor length skirt matched the underlaying solid white satin of the bodice. Her head piece was a simple white satin and tulle headband with tiny, Burgundy satin roses attached to the white tulle trailing down the middle of her back to her waist. She had opted against a long train since the wedding would be outside at the gazebo and she did not want to risk getting a train dirty. Her bridal party had matching gowns in Burgundy. They had chosen them together and agreed on gowns designed that were suitable for other functions. They agreed there was nothing worse than spending a lot of money on a gown you would only wear once. And all agreed they wanted something they would not cringe at in later years.

The bouquets she chose from a local florist for herself and her bridal party were also simple yet beautiful. The girls' bouquets included burgundy roses, white camellia, and Queen Anne's Lace. Each had wildflowers and Baby's breath with English Ivy cascading down from a ribbon wrapped stem and burgundy bow. Her bouquet had white roses in the center in place of the burgundy roses of the girls' bouquets.

The wedding was scheduled for two o'clock. Karen turned her head and noticed the time. She jumped out of bed! It was time to get busy. And according to Grace, to relax! How could she relax? Today was her wedding day! A day she had only dreamed about since she was a little girl! She had places to be, her hair to have styled, and a manicure from a salon just outside of town. She showered but did not wash her hair as she knew her hairstylist would be doing that.

Sara was up early so she could take care of a few business details before the wedding. She put her key in the office door lock, then realized it was unlocked. She opened the door cautiously and found Larry inside, looking at her family photos. She did not appreciate him being there without permission. She usually locked the door to avoid guests walking in when there was no need. It was odd that she had not locked the door, but she just shrugged, assuming she had been distracted with all the wedding planning and had forgotten. It was an easy, but inexcusable mistake, even with everything going on over the last couple of days. Larry greeted her as she stood at the doorway.

"Good morning Sara. I hope my being in here is okay. Grace mentioned this morning that it would be nice to have photos of your parents and grandparents displayed at the wedding reception. It would be a way to honor them and know that even though they are not with us in body, they would be there with you in spirit. I noticed the ones on the wall. Are these the only ones you have, or are there others that you would prefer? If you would like to use any, of course. It was going to be a surprise, but you've caught me." He shrugged his apology.

Sara believed him and thought it was a nice gesture on their part, although she was a bit uneasy with him in the office planning to take things without asking. She reached up and took the framed photos off the wall. "We can use these. I would have to look for any others and then take the time to frame them. It's faster just to use these. Thank you for thinking of including them." She handed them to Larry. "Is there anything else you can think of that we need? I need to meet with Heather and Cecelia to finish the decorating before getting ready for the ceremony. Will those be enough for what you want to do?"

"I believe this will do. Thank you so much. I'll put these with the rest of the decorations in the other room," Larry said as he carried them out of the office. He turned as he left and thanked her again. His eyes glanced a moment at the desk. Sara noticed his glance but thought nothing of it and told him she would see him in a few minutes at breakfast. She glanced around the room before walking out, making sure she locked the door this time.

By two o'clock, all the guests were seated on chairs that the girls and Ben had set up facing the gazebo. Each row of folding chairs had a single burgundy rose tied with a white ribbon on the end chair facing the aisle. White and burgundy tulle decorated with wildflowers framed the gazebo opening awaiting the bride and groom. A CD played a collection of love songs. Andy and the minister walked to their places at the gazebo entrance and waited.

The music changed. Heather began the slow walk down the aisle created between the set of chairs. Sara followed her in as they had rehearsed. Marc followed Sara and carried a white silk pillow holding the wedding bands attached with a loosely tied white ribbon. All eyes then turned to see Cecelia and Donovan's little girl as she skipped down the aisle, tossing rose petals from the wicker basket she carried. Her dress was a simple white gown that guests would soon notice matched the bride's gown.

The music transitioned to the wedding march immediately after the flower girl stopped and turned to stand in front of Sara. Larry and Karen stood waiting at the back for a moment. Customary to most weddings, the guests stood to watch as Larry and Karen, her left hand resting on his arm, her right hand holding her bouquet, walked together down the aisle.

Andy's eyes saw only Karen. He could hear his heartbeat. He started to sway. 'Bend your knees', that's what Grace advised him before the wedding began. He bent his knees to avoid fainting. His bride was beautiful. Her gown was as elegant as she was.

Karen felt Larry by her side but only saw Andy. The love of her life was waiting for her. She wanted to run like a child to be by his side. Larry, sensing her urgency, held her back. Larry escorted her to the steps of the gazebo where Andy met them. He placed her hand into her future husband's open hand, then gently kissed her left cheek, and stepped down to join his wife in the front row of chairs. Grace looked over at him and smiled before she and all the guests sat down.

Friends and family focused on Karen and Andy as they recited vows they had written to each other. They promised to love, cherish, honor, and always be there for each other in health, sickness, and through all that life may throw at them till death did they part.

Marc held up the pillow when it was time for them to exchange rings, then moved to stand on the bride's side by his mother, but sat on the ground instead, adding some comic relief to the serious event. Before they knew it, the minister pronounced them husband and wife and told them they could kiss. He then introduced them to their family and friends as Mr. and Mrs. Fairchild. They turned to face their guests with beaming smiles. They walked up the aisle holding hands – a symbol of their future together to always be side by side, never letting go of each other.

After the ceremony, the photo session filled the time needed to finish setting out the food for the buffet in the newly finished fellowship hall. The guests occupied this break by enjoying sweet tea or non-alcohol punch drinks, talking with other guests, and admiring the hall and decor.

Cecelia, along with a few helpers, had decorated the hall. They had covered the round tables with white fabric that draped over the sides. Each table had a centerpiece of a six-inch white pillar candle sitting inside a small wreath that matched the bridal bouquets. The bridal table was rectangular, with decorations matching the guest's tables.

The wedding cake, with its layers of red velvet, chocolate, and white cake, decorated in white and Burgundy roses cascading from the top around the cake to the bottom, and the topper of a standing crystal heart surrounded by white and Burgundy roses, sat on a separate table.

Andy and Karen made their grand entrance where they were greeted with cheers, whistles, and applause. Everyone raised their glass and cheered as the newlyweds walked to the bridal table.

Sara watched as the guests mingled with her family. She smiled as her baby brother and new sister-in-law spoke with their guests. Their smiles lit up the room. They looked so happy and so much in love. She watched other couples laughing and having a grand time, filling the room with idle chatter as they filled their plates and sat enjoying the Downtown Cafe and Catering's food.

From time to time, Sara heard clanging glasses encouraging the bride and groom to kiss, which they eagerly obliged. She missed that feeling. The feeling of young, innocent love. The feeling of being with that special someone, a soulmate. The feeling of being protected and taken care of. The feeling that she long ago lost. A bad memory, one that had hindered her life ever since. She shook those thoughts from her mind and stepped back into the room of guests and family. Her heart belonged to her family and the manor.

Andy and Karen were enjoying their special day. They stole some time away and took a walk down to the pond. They stood looking out into the woods where the leaves had changed into their wide variety of autumn colors. Some had already fallen to the ground in anticipation of winter.

“I'm so glad we chose to marry in the fall. I would have hated to wait until Spring. Karen, I love you with all my heart. Thank you for taking a chance and giving your love and your heart to me to share.” He reached out, drew her face to him, and gently kissed her. Karen was silent, but he could see the love in her eyes.

Hand in hand, they returned to the fellowship hall. It was time to say goodbye to their guests and family and head off on their honeymoon. Andy had kept the destination a secret but hoped his lovely bride would love it. Andy planned their first night in a hotel close to home because the honeymoon destination was almost a full day's travel by car.

The guests waved goodbye wishing them the best of luck and love as they drove off. Sara had given them a gift to open when they arrived at their destination the next day. In reality, it was a gift from Mama. She hoped it would sit well with them.

Clean up began as soon as the last guest left. Larry and Grace were staying an extra night and offered to help. Cecelia and Donovan stayed to help as well. Cleaning up would go faster with everyone's help. All the decorations needed to come down. The flowers found new homes in the great room and the guest's rooms for the new arrivals due the next day. They put the extra food away in the manor's kitchen. The cake top was wrapped and put into the freezer for the first anniversary. They placed the rest on the island for everyone to help themselves to the extras.

At one point, Sara noticed that Larry was nowhere in sight. She slipped away to look outside but did not see him. Maybe he had gone back to the manor to his guest room. She tried to stop thinking so much about him, but there was something about him that had her on edge ever since she had found him in the office.

It was late when she was able to sigh in relief. Everything was clean and back where it belonged. She would be ready for her new guests who were arriving in the morning. She returned to the office to double-check the details of the guest's registrations. She hoped to sleep in a little bit before they arrived.

Sitting at her desk, she reached for the registration book. As she did, she noticed the skeleton key was missing from the tiny basket where she had put it. She did a quick look over her desk but did not see it. The basket was there, but it was empty. How odd, she thought. She could have sworn it had been there that morning. She knew she had locked the office door the last time she left. She shook it off, thinking there had been too much on her mind. A good night's sleep would do her good. She closed the book after seeing the list for her next guests and headed out. She made doubly sure to lock the office door. She locked the front door, then walked through the kitchen out the side entrance and walked to her home.

Inside her own home, she felt relief. It was quiet. No one was making demands on her. The wedding was over. A lot of her stress was behind her. She would be able to sleep in peace. She changed into her comfortable clothes, but she opened a kitchen cabinet where she hid a bottle of white wine, before sitting down. It had been there a long time, since she rarely drank, and she had not touched it after Andy's arrival. She wanted to be a positive influence on him. He had enough on his plate staying sober. A temptation may cause him to falter.

She poured herself half a glass and put the bottle back on the shelf behind several other items. She swirled the drink around and took in its aroma, then sat down on her sofa to enjoy the evening. It was a rare, quiet, peaceful change to the hectic last few weeks. She lifted her glass in the air. “A toast,” she said to no one, “A toast to new beginnings.”

Exhaustion took over, allowing Sara to sleep soundly, providing visions of the ocean waves slowly rolling toward the shore, the sun shining, giving the earth warmth. It was a sign that all was well with life.

Sara awoke refreshed and ready to face the next phase of life at the manor. First, coffee. She thought Larry and Grace might have left already, but she made a full fresh pot in case they were still there. Otherwise, she would have made a single serving. After pouring herself her first cup of coffee for the day, Sara headed to her office to glance at the files one last time to see about her new guests arriving. It gave her a chance for that personal touch she had taken to heart when she saw her parents do the same thing.

The guests enjoyed that special touch. Snacks and flowers were one thing; knowing their names and a few details about them was another. With so many different guests over time, it was hard to keep track without a quick look. Sara made it a habit to add details about each guest to the files she kept, especially for the returning guests. Details about their children, grandbabies, their work, if they had sold their home, and anything else she heard that would be of interest. She had learned to be a good listener. God gave her one mouth and two ears for a reason.

She unlocked the office door and walked to her desk to pick up the files. She noticed the small basket when she picked up the papers. The skeleton key was back in its place. She felt a chill. What was going on? Someone had been in the office. The only people remaining after the wedding guests left were Heather, Ben, Marc, Cecelia, Donovan, Larry, and Grace. They all had stayed to help clean up the fellowship hall. She remembered everyone being there. Except for the time she noticed Larry missing.

Other people could have wandered into the manor at any time since they were at full occupancy for the wedding. So several people had access to the manor. None of them would have a reason to be in the office, and certainly no reason to mess with the key. None of them knew it was there as far as she knew. No one knew what her thoughts were about it. She had been the one who returned the photos to the wall. She shook her fears and suspicions out of her mind. She had things to do. Guests to bid goodbye to and others to welcome. And fresh coffee to enjoy first. She returned to the kitchen to pour a second cup. Something told her it was going to be a long day.

She jumped when Grace entered the kitchen. Sara regained control of herself and asked her if they wanted something to eat. Grace said she and Larry were going to grab something to eat along their way, that she had just come in to say goodbye and thank her for all her hospitality, adding that they hoped to visit again. Sara told her she looked forward to their next visit.

Larry had put their suitcases in the great room while he drove the car up closer to the front door. A few minutes later, they had everything packed in the car and were saying a final goodbye. Sara watched them drive away and waved one last time.

It had been nice to have them there, but there was something about Larry. She couldn't put her finger on it, but she couldn't shake her uneasiness about him. She would talk with Karen and Andy when they got back in a couple of weeks. Until then, life was going to go on – it always did.

Ben and Heather came into the manor with the two little ones. Sara reached out to hold little Maddex. He was changing every day it seemed and was so cute. She walked around with him in her arms and let Ben and Heather do what they needed to for the upcoming guests. They all had done most of the work the night before which allowed them time to relax for a bit.

While they waited, Sara said she had something to discuss with them. They were all ears.

"I know Andy isn't here, and we will wait to do this until he gets back, but I can discuss something with you. I'm not sure he even remembers the next phase in the will. Do you?" She looked at Heather as she posed the question.

"The part about not going up into the attic? I remember. Every time I go up into the supply room I look over at that door."

"Yes. I've had it on my mind a lot lately. It is time we contact the attorney to schedule an appointment. It was stated in the will to wait until Bella Rose Manor was remodeled, reopened, and profitable. And, of course, Andy being home. We reached those goals by mid-summer. Somehow fall has slipped by, with winter right around the corner. We are at full occupancy for about two more weeks. After that, we close for a few weeks again until after the new year. That would be the best time to investigate what is behind those doors."

"Can you wait that long? We've been waiting seven months already; since our opening."

"Well, we need to talk with Andy first, make an appointment to get the key, and then we can enter. However," she hesitated before choosing her words so she would not sound accusative. "Do you remember when I found the skeleton key?"

"I was there when you found it. You thought it might fit the attic door or something inside the attic. Why?"

"I was in the office organizing the desk during this past weekend." She noticed Heather looking at her with raised eyebrows. "Yes, I know; what was I doing organizing the desk with so much going on? I'm not sure. I needed some alone time, and the desk needed organizing. Anyway, I found the key again and put it in a small basket to put it in the top drawer. I got interrupted, and the basket with the key inside stayed on top of the desk. I had to leave the office, but you know I always lock the office door, right?"

"Yes, we have to ask you for the key to get anything out of there. I sometimes wish you would leave it open, but I understand you don't want our guests to access the business files. Continue."

"Well, yesterday, the morning of the wedding, I went in there, and the key was missing. The basket was there, but the key was nowhere to be found. I searched. This morning, when I went back in there, the key was back. Both times I had to unlock the office door to get in."

Ben looked at Heather, and they both looked at Sara. "Who could have gotten in there? The only people here overnight were Larry and Grace. We did have a full Manor during the wedding. So it could have been anyone," Ben said. "But it was locked, right?" Heather added.

"Yes, it was locked. The only other person who has been in there was Larry, yesterday when he asked about using the framed photos for the memorial table at the reception. The key was still there when he left. He was already inside, looking at the photos on the wall when I got there at that time. He said the office door was open. I was so preoccupied I didn't think anything of it. But you know me. I always lock that door."

"So we have a mystery key? Or a mystery ghost? You don't think that key has anything to do with the attic, do you? We've looked at the door to the attic. It takes a regular key, right?"

"Yes, we've looked. The key doesn't go to the door. I think it may go to something inside the attic."

"So, give the attorney a call tomorrow and see what we need to do to get in the attic."

"I will. We won't go inside until Andy gets back home, but I'm ready, aren't you?"

"I'm ready. Now time for more coffee." Heather rose to fill everyone's coffee mugs except her own. She was nursing her baby, and as much as she had hated not having coffee, she was doing her best to avoid the extra stimulation it could give her baby. She had slipped a few times, but Maddex was a perfect baby, and she was doing her best not to jeopardize anything.

Andy had surprised Karen by taking her to Lake Wallenpaupack for their honeymoon. He had rented a room at one of the other resorts near the lake known for years to be the lover's resort — with a heart-shaped hot tub in each room. The rose petals on the beds, along with chocolate and champagne, made it a popular honeymoon destination. He had requested sparkling juice instead of champagne, but otherwise, he wanted the best for his bride.

As they were about to walk into the room, Andy picked her up and carried her over the threshold. She laughed at him then kissed him as he set her down. She was thrilled with his surprise honeymoon destination. Even though she lived nearby, she had never been there.

Andy and Karen spent their honeymoon traveling around the lake region. They took an evening cruise on the lake to experience the colors of fall and the beautiful sunset. It reminded them of the one they had the evening they got engaged on the dike. They visited a few friends, had dinner out at her favorite places, and visited her resort for old time's sake. It had only been a few months since she had sold it and moved, but the changes Larry and the property manager were doing were impressive. All looked good to her. She felt she could rest easy when they went back to Tennessee.

Their honeymoon evenings consisted of fires in the fireplace, time in their private hot tub, and intimacy that left them wrapped in each other's arms until the morning light.

The last night of their honeymoon, Andy had arranged for them to have a party with Larry, Grace, and all of Karen's friends; complete with music, dancing, great food, and a simple wedding cake. It was his way of giving her a reception with those who had not been able to attend their wedding.

Andy knew it would be hard for her to leave, and he was surprised when she woke up and announced that it was time to go home to Tennessee. He wrapped his arms around her and told her again that he loved her. She melted in his embrace. Karen never dreamed that love could be like this. She never imagined being willing to leave her childhood home. But she was looking forward to experiencing this new adventure. Whatever it held for her she was ready as long as Andy was by her side.

Their final morning arrived. Andy and Karen looked around before putting their luggage and all the gifts into the car, then, seated inside with their seat belts buckled, Andy started the car. They looked at each other and in unison said, “Let's go.” Neither one looked back as they pulled out of the parking lot.

Someone had told her once that love changes everything, and now she knew they were right. Andy changed everything. It was time to start their new life together - in the mountains of Tennessee.

Chapter Thirty

Sara arrived at the attorney's office early. Would she ever get out of that habit of being early for everything? Mr. Williams was not in the office when she arrived but returned for their appointment and met her in the lobby. Together they walked down the hall to his office.

"How have you been, Ms. Fairchild?"

"Please, call me Sara. And I've been fine. We have been super busy at the manor as you may or may not have heard."

"I've heard you have had a full house since you opened. That is a good thing. How is everyone in the family doing?"

"Yes, having full occupancy is a good thing. The family is doing well. You know Andy came home. Well, he recently got married and will be home from their honeymoon later today. Heather and Ben had another baby. We've built a chapel on the grounds, which will officially open next year. We used it for the wedding but will do a formal grand opening in the spring. I'm going to enjoy slowing down a bit this winter. We are open except for a few weeks between Thanksgiving and Christmas and for a few weeks in January. We still have some open dates in December. I'm thinking of having a large Christmas gala, but I still need to discuss it with my siblings. We may wait till next year since time is so close to plan anything amazing."

When Sara finally stopped talking long enough to take a breath, Mr. Williams spoke. "You have been busy. I have a feeling those vacancies will be filled soon. And a Christmas gala sounds fun." He was selecting files out of his desk as he spoke.

"Here we go," he said as he held up her files. "Now, you are here today about the key to the attic, correct?"

"Yes, the will said that once we were up and running and profitable, we could get the key and finally get into the attic. I'm telling you it's been difficult not to break that door down at times when we were completing the remodel. Then we got so busy it would slip our minds. But I never forgot about it."

"Well, I have arranged with the bank for us to go over there from here to get the key. Here are the papers that go with the key. Susan left you a letter as well. She was very insistent that you do not get this letter until it was time. I do believe now is the time." He handed her the large envelope.

She took the envelope from him and saw her name written across the front in Susan's beautiful handwriting. She teared up but held her feelings from showing the best she could. Even as her mother aged, her handwriting remained beautiful. Oh, how she missed her parents.

"I will give you a few minutes to read it if you would like. Or, if you wish, you can wait to read it when you get home. There are no instructions as to when you need to read it."

He thumbed through the other papers in the file to ensure there was nothing else he needed to give her. He was watching her as she held it in her hand. He felt for her. She had been through a lot in her young life. He admired her for all she had been through recently. He thought that no one should have to deal with losing both parents, have major responsibilities thrown at you out of the blue, and have your life's direction changed forever for you. She had done a fantastic job dealing with everything. He knew she was under a lot of stress, but she handled it well. He knew she had her family by her side but getting them all home had been a struggle.

Sara could not get herself to open the envelope. "I think I will wait to read this until I get home. I may need more time to digest it than I will have here. And I know me, I will cry." She motioned to her eyes.

Mr. Williams nodded as he brought his thoughts back to what was taking place. He had only heard part of what she said. "Oh, I'm sure you will. You are a sensitive lady. Your parents meant the world to you. I miss my father, so I understand some of how you feel." He hoped that he had not sounded inconsiderate. Losing his father had been nothing like her losing both her parents so close together.

"Yes, we were close." It was all she could say without letting the tears fall.

"Are you ready to head to the bank to get the key?" He stood up and walked to the door. He held it open for her to walk past him. They walked through the lobby, where he told his secretary he would be back in about an hour. They walked together to the bank located three buildings from his office.

One of the tellers directed them to the bank president, who took them into his office. They looked at each other confused. They thought he would take them straight to the vault to open the safe deposit box.

The president told them that he had the next step that went with the will. Mr. Williams and Sara looked at each other and then at the bank president. They were silent as he continued.

"Susan left this file with me along with strict instructions. I have a note here that says I can only give you the key after each of her children has read the letters she wrote to you. Once you read those, I can give you the key that will let you open the safe deposit box."

"More stipulations from her! What is she doing, playing her version of treasure hunting? I am so confused." Sara stood up. She could feel the tears coming. Not quite angry, but feeling like it had been one step forward, and now faced two steps back. She had been so close to getting the key. She had told Heather she was going to get the key and bring it home. They were both excited that when Andy came home with Karen, they could get into the attic to find answers. And now this? Why? Now they couldn't get the key until Andy came home. Where would they have been if Andy had never come back home? Sara shook her head at that thought.

Mr. Williams stood with her and reached for her arm to calm her down. The bank president stood as well and handed Sara the note. "I'm so sorry. I know this is hard to understand. I asked her the same thing when she gave me this to hold. I told her she was childish about it. That she was treating you kids a bit rough in their time of sorrow."

"That she is. I hope once we find out what is in there, we will understand, but for now, I'm just pissed." She calmed down enough to say, "I'm sorry. I was not prepared for this. Not for any of this. Thank you for your time. We will be back once we have all read our letters." She walked out of the office with Mr. Williams close behind her.

"I'm so sorry, Sara. I didn't know there was another step to all this. I disagreed with her when she came in and set up the first step. But it was not my place to tell her how to handle her will or her children."

"It's not your fault. I'm not mad at you. I'm pissed at my mother," Sara took a breath and let it out with a huff. "I need to get home." She said as she swung around and headed to the door. She barely said goodbye as she rushed outside and down the steps to her car. Mr. Williams watched her as she drove away. He wished there was something he could do for her.

She was full of anger all the way home. She hoped she would be calm by the time she got there, but she knew she would still be upset, and Heather would pick up on it immediately. That's how sisters were. Plus, there was no key – yet.

Instead of going to the manor first, she went straight to her house. Ben and Heather could handle everything while she calmed down. She collapsed on her sofa and dropped the envelopes by her side. How much more could she take? How much more did her mother think they could handle? It was one thing to want all of her children to be together. But for what, to simply run the manor as a family? Why so secretive about the attic? Was there something so bad inside there? Something they may not be able to handle? Why had her mother put up so many roadblocks? What was she trying to teach them?

"Mama!" she called out in desperation. "What is it now?" She burst into tears. She buried her face in her hands, curled up with her legs under her, and cried until the tears started to drip through her fingers. She did not know how long she cried. She had no answers. As she dried her tears she glanced at the envelopes. She knew the only answers were inside.

After washing her face and getting a glass of cold water, she picked up the envelopes and collapsed on her sofa. She set the ones down that were for her younger siblings. She stared at the one with her name on it and the one with all their names listed. She knew she should wait for the others to read the one to everyone. So she set that one down on top of the others and opened the one addressed to her.

"Okay, Mama, what do you have to say that I had to wait to read?"

She pulled out the handwritten pages. The familiar beautiful stationary. The flow of her penmanship. She remembered her mother writing on that paper. Red roses and butterflies in blue. The memories were changing her feelings of anger into tears of sadness. Tears that blurred the words on the paper, so she wiped her eyes, then heard her front door open. She had forgotten to lock it.

Heather called her sister's name as she walked into Sara's home. She spotted her sister sitting on the sofa, facing away from her.

"There you are. Why didn't you answer your phone or your door? I was getting worried." She had reached the sofa, took one look at Sara, and sank to the seat beside her.

"What's wrong? Why the tears?" She wrapped her arm across Sara's shoulders and noticed the letter in her sister's hand. Then she spotted the envelopes beside her.

"What are these? Are these from Mama about the attic?" Heather sounded excited. This was good. Or at least it should have been. Sara nodded in response without saying a word.

"Why the tears? Is this not good news?"

Sara leaned into her sister and cried some more. She thought her tears were gone, but there they were. She sniffled and sat up, breaking off the connection with her sister.

"Mama wrote us each a letter. We have to each read our individual letters before we get the key. And we have a letter addressed to the three of us to read as well." She held up the envelopes. "I don't know what game she's playing, but this afternoon it made me angry. I think all the events from the last few months or years have finally caught up with me.

"I agree. You have been the typical older sibling. Everything fell into your lap, and you ran with it. You took the responsibility. Typical to the firstborn child, you stayed strong for the rest of us and everyone who came close. You let the rest of us help, but you took charge. After Mama's death, I promised to be by your side. Then my world changed instantly when that accident happened. Which I am still not convinced was because of a faulty transmission, brakes, or whatever that recall was. I still say we got hit by someone. I don't remember another car, but I remember a jolt. Anyway, after that, Andy finally came home with a girlfriend not far behind. And well, Sis, there has been stuff going on non-stop. You need a break."

"If you only knew."

"Knew what?"

Sara shook her head. She tried to wipe out the thoughts that had flown in about Andy, the key, Larry, her bad marriage. Everything flashed through her mind at once. "Nothing."

"Sis, is there more I should know about?"

"No, you're right. There has been a lot going on."

Heather picked up the envelopes and eased the letter out of Sara's hand. "Tell you what, Big Sis. This can wait. Everything else can wait." She waved them all in the air and did her best not to drop them.

"Heather, No!" Sara attempted to grab the letter back.

"Sara, Yes. It can wait. Andy will be home soon, and we can discuss it once they get settled. Until that time, I am going to put these in a safe place – My house! And you, young lady, are going to take at least a few days off to relax and enjoy yourself. Go somewhere, call up an old friend, visit them, go off alone, and make new friends. I don't care. But you, Dear Sister, are getting away from here for at least a week."

Sara started to protest, but Heather raised her hand. "Stop, no arguing. Go."

"I have to contact Mr. Williams tomorrow. I told him I would call to set up the meeting, and he is expecting me to call."

"Fine, but then you are out of here."

"Where will I go?

"As I said, I don't know, nor do I care," Heather said as she took the items of discussion and headed for the door. "Now, go wash your face, pour yourself some coffee, and find that suitcase I know you have in a closet somewhere. I want to say goodbye to you first thing in the morning and then not hear from you for at least a week!"

Sara watched as Heather left and gently closed the front door. She had taken all the evidence with her. It was so unlike her to be the dominant one. Her sister had always needed her. But she needed someone else to be the strong one for a while. That is what siblings were for. She started to cry again as she walked around her own house. They needed Andy to be home. Andy and Karen both needed to be here for this. Heather was right about that. Heather was also correct that it could all wait.

She started to cry again as she walked to her bedroom. Heather was right; she needed a break. Her shoulders felt the weight of the world. She cried, feeling some of the weight lifting. Yes, she needed to get away.

Sara set her suitcase out to pack in the morning and got ready for bed. She still had no idea where she was going but knew she had to be someplace other than Bella Rose Manor for a while. She curled up in bed, and despite everything, it did not take her long to fall asleep.

Breakfast was always served at nine o'clock sharp at the manor. She did not have to worry about that with Andy being away because she knew Ben was in charge for now. She planned to have her breakfast over by nine-thirty and be on the phone with her attorney to let him know she would not be there for at least a week.

The attorney answered at the second ring. "Good morning, Mr. Williams speaking."

"Hi Mr. Williams, how are you this morning."

"I'm well. How are you?" He sensed he knew the voice, but the noise from the construction work outside made hearing difficult, and he did not recognize who it was.

"Not so well. I took those envelopes home, and well, simply put, my sister caught me in tears. We talked, and now I need a place to hide for at least a few days. She says I need a week away."

"What? What are you talking about, Sara?" He recognized her voice but was confused by her statement. He stood from his seat and walked to the side of his desk. She had told him she would read the letters as soon as her siblings could be there. At least that had been the plan. When had it changed? Had she read them already?"

Sara took a deep breath while collecting her thoughts, "My sister says I need to take a vacation. 'Sister's orders', as she put it. Something about doing everything when she got injured, so now it was my turn. She said something about therapy sessions go a long way as well. I told her I'd take her up on vacation time, then if that did not work, I'd think about attending therapy. Now all I need is someplace to go. Someplace quaint, secluded, and ready to occupy. I have no idea where to look. As long as it is not a rundown hotel."

He instantly reacted. "I have a rustic vacation place in the country that is private and secluded. It is not so far off the beaten path you can't find it. It is well hidden in the woods. You are welcome to stay there for a few days, a week, or even longer."

"I can't possibly stay there. It's your place when you need a vacation."

"I won't be needing it for a while. I was up there two weeks ago. It did my body and soul good to escape my hectic life. There is no sense in letting it stand empty, which is why I let other people use it when I am not there. Why let it stand empty when I have people who want to stay in the mountains? I know a lot of people who need a get-a-way but can't afford a resort. Most do not want a resort; they want seclusion."

Randall stood and walked around his desk as he continued speaking.

"Now, it is not the Taj Mahal, but it will give you time to rest without interruptions. It has everything you may need except for food. It does have the basics like spices, condiments, bottled water. Take the foods you want to eat. It has a stove, oven, microwave, coffee maker, Keurig Machine, slow cooker, pots, pans, and dishes. About everything you may need. Sheets, towels. All fresh and clean. I even put clean sheets on the bed before I left.

"Thanks. I may take you up on your offer. Let me first talk with Heather. Since she is the one who insisted I take a vacation, she may have someplace up her sleeve of where I should go."

"You can use some time away by yourself. You've been through a lot, and none of it was things you expected. That adds extra stress to anyone. Believe me, I've seen many people buckle under less than what you have experienced."

"Thanks. I think."

"I mean it as a compliment. You are a strong and beautiful woman." The last part slipped out by accident, but it was true. She was beautiful. He hoped she would take it as a compliment and not a come on.

"Beautiful?"

"Yes, you are beautiful, even when you are angry."

"I'm so sorry you had to witness that."

"No problem. I've witnessed worse in my line of work."

"I'm sure you have." She was starting to feel relaxed. Her anger from the day before was still there, and she knew it would last a while. Chatting with her attorney was making her feel comfortable and more relaxed. She realized she should end the conversation. The offer of his vacation home was nice, but "no," she thought, "I'm done. I'm done being angry. Done being suspicious." She silently willed herself to be calm.

"Mr. Williams, I've made up my mind. I will take you up on your offer. When can I come for the key and directions?" She felt herself relax even more for the first time in months. Or was it years?"

"I'll do you one better, meet me for lunch. Oh, and will you please call me Randall?"

"Okay. Randall. I won't be leaving until after Andy and Karen return home, but I can meet you later today for lunch to get the key. You know, in case I decide to go sooner." She was planning to leave sooner but did not want to seem like she was running away.

"That's perfect. You can go when you want. Give me a few hours' notice, and I will have my cleaning company clean the place before you get there."

Sara caught herself smiling. Someone was looking out for her for a change. "See you at lunch at the cafe. Oh, and you may want to make that call to have it cleaned. I may decide to leave at midnight."

"See you then." He hung up the phone and leaned back in his chair as he called his cleaning service.

After he called his housekeeper and arranged for the impromptu cleaning of his vacation home, he put his feet up on the large mahogany desk and closed his eyes. A smile crossed his face. He had a date with Sara. She may only think of it as a lunch meeting, but there would be no work discussed. He had secretly liked Sara for years. From the first time he saw her, there was something about her. He had only been professional with her and her family during the time of their grieving. He knew she was not looking for more to add to her life during that time. Maybe someday she would be ready to move on. He hoped so.

Sara hung up her phone and looked around. Heather was right; she was long overdue for a vacation. Time for her to get some rest. As she entered her bedroom to get dressed, she caught her reflection in the mirror. She looked tired. Her hair was in much need of a trim, if not more.

Maybe while I'm on vacation, I'll go for the works she thought. She dressed for lunch, put some makeup on, threw her hair into a ponytail, and went to find Heather.

Heather took one look at her and knew something was up. It had been a while since her sister had put makeup on. But her ponytail? That did not go with the makeup; it would have to go.

"What's up, Sis? Going out?"

"I am having lunch with Randall to get a key."

"Key? Randall? THE Key?"

"No, no, the key to his vacation house.

"Okay, you lost me. Let's start from the beginning." She reached for her sister and dragged her to the sofa to sit down.

"It's nothing. I called Mr. Williams this morning to let him know we would wait to read the letters until after Andy came back. Then I told him you were sending me away on vacation.

He asked me where I was going, and when I told him I had no idea, he offered his vacation house."

"His vacation house, nothing else?"

"No, nothing else. Why would you think otherwise?" Sara looked shocked.

"Let's see. You are a woman. He is a man. You are about the same age. You are both single. You do the math. Oh, and do not forget - he is good looking."

"Heather!" she said as she tried to hide her tell-tale face. She almost felt like a teenager and could tell she was blushing.

"You will sit down for a few more minutes and let me fix your hair. You are not going with that hairstyle. Those are for when you are working in the garden or mowing the yard, not for a date."

"It's not a date." She protested while she sat still, letting her sister fix her hair and touch up her makeup.

Randall arrived at the Cafe at the same time that Sara pulled up to park across the street. He waited for her at the entrance, then held the door for her.

They followed the hostess to a table in the back where few people were seated. Their lunch crowd was starting to arrive, so it only took a few moments to fill up all the tables.

They placed their order for the meal at the same time they ordered their drinks. They both lived in the area and were regulars at the cafe, so they knew what they liked. Sara was surprised when they both ordered the chicken salad with cranberry and walnuts on a crescent roll. Most men went for something more filling. Of course, they both also ordered the fresh brewed sweet tea.

Their conversation automatically took on a business feel, which Randall told himself it would not. It was Sara who changed the subject and asked if he had family in the area.

"No, most of my family is from Pennsylvania. I am the only one who moved away."

"Oh? PA? What part?"

"Southeastern area near Reading? Have you heard of it?"

"I have heard of it. I don't remember why at the moment, but I've heard of it. You know Andy and my parents used to spend time in Pennsylvania, at Lake Wallenpaupack. In fact, that is where he met Karen. That's a long story."

"You can tell me that long story sometime." Randall was hanging on every word she said. He loved hearing her voice and watching her as she spoke.

Their lunch arrived, and as they began to eat, they were quiet. When Sara and Randall finished eating, Sara wanted to stay and chat more, but she knew he had to get back to work, and she had to get home. Plus, people were waiting in line for an empty table. Randall must have sensed her thoughts.

"Let's leave, so they have a place for the next patron. They get busy here at lunchtime."

"It helps that they are only open for the lunch crowd. I never did quite understand that, although the Downtown Cafe does make a good lunch. That's part of their charm. The catering business they started this year is going well too. We used them for the wedding reception."

"Yes, they do. I bring my clients here from time to time. I've not had the opportunity to use the catering service." They made it through the crowd to the front entrance. Randall offered to walk her to her car, and she accepted. She was not ready to say goodbye.

"I know the purpose of the lunch meeting was to give you the key, but I was wondering." He hesitated. For some reason, he felt like a teenager asking a girl out on a first date. "I was wondering, when you get back from vacation, would you consider going out to dinner and maybe a movie with me?"

Sara raised her head to look into his eyes and smiled. "I'd like that."

He opened her car door so she could get in. He told her that if she had any issues at the house, call him day or night and let him know, he would send someone to fix the problem, or he'd come and fix it himself. He closed the door and they said goodbye through the opened window.

As Sara drove home, she looked forward to her vacation. According to Randall, the place was about an hour away in the mountains with other vacation houses that shared a community pool and clubhouse. It was close enough to town for her to go shopping, have her hair and nails done, or go for a walk and people watch. She could relax and enjoy the quiet tranquility of peace if that were all she wanted to do.

As she drove up the lane towards Bella Rose Manor, she admired the rose bushes that still had a few blossoms. She smiled when she saw the tree her grandfather had planted as a seedling when he and her grandmama had moved there. She looked up ahead and spotted Andy's car.

"Perfect," she spoke out loud. "They are home, and I can leave in the morning if I want."

Suddenly realizing she was not ready to face her family, Sara pulled into the parking area by the walking trail, where guests often stopped to hike or have a picnic. She got out of her car and walked along the path to the overlook with a view of the mountains. She gazed at the beauty while feeling how blessed she and her siblings were. So many families lived far away from each other. Her family lived almost under the same roof. They had come a long way since their parents' deaths: the accident, Andy coming home after running away - again, the new baby in the family, and a wedding! Everything had been accomplished while doing a remodel complete with an expansion, reopening the manor, and already making a profit.

Yes, they were blessed. All Sara wanted to do now was talk with her siblings and officially welcomed Karen into the family. It was time to start fresh, time to open the letters from Mama and see what adventures awaited.

Sara climbed back into her car and started the engine. She turned the wheel and headed down the lane - to the vacation house. She would call her family later. Now, it was her turn to run away. She smiled as she turned off Bella Rose Lane onto the main road.

She glanced in her rearview mirror as she drove away from the estate. Pushing the accelerator to reach the speed limit, she chuckled at the thought that came to mind, her brother had been right –

"Yes, *Leaving Came Easy*."

Epilogue

Sara enjoyed her time away. She called her family to let them know she was taking the vacation that Heather had suggested. They did not ask where she was going, nor did they ask when she would return. They knew their sister would be fine. They also knew she would not be away for long.

The family had reached the place in their lives where nothing was missing. The siblings had found each other; nothing else mattered. They were together like their mother wanted them – home. The manor was profitable. Life was good. They could wait for their next adventure, and if it never came, so be it. Life was finally good for each of them. God truly had blessed.

There are times throughout our lives when we feel something is so important that we cannot wait for it. Later we realize that it was not important at all. We understand that God would have made whatever it was happen sooner if it had been so vital. There are times when God calls us to take time to relax, reconnect inwardly. A time to decide what is most important to us. Later we can look back and see that Leaving Came Easy. Sometimes leaving means running away; other times, it means leaving your troubles and worries behind and focusing on the positive in life and living.

For Sara and her family, God put many things in their lives to keep them distracted from what they first thought was most important. They found, in the end, that the goal had always been to reconnect with family. To find true love, build a family, make new friends, and cherish what the older generation shared of their lives. Now it would be their turn to teach the new generation by example, what was meaningful – Family, being there for each other, and love.

ACKNOWLEDGMENTS

With much gratitude to Will Wyckoff for his encouragement to start writing again. By reading his three books I was inspired to continue my own journey.

To Connie Mulligan for being eager to read my first rough drafts. I admire her courage to read through all the mistakes and still want to read more.

To my friends and family who patiently waited for this first book to finally make it to publication. And who now wait for the rest of the trilogy.

To Joshua Daughrity for his help in formatting and giving me confidence to continue getting this book out there.

I am blessed to have all of you in my life. Thank you.

About the Author

Phyllis Dewey has a passion for writing that began when she was just eleven years old when she wrote her first poem. Three of her poems are published in different Anthology Books. She stopped writing for several years while being busy school, her growing family, and work.

In 2019 she returned to her love of writing with a simple story idea that became the trilogy: The Mysteries of Bella Rose Estate.

She has a college degree in social work/mental health. She draws on her experiences in that field as well as her own life adventures in her writings.

Her passion for writing continues as she is currently working on completing the trilogy and working on two non-fiction books.

Ms Phyllis lives in east Tennessee, enjoying time with her family and friends. She also enjoys her flower gardens and photography hobbies, and the view of the mountains from her home.

www.ingramcontent.com/pod-product-compliance
Lightning Source LLC
Chambersburg PA
CBHW030157200626
46812CB00017B/2270

* 9 7 8 1 7 3 6 4 3 4 7 0 3 *